rd-bitten stuff, anti-Newbolt and ...

Times Literary Supplement

"Robinson is a better storyteller than Jeffrey Archer, Ken Follett or Wilbur Smith . . . His is a rare achievement, difficult to attain and one not much striven for in the current literary output, the creation of poetry in fiction"

TIBOR FISCHER, *The Times*

"Robinson has a narrative gift that sets up the hackles of involvement. A rare quality"

PAUL SCOTT

"Nobody writes about war quite like Derek Robinson. He has a way of carrying you along with the excitement of it all before suddenly disposing of a character with a casual, laconic ruthlessness that is shockingly realistic . . . As a bonus, he writes of the random, chaotic *comedy* of war better than anyone since Evelyn Waugh"

MIKE PETTY, *Independent*

"Robinson mixes the action with cynicism and hard-bitten humour that has you halfway between tears and laughter. Biggles was never like this"

Express

D0238475

Novels by Derek Robinson

THE R.F.C. TRILOGY*

Goshawk Squadron
Hornet's Sting
War Story

THE R.A.F QUARTET*

Piece of Cake
A Good Clean Fight
Damned Good Show
Hullo Russia, Goodbye England

THE DOUBLE AGENT QUARTET**

The Eldorado Network
Artillery of Lies
Red Rag Blues
Operation Bamboozle

OTHER FICTION**

Kentucky Blues
Kramer's War
Rotten with Honour

NON-FICTION

Invasion 1940

* Available from MacLehose Press from 2012/13
* * To be published in ebook by MacLehose Press

Derek Robinson

HULLO RUSSIA, GOODBYE ENGLAND

MACLEHOSE PRESS
QUERCUS · LONDON

First published in Great Britain in 2008 by Whistle Books
This edition published in 2012 by

MacLehose Press
an imprint of Quercus
55 Baker Street
7th Floor, South Block
London W1U 8EW

A CIP catalogue record for this book is available
from the British Library

ISBN 978 0 85705 092 2

2 4 6 8 10 9 7 5 3 1

Designed and typeset in Minion by Libanus Press, Marlborough
Printed and bound in Great Britain
by Clays Ltd, St Ives plc

To Joanna

PART ONE

STOOGING AROUND

CORKSCREW

1

"I am the Lord thy God," said Air Commodore Bletchley. "I say to this man, Go, and he goeth; and to another, Come, and he cometh . . . Do sit down. Cup of tea?"

"No thank you, sir."

"Good decision, it's pure poison. How d'you fancy a posting to Greenland?"

Bletchley had an office in the Air Ministry. If he lost any more weight he would be too thin. His hair was grey and years of brushing had beaten any insolence out of it. His hands rested on his desk, one of top of the other; his body didn't move. His eyes were as bright as his buttons and his voice was crisp and brisk. He made Silk nervous.

"I don't know much about Greenland, sir."

"It's towards the north. Somewhat icy. Sunstroke is not a problem. You'd be an airfield controller. Last chap got killed by a polar bear. They stand nine feet tall and run like the wind."

"Good God."

"The chap before him went insane. He kept seeing animals at the foot of his bed. Guess what they were."

"Um . . . pink elephants?"

"Polar bears. With green spots. Imagine that." Still Bletchley was motionless. "Or I could post you to Bombay, India. Our psychiatrist there needs help in assessing the dementia of aircrew. Does that interest you?

"All pilots are a bit demented." Silk was beginning to get the measure of Bletchley. "You've got to be a bit demented to want to fly."

"Bombay is unlike Greenland. The Indians have twenty-nine words for typhoid fever and seventeen for malaria. The flies breed by the billion."

"If they like it so much," Silk said, "they can have it, sir."

"That leaves the Aden posting. Crash investigation officer. Right up your street, Silk. Lots of action, thrills, drama."

"Action, sir? At a crash site?"

"From the Arabs. They regard the wreckage as their property. You have to fight them for it."

At last Bletchley moved. He cocked his head an inch to the left.

"So either way, it's death," Silk said. "Just a matter of deciding whether to be frozen, baked, or shot into little pieces by ten thousand fanatical fuzzy-wuzzies. Sir."

"Or I could post you to Washington D.C., and you could make a morale-boosting tour of American war industries."

Silk had had enough. He didn't care what the air commodore said or thought or did. He relaxed, and looked away, and spun his hat on his forefinger. "You're pulling my pisser, aren't you, sir?"

"I am the Lord thy God, Silk, and when I say to thee, Go to Washington, thou goeth. Starting now." He clapped his hands, once.

Silk stood up. "Washington. Bloody hell. Why me?"

Bletchley left the desk and took him by the elbow. "One: you're a double-tour-expired decorated hero, so we're not going to let you kill yourself. Bad publicity. Two: the U.S. Air Force sent James Stewart over here, in uniform, flying bombers. We need a counterweight over there. You're not James Stewart but in a bad light you might be David Niven's younger brother. And three: if you stay here

10

you'll only make a thundering nuisance of yourself. Off you go."

Silk went into the outer office. An elderly flying officer saw the look on his face. "Polar bears?" he said. "Everyone gets polar bears."

"Is there a reason?"

"He spent too long with the Desert Air Force. Too many good types bought it in order to help win a bit of desert that looks like any other bit of desert, and in the end he went sand-happy. Wore a loin cloth, told everyone he was Florence of Arabia. Desert Air Force sent him home to be cured, Air Ministry gave him a desk which he hates. And now he plays his little games."

"So . . . am I going to America, or not?"

The flying officer gave him a large envelope, heavy with documents. "Sailing from Liverpool, the day after tomorrow."

"He knew that, all along."

"Look, Bletchley's no fool," the flying officer said. "He gets the postings right. He does it in his own way, that's all." He glanced at the purple-and-white ribbon on Silk's tunic. "Nobody gets a medal for cracking up, do they? Give your life for your country, and you might get a gong. Give your sanity, you get damn-all."

On the train back to Lincoln, Silk thought about that. He wondered if Bletchley had known what was happening to his mind as he became sand-happy in the desert. Or was madness like malaria, a thing that took charge silently and secretly? Crept into your mind like an earwig crawling into your ear? Nothing lasts forever. Keep stretching an elastic band, and it snaps. Maybe Bletchley's sanity simply wore itself out. Could a weakness like that be inherited? There was great-aunt Phoebe on his mother's side, rumoured to be only tenpence in the shilling.

Silk was glad when he reached Lincoln, drove to the cottage and told Zoë he was posted to Washington. She wept.

It startled him. Women were so damned unpredictable. But after two minutes her tears suddenly stopped, and she was back to normal. Proved nothing, of course. Great-aunt Phoebe looked perfectly normal when she wasn't hiding the spoons up the chimney. What a day.

2

That was in 1943. A bleak year everywhere. The U-boat war in the Atlantic was a brutal business. In Russia, both sides counted their losses in whole armies. Fighting in the Pacific had developed into a bloody slog. In Britain, U.S. bombers were attacking Germany by day and paying a heavy butcher's bill for it. R.A.F. bombers raided by night. They'd been in action for more than three years, so the job prospects were well known, although not advertised.

There was a large element of luck. Bomb Berlin or the Ruhr and you might suffer ten per cent losses; keep that up and ten raids would wipe out the whole unit. On the other hand, leaflet raids over France were easy meat: you might lose only one per cent, perhaps none. But an operational tour in Bomber Command meant thirty missions, mostly over Germany. The grim arithmetic of war meant that only a minority of crews survived a full tour. A second tour was twenty missions, and the odds against surviving both tours were not worth thinking about. Silk never thought about them. Waste of time. From the start, he let life and death happen all around him, and that included Tony Langham marrying Zoë. The wedding was in Lincoln cathedral. Silk was his best man. Obviously.

Silk and Langham were a double-act. Joined the R.A.F. together, trained together, got their wings on the same day, joined 409 Squadron in nice time to fight World War Two. Silk thought Tony was very lucky to get Zoë, she being intelligent and young and rich, with a figure that made grown men on the other side of the street walk into lampposts.

Their happiness was a poke in the ribs for Silk. Life was for living, not flushing down the toilet. 409 was based at R.A.F. Kindrick in Lincolnshire; Langham and Zoë rented a nearby cottage and kept open house. Silk dropped in whenever ops allowed, took his meals there, played cards, had a bath, slept on the couch, left some clothes. "It's fun," Zoë told him. "Find yourself a popsy, Silko. Get married, be happy."

"Someone like you?"

"Someone you like. And don't frown. It gives you wrinkles."

"Signs of maturity and wisdom, darling. Don't worry, Tony will never get them."

He was right about that. A month later, Langham went down over Osnabrück. No parachutes were seen.

Silk drove to the cottage. Empty. People told him she'd gone to London. 409 was glad of that: nobody wanted a black widow hanging about the airfield: it was bad luck. He tried to write a letter, couldn't find the words. A terrible shock? Not true: crews got the chop every night. Awfully sorry? That wouldn't make her feel any better. He gave up. Best to forget them both.

Then, almost a year later, Zoë turned up at Kindrick. She never explained why, and Silk didn't ask. Meeting her was a pleasant surprise and falling into bed seemed very natural. Those were two small and happy facts. Against them stood the large fact of the war. Silk knew that his future was never a problem, because he had no future. When Zoë went back to London he could kiss her goodbye and forget her. Ops were his life, not women. It didn't work.

They met again. She told him that, when Langham died, she had been pregnant. They had told nobody, and without Langham she had no reason to stay in Lincolnshire. Now she had a baby, a girl called Laura. Silk didn't know what to make of that discovery. He wondered if he had a moral duty to Zoë, as Langham's best friend, and immediately knew that was bullshit. Maybe he was in love. Would that explain why she refused to get out of his mind? It annoyed him, her persistent presence. He hadn't planned to fall in love. It was a damn nuisance. This was a ridiculous state of affairs in the middle of a war. He got forty-eight hours leave and went to London to straighten things out.

They were in her Albany apartment, drinking gin. Little Laura was far from the dangers of London, being cared for by her grandmother at her house in the Cotswolds. Langham had wanted a daughter, and Zoë was quite proud of the baby, but motherhood did not dominate her life.

For Silk, it had been a slow and tedious rail trip, and now that he'd arrived he wasn't at all sure what he wanted to say.

Zoë was bored with the war. "Have you seen the underwear the shops are selling?" she asked Silk. "No, I suppose you haven't. Quite brutal. Totalitarian. Suitable for Jugoslav lady partisans, I suppose, but personally I'd sooner go naked."

"It's the price of victory," Silk said.

"Too high."

"What a damned shame. We'd better have a ceasefire, while I ask Air Ministry if they can spare a parachute or two. How many square yards of silk d'you need to gird up your delicate loins?"

She stared, not quite smiling. "Why are you so angry?"

"I'm not *angry*." He tried staring back, and couldn't do it, and drank gin instead. "You're the one who's fed-up."

Zoë went to close the curtains. As she passed behind him, she tickled his neck and saw his shoulders stiffen. "There you go again," she said. "Always looking for a fight."

"I don't like being touched."

"Yes you do. You're absolutely itching to be touched." She sat down and crossed her legs. Since he couldn't look at her face he looked at her legs. Stupendous was the word that came to mind. They wouldn't last, of course. Nothing lasted. By the time she was ninety . . . He couldn't complete that thought. Zoë was talking.

"I told my gynaecologist about you yesterday. He's not surprised you're permanently angry. He says that subconsciously you believe I killed Tony."

"Bollocks."

"Yes, he said you'd probably say that. But Tony was your pal, and then I came along, and who else can you blame?"

"For a gynaecologist, he's a bloody awful trick cyclist."

"Now you're angry with him."

"I don't give a toss about him. Or Langham. Or you."

They sat in silence. The only light came from the gas fire. Silk was sprawled on the couch. *Well, that's well and truly buggered everything,* he thought.

"He's really an awfully good gynaecologist," Zoë said. "What you call my delicate loins are in perfect working condition."

"Oh, Christ Almighty," Silk said weakly. He had run out of rage. "Romance. Bloody romance. That's not fair."

"Come on, Silko." She helped him up. "The bed is in the bedroom. Convenient, isn't it?"

3

Silk vetoed Lincoln Cathedral and they got married at Marylebone Road Register Office. Freddy the navigator was one witness. Zoë's gynaecologist was the other. Silk had not liked that choice. "He'll be there as a friend," Zoë said. "And if you had any idea how much he charges by the hour, you'd feel flattered."

"If he so much as smirks at me, I'll thump him."

"Goodness, you are touchy. I'll tell him to look grim and dyspeptic. Will that suit you?"

The ceremony went off smoothly. They left the office and stood in the street, congratulating each other. "Well done, Freddy," Silk said.

"All I did was bring the ring, old boy."

"But you did it with such *panache*," Zoë said.

The gynaecologist had brought champagne and glasses. "Now," he said. "Before the gloss goes off the union." He thumbed the cork off a bottle and it hit a passing major in the Polish army on the left ear. The major got the first glass. He kissed Zoë, and then kissed Silk. He proposed a long Polish toast, and stayed to the last of the champagne. "We could do with you in the rear turret," Freddy told the gynaecologist.

* * *

No honeymoon. Wartime Britain was not the place for that. All the hideaway hotels had been requisitioned by the War Office as headquarters for infantry training exercises. Silk and Zoë went to the same cottage, midway between R.A.F. Kindrick and Lincoln, where she had lived with Langham. It smelt of mould.

"You'd think the landlord would have lit a fire, or something," Silk said.

"I'm the landlord," Zoë said. "Didn't I tell you? After I lost Tony, I didn't want any squalid strangers living here, so I bought it."

Silk stared. "Tony bought it. And then you bought it."

16

She breathed on a mirror and wiped it with her sleeve. "I hope that was a joke."

"Sorry. It just slipped out."

He took their bags upstairs. In the bedroom, on a windowsill, lay the dried remains of a pigeon. Got in somehow, down the chimney perhaps, couldn't get out. He picked it up by a tiny claw and carried it downstairs. "Dead bird," he said. "Sort of symbolic, isn't it?"

"No."

"Oh." He went out and tossed the pigeon into some nettles and came back. She was reading a newspaper that was brown with age. "He's dead, you know," Silk said. "They don't come any deader than old Tony. I hope you're not turning this place into a shrine. I can't live in a shrine."

"We must have a party. Tomorrow. A sodding great pisser of a party. Open house for a week."

"I can't live in a pub, either."

"I can. An alcoholic shrine. Like Lourdes, only with gin galore. You'll love it, darling. Which reminds me: it's nine hours since we made whoopee."

"Scandalous. Just when the government keeps nagging us not to waste anything."

He followed her upstairs, taking off his tie, undoing his collar stud, his shirt buttons, his cuffs. Already his pulse was beginning to race. "You think sex solves everything, don't you?" he said. He tugged at his laces. One got knotted. He used both hands and dragged the shoe off and threw it into a corner. "Sex doesn't make the world go round," he said. "It makes it go slightly elliptical." She laughed. That was reward enough. And there was so much more to come.

* * *

17

Marriage was a new and delightful experience. Ops were not. Ops continued to be the hard labour of dumping loads of high explosive on German cities, night after night, while flak and nightfighters tried to blow the bombers to bits, preferably before they dropped their loads. Sometimes a nightfighter went down in flames, hit by an air gunner or occasionally by friendly flak. Sometimes a crippled bomber exploded and took another bomber with it. Highflying German aircraft dropped pyrotechnic displays called "Scarecrows" that resembled burning bombers, or so it was said. Other pilots rejected the idea: the night sky over Germany had victims enough without playing the fool with stupid bloody fireworks. That was true. Ops hurt Germany, but the pain had to be paid for.

In 1943, when he was well into his second tour, Silk knew that a few of the men on their first tour had mixed feelings about him. They were amazed that he and his crew had survived so long, but they suspected that this might be at the cost of crews who had failed to return. There was only so much good luck to go around. Silk was getting an unfair share. What was his trick?

He had no trick. He was a good pilot and he kept learning from experience. This was something you couldn't teach the newcomers. After an op, if there was an empty table in the mess, chances were the missing crew was inexperienced. Silk didn't let it worry him. Nobody said the chop was fair. Equally, nobody said dodging the chop was fair. You made the most of life while it lasted. Silk's new life was flying.

He liked the Lancaster. It was his workplace, his office. Every time he opened all four throttles and turned the Merlins' roar into a thundering bellow and felt the controls become alive and the undercarriage hammer the tarmac until finally the bomber came unstuck and the engines stopped shouting and began singing: every time that happened, he felt privileged.

He knew the price of that privilege. From the outside the Lancaster looked formidable. From the inside it was a long alloy tube stuffed with explosives and aviation fuel. Silk had seen too many Lancasters falling out of the night sky over Germany, burning like beacons. All aircrew believed that some other poor bastard would get the chop, not them. All aircrew except Silk; until one night they flew to Stuttgart, and even Silk began to wonder.

4

He'd been there before. About five hundred miles from base to target. The flight plan would include plenty of twists and turns, all with the aim of keeping the German fighter controllers off-balance, hoping to con them into scrambling their night fighters over the wrong city. These detours would add a hundred miles to the op. A fully loaded Lancaster could cruise at 180 or 190 miles an hour, depending on wind strength and direction. So Silk's crew expected to spend four hours or so over Europe, mostly over Germany.

It was a biggish raid: 343 Lancasters. The bomber stream began to cross the North Sea at 10 p.m. Silk was at fifteen thousand feet, still climbing, eating a corned-beef sandwich. Things began to go wrong. The port outer engine was losing revs. With unequal power, the Lanc was edging to the left.

Silk dropped his sandwich and applied a little rudder to straighten the bomber. He throttled back the starboard outer to equalize the action, and he looked at Cooper, the flight engineer. "Your rotten engine is mucking me about, Coop," he said.

"Temperature's okay, oil pressure's normal. Electrics are working. Could be we lost a cylinder but I don't think so."

The port outer got no worse but five minutes later the starboard outer lost some power and from then on, at one time or another, each of the four engines gave trouble, and the Lancaster couldn't keep its place in the stream.

Silk concentrated on flying the aeroplane. He trusted Cooper to nurse the Merlins and keep the airscrews churning. The Lanc was a frighteningly complex machine. Sometimes – not often – Silk had watched his ground crew at work, exposing the criss-cross networks of tubes and cables and rods: hydraulic, pneumatic, electric, oxygen supply, flying controls, fuel system, ammunition ducts, de-icing system, fire extinguisher system, intercom, engine controls, bomb fusing system, cockpit heating, and a whole lot more. It didn't pay to think of the things that might go wrong. He left the ground crew to it.

The Lanc was over Holland when Cooper said: "Dirty fuel, skip."

"You sure?"

"Pretty certain. Explains why the engines go sick and get well and go sick again, well again."

"How can petrol be dirty? They filter it when they fuel the kite, don't they?"

"Maybe the tanks got dirty."

"Come off it, Coop."

"They clean the tanks every time a Lanc has a major overhaul, skip. Why clean them if they're not dirty?"

The port inner coughed and backfired and made a stream of sparks, and went back to business.

"I hate to get this far and quit," Silk said.

"Nav to pilot," Freddy said. "New course in one minute."

"Thank you, Freddy. Deeply appreciated."

"You could have had it ten minutes ago, skip, but you're so damn slow."

Silk didn't quit. If he turned back now he would be cutting across the bomber stream and then flying against it. Not a pleasant thought. His present situation was bad enough, drifting back through the passing stream. The rear gunner was searching the blackness for any oncoming bomber. Silk's machine was trailing a long slipstream of broken air. A following pilot should feel the warning tremble at 600 yards' range and be rocked by turbulence at 400 yards. But what if the other Lanc was not behind but alongside? Changing direction, changing height. Cruising at 180 m.p.h., a Lanc covered 88 yards a second. Even a gentle nudge would be enough to weld two aircraft into a blazing memorial to dirty fuel. Once already, Silk had been forced to bank steeply to escape the shape of a wandering Lanc that had lurched out of black nowhere and vanished into the same nowhere just as quickly.

All the same, he decided it was safer to stay in the stream. There was the added protection against enemy fighters. The risk of collision was acceptable because a stream was not a close formation. Bomber Command did not attempt that kind of insanity at night. From head to tail, the stream of 343 Lancasters made a column about sixty miles long and three miles wide. Each navigator knew the route and the turning points. He'd been told to be on time so that the whole force would bomb the target as a mass, saturating its defences, in and out in twenty minutes. If any crew straggled or strayed, that was their funeral.

Silk's dirty fuel kept him drifting back. He could never rest. His eyes felt strained and weary from the labour of always searching the night, with nothing to focus on. Finally, Freddy told him they were thirty minutes late, which meant they must be clear of the stream. Later, Silk saw the target ahead. When he reached it, his was the only Lanc over Stuttgart. The city was burning hard. He bombed it and stayed on a straight and level course for the camera, although he knew his bomb-bursts would be lost in all that flame and fury.

Freddy stood beside him and looked down at Stuttgart. Normally he never left his navigator's position behind the cockpit; this was a brief reward. "Crikey," he said. "Someone's been playing with matches."

The rear gunner shouted: "Corkscrew port!"

Freddy reaching out to grab something, anything, but his fist closed on air, the floor slanted, his boots skidded sideways and his head whacked metal. Sparks chased across his eyes. The Lanc was banking steeply and plunging so hard that he feared it must be damaged, out of control, crashing. Through a haze of dust he saw Silk's boots on the rudder pedals, his hands on the control column. Hands and feet moved, violently. The Lanc got slung from a hard left-hand bank to a hard right-hand bank, from a steep dive to a steep climb. Freddy felt as if he'd left his guts behind. The sparks drained away. He saw tracer pulsing in the night. Then the Lanc corkscrewed left and plunged again. The wings must fall off. Freddy counted his last seconds, got to five and Silk threw the Lanc from left bank to right bank and it went up like a lift. *It's not a bloody Spitfire,* Freddy thought. *Still, the engines must be okay.* The Lanc plunged. *No bloody night fighter can catch us like this,* Freddy thought. Silk corkscrewed again.

* * *

They were the last aircraft to land at Kindrick.

Every Intelligence Officer had a nickname. At 409 he was called Skull because his head looked a bit like one and it was full of brains. After he had asked his usual questions, he said: "Anything unusual happen?"

"Silko corkscrewed us halfway across Germany," Freddy said. "Is that a new world record?"

"It was only over Stuttgart," Silk said. "Routine evasion. Shook off the Jerry."

"Nearly shook off the tail unit," Freddy said. "I only mention it because the operating manual forbids aerobatics. Should we tell the manufacturers?"

The I.O. screwed the cap on his fountain pen. "Let's not," he said. "It'll be our little secret."

As they went out, Group Captain Rafferty, the station commander, said, "Damned good show." Every night of ops, Rafferty stayed up until the last crew had landed at Kindrick or until there was no point in waiting; and he always said the same thing. He was right. Just to bomb the target and fly home again was a damned good show.

The aircrew meal was always bacon and egg. Freddy slid his egg onto Silk's plate. "That's for getting us home," he said.

Silk was too tired to argue.

"I nearly shot down the night fighter," the rear gunner told Cooper. "Give me your egg."

"Tell you what: I'll eat it for you first," Cooper said. "Then you can have it tomorrow."

"That's in very poor taste," the rear gunner said.

"Not if you put lots of Worcester Sauce on it," Cooper said. "Brings out the flavour a real treat."

"Rotten shots," Silk said. They looked at him. "Stuttgart," he said. "Just us, and all their flak and fighters. Pitiful. If that's the best they can do, they don't deserve to win the damn war."

Nobody argued.

*

The flight engineer and the rear gunner didn't finish their tours. On a day when Silk's crew were off duty, not required, the engineer in another Lanc walked into a glass door, split his scalp and got double vision. Cooper volunteered to take his place and the bomber went down over Kassel. And of course the tail was always the most dangerous position in the aeroplane. Silk was bringing them back from a raid on Bremen when his rear gunner caught a glimpse of a Messerschmitt-110 a fraction of a second too late and a burst from the night fighter killed him. Silk saw tracers going past and he corkscrewed. Already both rudders were a mess, but the corkscrew was so violent that the fighter overshot the Lanc and, in the ocean of night, never found it again.

So, against all the odds and against his expectations, Silk completed his second tour.

* * *

He was the first pilot on 409 Squadron to accomplish this. There had to be a party.

The Group Commander came, made a speech, congratulated Silk on his second D.F.C. Nobody was surprised, everyone cheered.

Rafferty made a speech. He denied the foul slander that the only reason Silk had achieved his double tour was because the Huns knew he would make a bigger bloody nuisance of himself back here than over there. Laughter and prolonged applause.

By now, the beer was at work. Wisely, the Squadron Commander said only a few words. "Sixty ops is a lot," he began. "Silko did it in units of ten. This was because he can't add up to more than ten without being arrested for indecent exposure." A wave of laughter, then a second wave from those who had been slow to get the joke. "But he deserves all our admiration. And we deserve to know the secret of his success, so we can bottle it for the Mess!"

Warm applause. Silk stood on a chair. "I remember the first time I met Bomber Harris," he said. That silenced them. Most had never seen the head of Bomber Command, a burly, unsmiling air chief marshal whose goal was to win the war by flattening every German town and city. This would make invasion unnecessary. His determination was respected. His power was feared. Presumably his wife loved him. Nobody else did, which suited him fine. He didn't want love, he wanted the steady tramp of high explosives down every German street, followed by the patter of a million incendiaries.

Silk continued: "I said to him, 'Who are you?', and he said, 'A.C.2 Harris,' and I said, 'That's amazing. Why are you only an A.C.2?' and he said, 'Because there's no such rank as A.C.3' Very witty, Bert was . . .'"

More laughter, cut short. Nobody wanted to miss a word.

"Bert Harris and I were friends from the start," Silk said. "He was sweeping the hangar floor, using the intelligence officer's silk knickers for the purpose, nothing's too good for Bomber Command, and I knew at once this man was going places. In fact I said, 'You've got the stuff of greatness in you, Bert', and he said, 'What a relief, I thought I was six months pregnant.'"

That went down well. Even a visiting air vice-marshal smiled.

"I wasn't flying that day. I was dressed as usual, just a tweed skirt, tight sweater, rather daring, I suppose, and a gypsy headscarf. So I asked Bert, 'D'you know who I am?' and quick as a flash he said, 'Juicy Lucy from Lincoln, and have you got change for a shilling?'"

That went down very well, except with the air vice-marshal.

"None of that's true, I made it all up," Silk said. Groans of disapproval. "Even the silk knickers. Intelligence is *tight*, you know that, they *never* give anything away. Actually, I borrowed them from a chap in the Provost-Marshal's office. Awfully sweet fellow."

A storm of derision. The Provost-Marshal's office investigated crime, such as using aviation fuel in a private car. By now, the air vice-marshal had stopped smiling. He was talking to Rafferty.

"Where was I?" Silk said. "Oh, yes. You all know Bert Harris, full of merry quips and banter. So I said to him, 'Come on, Bert, tell me a witty joke, something I can use to make my crew laugh on a really filthy night over Bremen when the flak's as thick as pigshit.' Bomber Harris turned to me, and quick as a flash – and witty with it – he said, 'Why don't you fuck off?'" The roar of laughter made the air vice-marshal flinch. "Bloody good advice," Silk said. "And that's exactly what I've been doing for two tours: fucking off as fast as I could." The C.O. was tugging his tunic. "For my next trick . . ." Silk began. The C.O. tugged harder and Silk fell off the chair. Everyone cheered.

The C.O. helped him up. "Christ, Silko, I shall be bloody glad to see the back of you." Elsewhere, "For He's A Jolly Good Fellow" was being sung lustily. "Now get yourself good and plastered and stay as far away from that air vice-marshal as possible." He gave Silk a beer and moved off.

Rafferty came over with a bundle of congratulatory telegrams. "Very amusing speech, flight lieutenant," he said. "It rather explains why you never made squadron leader. And never will."

"Thank you, sir. I never trusted squadron leaders. Ambitious buggers." Rafferty grunted. "Of course, group captains like yourself are scholars and gentlemen and a boon to the Service."

They were silent for a moment, looking at the crowd.

"That bloody fool of an A.V.M. wanted you placed under close arrest," Rafferty said. "I talked him out of it, this being your big night and the boys getting tanked-up."

"I couldn't make a proper speech," Silk said. "Not my style."

"Well, you've had the last laugh. From tomorrow, you're off 409 Squadron. Where next, I don't know."

"Two tours have got to mean something," Silk said. "Any old cockpit will do. Not Training Command. I've done that. Ropey old kites. Terrifying."

"You'll do what you're bloody well told, Silko. The war is not for your benefit."

"They can't ground me. If they ground me, I swear to God, I'll desert and join the Luftwaffe."

"There you go again," Rafferty said wearily. "The wrong way down a one-way street."

Silk sipped his beer. It tasted thin; he didn't want it. He felt flat. How could he have been so lucky and yet end up so flat?

SWEET BLIND O'REILLY

1

On the morning after the squadron party to celebrate completing his second tour, Silk put his bags in his little lemon-yellow Frazer-Nash and drove to the cottage. He didn't say goodbye to anyone, not even his crew. He had said goodbye, silently, to each of them, long ago.

It would be fun to be kissed by Zoë, to tell her about his second D.F.C. and let her read all the telegrams. Then they would celebrate with a bit of rumpty-tumpty. Or a lot. He had two weeks to kill. She wasn't there.

He dumped the suitcases. Maybe there was a note on the kitchen table. Nothing. Maybe she was asleep, hadn't heard his voice. *You're getting bloody desperate, Silko*, he told himself. He tramped upstairs, making the treads creak, and found the cat asleep on the bed. She was a little cat, black with white paws, and she made the bed look very big and very empty. "I bet you're glad to see me, puss," he said. She opened her eyes a crack and studied him. "Silko," he said. "D.F.C. and Bar. Remember?" She yawned.

He sat on the bed and tickled her stomach. She stretched and doubled in length and rolled onto her back. "I can make Zoë do that," he said. The cat showed her claws and made an upside-down grin. "Not that, though," he said.

He went downstairs, boiled a kettle, made a pot of tea. He was looking for milk when the thought occurred that Zoë might be ill, suddenly stricken, lying in hospital in Lincoln. Stricken . . . That was a damnfool word. Nobody in England had been stricken since the Black Death. For no reason, it reminded him of the writing bureau in the sitting room. Might as well check it out.

Nothing there.

This was like coming home to the *Marie* bloody *Celeste*. He opened the top drawer of the bureau. Full of stationery. In the bottom drawer he found his letters: three bundles, each tied with a ribbon. So she cared enough to keep his not-very-brilliant letters. Why was that a surprise? But it was. It made him feel suddenly valuable. An uncomfortable feeling.

He stood in the middle of the room and tried to make sense of his life. It seemed to have purpose without direction. Or was it direction without purpose? Bollocks. Too early in the day for that sort of tosh.

Silk put the bundles of letters back in the bureau drawer, at first trying to make it look as if they had never been disturbed, then getting annoyed with himself for wishing to hide something from his wife when it was perfectly harmless, even likeable; so he turned the bundles sideways, making the change obvious. Why? Stupid thing to do. He slammed the drawer. It jammed, half-shut. "Sweet suffering buggeration!" he shouted. He raised his foot to kick the drawer just as the cat came into the room, yawning. He balanced on the other foot. "I suppose you want some milk, puss," he said. The cat sniffed the raised shoe. "It's a long story," he said.

They went into the kitchen, and he watched the cat drink some milk. It sat and washed its face. "Bloody good show," he said. "You deserve a gong."

He changed into some old clothes and went out and did what he usually did when he felt flat: he bashed the garden. Zoë couldn't find a gardener in wartime, so brambles and nettles and giant cow parsley had a free run. Silk hacked and slashed with a billhook, his favourite weapon. He dragged the stuff into a heap and lit a bonfire. It made a lot of smoke but very little flame. "Couple of nice 110-pound incendiaries, that's what we need," he said. He was poking newspaper into the heap when a car arrived. Zoë's taxi.

She was wearing a deep red outfit, just a slim skirt and single-breasted tunic, almost military in style, and a modest black cap with a short veil. The cottage was shabby, the garden was wrecked, even the bonfire was not a success; but in Silk's eyes all the colours brightened now that Zoë was there. *Lucky, lucky me,* he thought.

"London is the purest hell," she said. She made it sound like rain at Ascot. "Weak gin, and a choice of shepherd's pie or spam fritters. You look very dashing, darling." She kissed him, full throttle. His hands were filthy, so he did not embrace her. She kissed him again. "What lovely lips you have. Could you get changed, darling?

"Where are we going?"

"Lunch, obviously. With the bishop of Lincoln." She picked a dead leaf from his sweater. "We're organizing the Salute For Stalin Week. I've got five thousand ladies knitting socks for the Red Army. You will make a speech, won't you, darling?"

"Dozens. I've got another D.F.C."

"Silko, what perfect timing."

"And I'm off ops. I'm grounded." That surprised her. Eyebrows went up, lips parted. "*Well*," she said. "I mean, sweet blind O'Reilly, Silko. Grounded? For good? Honestly?" The bonfire crackled. For years afterwards, whenever he heard a fire crackle, it brought back that day, that moment when he and Zoë looked at each other and realized the disaster of death was postponed. It had been pointless to think about years of married life while the nightly chop was waiting over Germany. Now they were totally, inescapably married, probably for a very long time. She was enormously relieved. Two years ago, when Tony died, grief had been dumped on her like a freakish cloudburst, and she had found it an ugly, exhausting experience. One load of grief was enough; she couldn't take another. It was simply unacceptable. Her mother had buried three husbands and all she'd got out of it was money and gallstones. And a title. So: *grounded* sounded fine. Silko looked good, tousled, a bit piratical with bonfire smudges on his face, and amazingly, wonderfully alive.

"The bishop won't mind if we're a little late, will he?" he said. She took his arm and they strolled to the cottage. "You can tell him we were consummating our holy union. The church is very hot on that."

"Two gongs," she said. "I married a man with two gongs."

"One's called Rumpty and the other's called Tumpty. Knock them together and they chime the hours."

That's better, she thought. Silko had survived, and she had five thousand ladies knitting socks for Stalin. Little Laura was safe in Dublin, which was neutral, being cared for by an aunt. Time to make whoopee. The bloody silly war could wait.

2

Silk enjoyed his leave. There was nothing to look forward to, nothing to plan, nothing to avoid: no Stuttgart, no Bremen, no Essen, especially no Berlin.

Zoë's involvement in Salute For Stalin Week brought with it a supply of petrol coupons. They drove around the Lincolnshire towns and villages, giving pep talks to Women's Institutes and Mothers' Unions, to Gardening Clubs and Townswomen's Guilds. He stood behind her, in uniform, looking handsome yet modest, while she savaged the *Wehrmacht*.

"We always knew the Hun was gutless," she said. "Now his guts are strewn across the bloody battlefield of Russia. Stalin's gallant troops are stamping out Hitler's vile stormtroopers, stamping them out with strong Russian boots and warm English socks! From you! Think as you knit – think that your needles are stabbing the heart of Nazi Germany!" And so on. The ladies enjoyed it enormously. Silk added a very few words. "Any one of you could fly a Lanc," he said. "Piece of cake. I couldn't knit to save my life. Damn good show. Wizard prang." He smiled, shyly. They loved him.

Ten minutes later he accelerated away in a crackle of exhaust from the little Frazer-Nash while Zoë fluttered a handkerchief to the waving hands.

Two or three talks a day. The rest of the time they motored around the county, stopping occasionally to look at a ruined abbey or to stroll along a riverbank that had picturesque swans on one side and inquisitive cattle on the other. Then lunch. Zoë knew all the best black-market restaurants, and they knew her. If the weather turned foul, she navigated Silk to the nearest big house. One day, in a cloud-burst, it was Tattershall Castle. "What a pile!" Silk said. "It's like the Tower of London." Rain was lashing the windscreen, melting the battlements. "It's got a *moat*. Are you sure you know these people?"

"Felicity was at Cheltenham Ladies College with me." Zoë leaned across and punched the horn. "Rode in a point-to-point without permission, got the sack. Came second, though." More horn. "Ah! Results." Servants appeared with golfing umbrellas.

"Have you been here before?"

"Finest lavatories in the county, Silko. Your tubes have a treat in store."

Felicity gave them tea. Later, Silk peed into a superb lavatory and told his bladder how lucky it was to be in a fifteenth-century castle with twentieth-century plumbing. Then he told himself how lucky *he* was. Zoë could have smiled at any one of a thousand men, cleverer, better-looking, braver, and the chap would have jumped at the chance. Silk looked in the mirror. Double D.F.C. No visible scars. Zoë was no fool, so she must have found *something* special in him. That was good enough.

Life with Zoë was all fun, and that was rare in the middle of a war. Money helped. Lots of money helped a lot. He slipped easily into her lifestyle. They fell easily into bed. As they lay together, joined snugly at the loins, he heard the squadrons circling, making height, and he thought: *I've done all that, so I deserve all this.* Next day the telegram arrived. Report to Air Commodore Bletchley at Air Ministry.

YOU CAN SHOVEL ALL YOU LIKE

1

The air attaché at the Washington embassy was Group Captain Hardy, a stubby man in a light grey suit. As they shook hands, he made a rapid study of Silk's face. "No visible scars, thank Christ," he said. "The last man London sent us had first-degree burns and a lisp. No use at all. Imagine showing him to American mothers. Your boy goes for aircrew and comes back looking like overdone steak and talking like a pansy."

"Very inconsiderate of him," Silk said.

"Spare me your wit. It won't ring any bells over here. I was a pilot once, I know all about crashes, I felt sorry for the poor devil. But this isn't Europe, it isn't even a different country, it's a different *world*." They followed the porter to Hardy's car. "The ambassador wants a quick word. Then we've got you a hotel room. Not de luxe, but Washington's stuffed to the gills with people, and it's only for one night."

The ambassador was tall and slim, and he made Silk feel that his arrival was the high point of the day. "I do congratulate you on your second D.F.C.," he said. "We are privileged indeed. It can't be right that you are still only a flight lieutenant."

"Natural phenomenon, sir. Like the eclipse of the sun."

The ambassador smiled. "Jolly good . . . But it won't do. Americans feel shortchanged by any rank less than squadron leader. We leaned on Air Ministry and you are now an acting squadron leader."

"Let's get that third ring sewn on lickety-split, shall we?" Hardy said. He helped Silk take off his tunic and he left the room.

"Three things I feel you should know," the ambassador said. "Steer clear of the race business, Negroes, segregation, their Civil War – it's a minefield, and it's *their* minefield, so leave it to them. Homosexuality is another hazard. Americans believe it's compulsory in England. They fear for their manhood; that's why they shout so much. When in doubt, ask them to explain their gridiron football. They like that. And above all, never discuss politics. Your wife is doing truly splendid work in the Salute For Stalin campaign, isn't she? Say nothing of that. Americans tolerate Russia as long as it's six thousand miles away. Here, they consider Socialism a transmittable disease, like cholera." He smiled. "All tickety-boo?"

"Yes sir." But this wasn't what Silk had expected. The song about America said *Anything Goes*. Obviously, anything didn't go. "Complicated, isn't it?"

"Keep it simple, squadron leader. Just say we're winning, because we're best. Which, of course, we are."

2

Hardy had breakfast with him at the hotel. "Here's your speech," he said. "Memorize it. Stick to it. Stand up, speak up, shut up. Can you manage that?"

"Piece of cake." Typed, double-spaced, with wide margins, it made half a page. "One thing wrong: I never flew a Liberator. Have to change that."

"You flew a Liberator, Silk. Today's factory makes gun turrets for Liberators. They're not going to give up ten minutes of their lunch break to be told what a wonderful kite the Lanc is."

They drove to Baltimore, Maryland. The plant was vast. Half the workers were women. A manager introduced Squadron Leader Silk as one of Britain's knights of the sky who took the battle to the heart of the Nazi homeland, and the roar of applause startled him. The speech was easy. He told them the U.S. Air Force and the Royal Air Force together delivered a left-right punch that had Germany on the ropes, and they cheered. He said the Allied formula was simple: we're winning because we're best. They cheered. He said he'd flown the Liberator, he'd sat in its magnificent turrets, fired those 50-calibre guns, seen the havoc they caused, and every man and woman here should feel proud . . . the rest was drowned by a storm of cheering.

In the car, Hardy said: "Seven out of ten. Don't rush it. And don't grin. You're David Niven, not Jimmy bloody Cagney."

"Where next?"

"Allentown, Pennsylvania. Bomb factory. Same speech, tailored to suit the audience. Any ideas?"

Silk thought. "I could say the bomber's only as good as the bombs it drops."

Hardy grunted. "That's a start." He turned on the radio. "Ah . . . gospel music. I'm rather fond of gospel music."

3

At the end of a week they had worked their way through Connecticut, Rhode Island, Massachusetts, and New Hampshire. Silk had made fifteen speeches, praising the manufacture of everything from radios and bullets to flying boots and navigators' pencils. At night they stayed at the nearest air base. "Don't you find this boring?" Hardy asked.

"Compared with what? Flying home from Berlin with one engine on the fritz and a cookie hung up in the bomb bay? Yes, I suppose it is rather boring."

"Well, I've had enough. You don't need me. I'll take you back to Washington and put you on a plane to Chicago. You'll love the Midwest. It's ten times more boring than the East."

For the next two months, Silk toured factories making war material in Illinois, Indiana, Michigan, Wisconsin, Iowa, Nebraska, Kansas, Missouri. An officer from the Chicago consulate planned the itinerary, arranged the transport, paid the bills, organized the overnight laundry, quietly reminded Silk which state they were in just before he stepped forward to say how privileged he felt to be in it. They visited forty-two factories, Silk gave fifty-three interviews to radio stations and local papers, was photographed several times a day. If he felt lonely he wrote home: short, jokey letters. If he could find a little fluffy baby-toy for Laura, he sent that too. Did they ever arrive? He never knew. If Zoë ever wrote back, the mail never caught up with him.

At the end of the tour, a reporter asked him what he thought of America. He had answered that question a hundred times. Maybe a thousand.

"I had a dream last night," Silk said. "I was on a train crossing America, except it was going in circles, and I was in the locomotive with a shovel, stoking the furnace. And the engine driver said, 'There's good news and there's bad news. The bad news is you've got nothing to shovel but bullshit. The good news is you can shovel all you like.' Then I woke up."

"Don't print any of that," the consulate officer told the reporter.

"It's an old R.A.F. joke," Silk said. "Not very funny."

"The squadron leader is tremendously impressed by the energy and enthusiasm he has found everywhere," the officer said. "Against the forces of freedom, the enemy stands no chance at all."

The reporter left. "Sorry about that," Silk said. "Sometimes I have this odd sensation of being two people, in two places. I'm over *here*, watching myself make another speech over *there*. And I don't know which is the real me."

"You're doing brilliantly. Let's get a drink."

Next day he put Silk on a plane to Los Angeles. The man from the L.A. consulate met him. He was somewhat in awe. "You've made a tremendous impression back east, squadron leader," he said. "It feels like every war plant in California wants you."

"How many is that?"

"Around five hundred. Not all making aircraft, of course. Some are equipping the army or the marines. Still, it's all the same war, isn't it?" Silk could think of nothing to say. He looked away. "Ah! Now I see it," the man from the consulate said. "The eyes, and the mouth. A clear resemblance. That's very useful."

"Resemblance?"

"David Niven. The Washington embassy mentioned that you're related. Younger brother, is that right? Niven's awfully popular in Hollywood."

Silk rested against a pillar. "You can shovel all you like," he said. His legs slowly folded until he was sitting on the floor. "Five hundred fucking factories."

"More or less," the man said. "That's what you asked, wasn't it? You'll be visiting fifty. Only fifty."

"Can't do it." He slumped further. "I'll just lie down here and die."

"For God's sake . . . Stand up, squadron leader, please. There are photographers . . ." A couple of people had stopped to stare. "It's the heat," the man explained. "He'll be fine in a moment."

With their help he got Silk into his car. Silk said nothing on the way to the hotel, or in the elevator. He sat on the edge of his bed, too tired to take his shoes off. "You can lead a horse to water," he said, "but what does it get you?"

"Rest," the man advised. "You need rest."

"It gets you wet feet," Silk said. "But don't tell anyone."

"I'll pick you up at ten tomorrow morning."

When he arrived, Silk was wandering about the room, naked, reading the Gideon bible. His body was covered in a bright red rash. "The hotel doctor doesn't like the look of it," Silk said. "Personally, I think it's hideous. What do you think?"

The consulate cancelled Silk's tour. It sent a specialist in skin conditions, a burly, amiable American with a touch as delicate as a concert pianist's. Throughout his very thorough examination he chatted with Silk about England, and bombers, and where he'd been in America. It was a relaxed and comfortable conversation. "Do you see a lot of people like me?" Silk asked. "Red all over?"

"Well, there's Hollywood, of course. Movie-making can be hard on the nerves. All that make-up doesn't help."

"I knew a chap who wore make-up. Polish pilot. A touch of rouge on the cheeks, and he always slept in a hairnet. Brave as a lion. What we call a press-on type. Got the chop, of course. Over Osnabrück."

"Was he a good friend of yours?" the doctor asked.

"Certainly not," Silk said. "Chap gets the chop over Osnabrück, he's no friend of mine."

"Eyes wide open." The doctor stared into one, then the other. "Clear as gin . . . You play any sports?"

"Sex. Lots of sex. Not enough, though. And none at all, recently." He walked over to a full-length mirror. "You don't get as red as that from a touch of rouge," he said. "Looks more like a bucket of blood."

"I'll be back tomorrow. Drink lots of orange juice. It won't stop your rash, but it helps our economy."

4

Silk never saw him again.

There was a strong English colony in Hollywood which did its duty by providing hospitality for any compatriot in uniform who was passing through Los Angeles. Ronald Colman was accepted without question as the leader of the colony. He had played the perfect Englishman in so many hits that he was the unofficial British ambassador on the West Coast. His male secretary tapped on Silk's door, didn't even blink at what he saw, explained that Mr Colman thought Mr Silk might feel more comfortable as his guest in Beverly Hills. Stroll in the grounds, swim in the pool, watch a little cricket . . .

"Can't wear my uniform," Silk said. "Odd, isn't it?"

"Try this." The secretary had brought a pure silk dressing gown. "Belongs to Myrna Loy, but she has plenty more."

"Crikey." Silk slipped it on, warily. It felt like a cool evening breeze. "Strewth . . . Can I go out like this?"

"With your figure, I think you can carry it off."

The car was a white Rolls. When it stopped at lights, some passers-by shaded their eyes and waved. Silk waved back.

"What if they want my autograph?" he asked.

"Just write Errol Flynn. That's what I do." The white Rolls seemed to know its way home. With only a little help from the chauffeur, it strolled up a driveway and circled what Silk took to be an unusually handsome country club but which turned out to be Ronald Colman's home. His secretary had not been joking about cricket: the lawn was big enough. Sprinklers tossed small rainbows back and forth. Mexican gardeners hunted down weeds.

The Rolls stopped at a fake-Tudor cottage under a group of big shade trees. "Everything you need is in here," the secretary said, "and if it isn't, just pick up the phone. Mr Colman returns from the studio at six. Cocktails by the pool at seven."

"What should I wear?"

"Anything. An air of quiet confidence would be fine."

Silk searched a chest of drawers and found a pair of shorts, so flimsy that he wondered if they too belonged to Myrna Loy. He put them on. Not too painful. The kitchen was well stocked. The bathroom had a dozen towels, the thickest he had ever seen.

He went out and walked around the cottage, and saw a lush tropical bush where a hummingbird was doing its act. It glowed like a jewel. The wings were a blur, the tiny body shimmered with a golden green, a crimson, a purple, a bronze. This wasn't flying the way Silk flew. The hummingbird stood on thin air and tickled the depth of a blossom with its probe, an action that was pure sex without the embrace. Silk blinked and the creature had gone.

He moved on and found it again. Or maybe its pal. Another blossom was in luck. Next to this genius, an aeroplane was just a truck with roaring propellers. Other hummingbirds visited other bushes. He studied them until his eyes began to lose focus.

The day slipped away, pleasantly, painlessly. He sat in a garden chair. After a while, a yellow butterfly as big as his hand landed on his knee. Its antenna uncurled and tasted the red skin. "Mustard?" he asked. "Horseradish sauce?" It flew away, dodging imaginary enemies. "Drunk on duty," he said. "Court martial."

Later, he walked through the trees to the cricket pitch, moving from one piece of shade to another. There was a white wooden pavilion with a scoreboard. He went inside and at once the cool gloom swamped his senses. Cricket gear lay scattered about, just like school, and that special smell, what was its name? You rubbed it into the bat to preserve the wood. His damn stupid brain knew the word but it was being bloodyminded. He picked up a bat and swung it. Whoops! There was that schooldays smell again, ten times stronger. How idiotic, six thousand miles from home, in Los bloody Angeles, to get ambushed by the smell of cricket!

He dropped the bat and walked back to the cottage. His suitcases were in the bedroom. Somebody had gone to the hotel, packed his clothes and brought them over. Thanks very much. Awfully decent. They wanted him to relax. He hadn't relaxed in four years. Flying Hampdens, then Wellingtons, then Lancs, it didn't pay to relax. He put an Artie Shaw record on the gramophone. Relax and you might fly into a stuffed cloud. He looked at his watch. Eight hours' difference. Back at Kindrick the crews would be getting ready for ops, maybe. Not relaxed, certainly. Guts as tight as fiddlestrings. Artie Shaw was relaxed, music just tumbled out of his clarinet like . . . He couldn't think what it was like, until he remembered how a stream of incendiaries looked as they tumbled into a searchlight beam and scattered, pretty as confetti. Artie Shaw seemed to have an endless bombload, his stuff kept tumbling and tumbling. Now Silk felt too tired to stand. This relaxation business was exhausting.

As he stretched out on the bed, the word came to him. Linseed oil. Thank you, brain. About bloody time. He fell asleep.

5

Drinks by the pool. Ronald Colman welcomed Silk like an old pal who'd been away for a week, said nothing about the bright red rash, just gave him a half-pint tankard. "It's called Buzzard's Breath. Don't ask what's in it," Colman said. "The President of Mexico sold me the recipe. State secret, he said." Silk drank deep. It tasted like liquid moonlight with firecrackers, a bloody silly turn of phrase, very unSilklike, must be caused by his vulnerable condition, so he took another swig to wash it away.

"What d'you think?" Colman asked.

"It's a far cry from linseed oil," Silk said.

Colman smiled. "Indisputable," he said. "Come and meet Ginger." Who turned out to be Ginger Rogers. She was very easy to talk to. She made Silk realize that he was a very interesting chap. Somebody kept filling up his tankard. Later there was food, delicious food. He made more friends, people with famous names. Ginger walked him back to the cottage, kissed him goodnight. See? That's what a double D.F.C. gets you. Almost worth the effort.

* * *

A week passed, painlessly.

The consulate seemed to have forgotten about him. The war was making steady progress without his help. He slept a lot, swam a bit, played some casual tennis with a man who talked like Charles Boyer and turned out to be Charles Boyer. People were always dropping in at Colman's and they were nearly all Famous Names. Quite soon, Silk stopped thinking of them as Hollywood stars; they were just Ronald's friends. A chap who has been kissed goodnight by Ginger Rogers grows up fast. The possibility that they might feel privileged to meet a battle-scarred squadron leader never occurred to him. He didn't talk about ops and they didn't ask.

The rash faded a bit and his skin felt slightly less anxious. He could take a shower and walk away intact, provided he was careful with the towel. He had the use of a Cadillac convertible. Joan Fontaine asked him to take her shopping. She picked out a lot of clothes that were just right for him. No money changed hand, no cheques were written, nobody seemed concerned, the stores had people who carried the purchases to the car, and Silk realized he had strayed into the Shangri-la of Hollywood where money didn't talk because it didn't speak the language. If you were in, money wasn't necessary; if you were out, money wouldn't help. That was how it seemed to Silk; but he wasn't thinking very hard, he was just letting himself be sucked into the slipstream of Ronald Colman and friends.

They took him to the races, a private box high in the stands; to the movies, a private preview, invitation only; to Romanoff's, dark as a speakeasy, for lunch. He stopped saying thank you. He didn't feel especially grateful. Not getting blown to buggery by a German night fighter was partly down to luck; well, so was this holiday. Everything in life and death was luck.

One day he stayed in the cottage and wrote to Zoë about his luck. After two pages he stopped and read the letter. What a load of self-important guff. It was stiff and jokey and shapeless; he could imagine her mounting impatience with it. He tore it up and burned the bits. Then he wrote something simple and safe:

> *Darling Zoë,*
> *A lot has happened since I last wrote from, I think, Kansas. Much of it was the same thing over and over again: another factory, another speech, although of course it was always the same old gung-ho speech with local variations. (Gung-ho means bloody good show, keep up the good work. You probably know that.)*

Now I'm in California on sick leave with a boring condition which would be total sunburn if I'd been in the sun. As I haven't, the quacks are baffled. I'm in a sort of rest home for heroes, run by English movie actors, damn good types. God knows when I'll be ordered home. I'm sure you're holding the fort brilliantly. Stalin's troops seem to be hotfooting it after the frightful Huns, no doubt helped enormously by your ladies' warm socks.

Much love from me and my two gongs, Hanky and Panky. Kiss Laura for me – if you can.

Silko.

Good enough. The bit about the rest home was a white lie. Was he afraid Zoë might think he was bonking Hedy Lamarr? That didn't sound like a happy marriage. What had happened to true love and complete trust and all that cobblers? "Bollocks," Silk said. He addressed the envelope and set off to the house. Colman would have someone who could stamp it and mail it. On the way he met Barney Knox, and that changed everything.

6

The man was carrying a butterfly net. When they were still ten yards apart, he said to Silk: "I was playing poker with the Andrews Sisters, they can read each other's minds, I swear it, they took a week's pay off me in ten minutes flat, so I told them I was going on a butterfly hunt, and hey, look, the butler gave me this. You're the squadron leader. I'm Barney Knox." They shook hands, gently: he could see the rash.

45

Knox was tall, with close-cropped hair. Some time ago, his nose had been in collision with something hard; faint white surgical scars showed around his cheekbones and forehead. Silk had seen that sort of marking before. It often followed a forced landing, when the instrument panel went backwards and met the pilot coming forwards.

"Our host told me all about you," Knox said.

"Did he? Very clever of him. He doesn't know all about me."

"Right. He told me two things. One is you're bullshit-proof."

"Evidently you didn't believe him."

"The other's anger. You're a very angry man, Mr Silk."

"More bullshit."

Silk walked on, and Knox went with him. "Letter to England?" he said. "Give it to me and I'll get it on a plane tonight. Otherwise it'll take a month." Silk stopped. "No bullshit," Knox said.

"Why should you care? And who the hell are you?"

"I'm a guy who flew B-24s in England, what you call Liberators. I'm flying one this afternoon. Test flight. Want to come along for the ride?"

Silk scratched his head with a corner of the envelope. His scalp flinched, a warning sign; so he stopped. "Not in uniform. I can't wear uniform."

"Flying overalls okay?"

Silk gave him the letter. "Why bother? What's in this for you?"

"Wrong question. You should be asking what's in it for *you*. And the answer's not down here with the butterflies."

7

The Liberator looked fat. It squatted on its tricycle undercarriage, close to the ground, as if its size and weight were pressing it down.

Silk was biased, he thought the bomber was a tub of lard compared with the tight lines of a Lancaster, but he sat in the co-pilot's seat and said nothing for the first half-hour, while Barney Knox did his pre-flight checks and got airborne and climbed to eight thousand feet, following the Pacific shoreline southwards. He went through a sequence of manoeuvres and made notes on his knee-pad. Then he briefed Silk on the controls, the taps and switches and dials. "She's yours," he said. "Leave the fuel to the flight engineer. Just throw her about a bit."

It was hard work. The Liberator was agile enough but it had to be kicked and shoved every inch of the way. Four Pratt and Whitney engines gave buckets of power, yet the aircraft felt heavy. Even flying straight and level was perpetual work. Instability seemed to have been built into the design. Nevertheless, flying the beast was the best thing that had come Silk's way in months.

Knox took the bomber home to its base, just outside Los Angeles, and landed with only a slight bounce. They got out. Silk took a deep, refreshing breath of high-octane fumes. He pinched his nose and blew hard and his ears popped. A sudden world of fresh sounds arrived. A small wave of happiness came with them. He felt hungry. He hadn't been truly hungry in a long time.

"Don't tell me what's wrong with the B-24," Knox said. "The nose is so long that it blocks the pilot's view, and sometimes the automatic pilot forgets its manners and flies aerobatics, and you want to land but the goddamn nose wheel won't extend, so now the flight engineer has to crawl into the nose-wheel compartment and wrestle the bastard down which shouldn't take more than five minutes provided he remembered to bring his toolkit, by which time the airfield defences will have blown us out of the sky from sheer boredom. I know it all. She's a bitch, but she's *our* bitch and

I love her. Don't talk to me about your lovely Lancasters. This bitch can hit a target a thousand miles away and bring her crew back safe. Now, one question. You want to fly with me?"

"Yes." They shook hands. "Can you clear it with the consulate?"

"From what I hear, they'll pay us to take you off their hands."

"What a peculiar war it is," Silk said.

8

Colman was working late at the studio. Silk left a note of thanks, packed his things, and Knox drove them back to the base.

Next morning, he was having breakfast when Knox came and sat opposite him. "Shaved yet?" he asked.

"Yes." Strange question.

"Did you look in the mirror? The rash has gone."

"Good Lord." Silk felt his face. "I forgot all about it." He looked at his arms, unbuttoned his shirt and squinted at his chest. "All gone. Gone as fast as it came. Extraordinary."

"You reckon? I don't. Everybody says hail the much-decorated squadron leader, what a hell of a flier, but you don't fly. It's the only thing your body wants to do. You keep talking about flying, you never do it. Your skin goes on strike. Won't wear the wings."

"So . . ." Silk leaned back and stared at the ceiling. "You're saying I did this to myself?"

"And now you've undone it. You're a natural-born pilot, Silko. You're good for one thing only, and that's flying. You and the airplane are in love. I may cry." A waiter put a plate of blueberry pancakes in front of him. "How would you like to demonstrate the corkscrew to a bunch of trainee fliers?"

Silk drank some coffee. "One day I must tell you about my great-aunt Phoebe," he said.

"Did she fly?"

"She thought so. That's the important thing, isn't it?"

WHY THE HELL NOT?

1

Silk spent the rest of the war on attachment to the U.S. Army Air Force. Barney Knox was a colonel with a good record as a formation leader over Germany. Now he had a roving commission to travel around the many aircrew training schools and tell them stuff he wished he'd known on his first bombing mission.

They developed a Pat-and-Mike routine. To a class of trainee pilots, Knox said: "Who here has seen a corpse up close?" Three hands went up. "Shot to death?" Two went down. "See here." He passed out some 8-by-10 prints. "My old command," he said. "Consequences of flak. Or fighter attack." Some trainees glanced and quickly passed the pictures, others kept looking. "Battle damage happens," Knox said. "You better be ready."

"Each of you has eight or nine pints of blood in him," Silk said. "All of it gets pumped around your body three times a minute. If a crewman gets badly hurt..."

"Arm blown off," Knox said.

"... he'll lose blood twice as fast because in a crisis the heart pumps twice as hard."

"Three pints looks like six gallons," Knox said.

"Your casualty is swimming in blood," Silk said. "And screaming. Crewmen are panicking."

"First thing you do?" Knox asked.

Total silence. Grim faces. This wasn't why they volunteered.

"Disconnect the casualty's intercom," Silk said.

"Restore silence!" Knox shouted.

"Rear gunner's trying to report enemy fighters three o'clock high," Silk said, "but he can't because . . ."

"Shit, you know why," Knox said. "Questions so far?"

Nobody was in a hurry. Then a trainee raised his arm. "Sir: the casualty—"

"Casualty's dead, son. Question is: will your ship live?"

Later, they took up a few trainees in whatever bomber was available and Silk corkscrewed the aircraft. Back on the ground, there were many questions. Someone always pointed out that corkscrewing in close formation was suicidal. "You won't always be in close formation," Knox said. "Hell, some days we ended up in no damn formation at all."

"Look at it from the enemy's point of view," Silk said. "He likes to get in fast and fire and get out fast. To follow a corkscrew he's got to slow down and stay close, which brings him near my gunners. No, thanks. He'll scram. Look for easier pickings."

"The squadron leader knows," Knox said. "He's done it."

Next day they moved on. They flew in a Harvard single-engine two-seat trainer. Knox said he won it in a poker game. Maybe he did. They cruised across America, from one aircrew school to another. "You learn success," Silk told pupils. "Good. But it also pays to practise failure. What can go wrong? Before take-off, I always wrote the courses *to* target on my left hand, courses *from* target on my right. I wrote big. My navigator gets the chop, I don't want to guess where to steer next."

"And stay away from ships," Knox said. "All sailors hate flyboys. They'll kill you if they can."

*

2

They were in Virginia when Knox asked Silk if he'd like to make a call to England. Silk said it was a nice idea, but wasn't the transatlantic telephone confined to official military business? Knox said, "You're military, I'm official, and besides I know a guy." An hour later Silk was talking to Zoë. She was in her Albany apartment. "Should you be in London?" he said. "I worry about all those flying bombs."

"Yes, nasty. And the rockets, too. We're not supposed to know about rockets. The government keeps saying it's just another gas main exploding. Not very clever, are they? That's the worst thing about war. One gets treated like a child. Laura's safe and sound, of course, and fat as an Irish pig. Are you well?"

"Never better. Lots of flying. Lots of oranges."

"Haven't seen an orange since . . ." She sneezed. "Damn . . . Another cold coming on. Eddy Skinner got killed."

"Tough luck." That was what he always said. "Eddy who?"

"Oh, I forgot. You didn't know him. He was in the Grenadiers. Not that it makes any difference. London's awfully dreary without you, Silko. When are you coming home?" The line was cut, no warning, he was left listening to a harsh buzz. He rattled the cradle and said: "Hullo? Hullo?" It was what they always did in the movies and it did nobody any good, then or now.

Knox said, "All well in the old country?"

"She wants me to come home."

"Sure. That's what they always want. Heard it a hundred times."

"You're married? I had no idea."

"Nor did Jessy. She fell for the uniform, wings on the tunic, very romantic. Then she expected me to come home every night to eat her meatloaf, drop my pants and do my husbandly duty. Thought

52

she could educate me out of flying. That's the difference between women and airplanes, Silko. An airplane kills you quickly, a woman takes her time."

"I don't think Zoë's like that." But a corner of his mind was thinking: *You don't really know what Zoë's like, she's a beautiful mystery, all you really know is flying.* Another part of his mind answered: *So why did you marry her, if you want to spend your life in the sky? Yes, but on the other hand . . .*

Barney was talking about a great new airplane from Lockheed. "It's coming into Washington D.C.," he said. "If we go now . . ."

"Why the hell not?" Silk said.

They borrowed a jeep.

3

There was a crowd at Washington airport, many of them newsmen. Knox had told Silk all he knew: the C prefix made the model a transport, it had four engines and it was said to be something special.

It arrived from the west, low; made a half-circuit; and came straight in to land. The crowd roared its applause. "That can't be a transport," Silk said. "Too beautiful." It was the first aeroplane he had seen that was as sleek and streamlined as a big fish. Nothing seemed straight, everything was gently curved. It had tricycle undercarriage and triple fins, and it was a shining silver. It turned at the end of the runway and taxied back and the PA system announced, "A new American record – from Burbank, California to Washington D.C. in exactly seven hours and three minutes!" The crowd cheered. Knox cheered. Even Silk clapped his hands quite warmly.

They got a close look at the plane, talked to a Lockheed representative, took a copy of a press release, and went for a beer.

"We have seen the future, and it flies," Knox said.

"It's a work of art, I agree. But it'll make a lousy transport."

"Grow up, Silko."

"Truly lousy. They'll crop the wings and enlarge the tail and add a bloody great cargo loading bay and it won't make two hundred knots. You watch."

"No, *you* watch. This war's got another year left in it, maybe less. What d'you aim to do then? Go back to England? Drop a rank? Flight Lieutenant Silk, boring the pants off everyone in the Mess?"

"There I was over Berlin," Silk said dreamily, "flak so thick you could get out and walk on it, and would you believe it, the port wing fell off. 'Damn,' I said."

"Seven hours, three minutes," Knox said. "You realize what that means? Breakfast in LA, dinner in New York. Coast to coast in a day! Who wants to spend three days and nights in a train? Or a week in a car, you arrive with your ass feeling like hamburger, very rare, hold the onion. Air travel, Silko, is gonna be big. Very big."

"And you reckon there's a job in it for blokes like you and me?"

"I've had two offers already."

A spark of patriotism burned inside Silk. "What makes you think I won't go home and fly for British Overseas Airways?" he asked.

"What makes you think Britain has an airliner?"

"There's the Sunderland."

"It's a flyingboat, for Christ's sake. Ten passengers at a hundred and twenty knots. This C-69 carries sixty at three hundred plus!" Knox waved the company hand-out. "A pressurized cabin, yet!"

"We'll build our own. Britain's got a bloody good aircraft industry—"

"Warplanes, Silko. You make warplanes. U.S. companies were

building big passenger aircraft five, ten years ago. Lockheed, Boeing, Douglas . . . This beauty already has a name. Constellation."

"Oh, bollocks," Silk said.

RUMBLED

1

When Germany surrendered, the U.S. Government gave Silk a medal and the Embassy sent him back to England. He asked for immediate demobilization and he got it. While he was at Air Ministry he called on Air Commodore Bletchley, to say goodbye.

"I hear you cracked up in California, Silk," Bletchley said. "Good choice. I blew a gasket in Libya, poor choice, everyone was more or less batty in Libya, it helped to pass the time, you lost your friends in the morning and lost your marbles in the afternoon. Not important any more. How did you get on with the Americans?"

"They like to fly, sir, and so do I."

"You're wise to leave the Service. Britain can't afford another war for ten years. Imagine spending ten years in clapped-out Lancs, dropping dummy bombs on the Suffolk ranges."

"Done that, sir. I hit Norfolk once. Similar spelling."

They shook hands. "Give my regards to your wife. She intends to enter Parliament in the coming elections, or so I read. Brave girl."

It gave him something to think about, on the midday train back to Lincoln.

Zoë was waiting there, with the Frazer-Nash. After American roads, English lanes seemed dangerously narrow and twisting. *This is worse than Bremen,* he thought; but they arrived intact.

He dumped his suitcases in the middle of the living room. He had forgotten how small the place was, how low the ceiling. He went out and stood in the garden. Flowers everywhere, a riot of colour.

Not like America. Zoë appeared, carrying two gin-and-tonics. "Bed," she said.

"I was looking at the hollyhocks."

"Awfully pretty." They touched glasses and drank. "But non-starters in the bed stakes."

In the bedroom, his fingers felt clumsy, fumbling with shirt buttons until Zoë, wearing nothing at all, told him to stand still and she rapidly stripped him. The bed felt pleasantly cool. Zoë felt blissfully warm. Silk had a brief memory of his sense of total relief and relaxation as the Lanc touched down after a long and dodgy op. Then he got down to business. After ten minutes it was obvious that business had shut down for the day.

"Buggeration. What a hell of a homecoming."

"Don't worry, darling. Not important." She very nearly said *It happened to Tony once,* but she stopped herself in time. "Just one of those things."

"Actually it's two of those things," Silk said, "Rumpty and Tumpty, remember? Each as useless as the other." Then he remembered the day when Tony told him he had the same problem, he couldn't keep pace with Zoë, the well had run dry. That was three years ago. In those days, Silk had lusted after her. Everyone had. But Tony had been his best friend, his only surviving friend. And sex was just an itch to be scratched, it was nothing compared with sudden death, three or four miles high, of which there was more than enough to grip the squadron's attention. Tony had solved his sex difficulty with special bath salts, or so he said, but the bigger problem caught up with him over Osnabrück.

Now Silk was in his bed and he knew how Tony must have felt. Utterly bloody useless.

"Hey!" he said. "Just remembered. Got some Benzedrine tablets somewhere. We used to carry them. Keep us awake on ops."

"Silko." She threw back the sheet and sat astride him. "You'd have a heart attack. I look awful in black. Who on earth is going to vote for a widow?"

"I was going to ask you about that." He linked his hands behind his head and enjoyed examining her breasts. "I had a joke about two upstanding members in one household, but it doesn't seem so funny now."

They got dressed, and had tea and toast in the kitchen. Zoë explained how she came to be a candidate.

She had gone to a party and met a major in the Education Corps, slightly drunk, offering odds of ten to one that Labour would win the General Election hands down. Most people were amused. Zoë asked why he was so sure. "Easy," he said. "What was the British army doing between Dunkirk and D-Day? A few divisions slogged their guts out in North Africa and Italy and Burma. All the rest – trained. Troops got bored. War Office invented A.B.C.A. – Army Bureau of Current Affairs. Lectures, film shows, debates. What are we fighting for? Millions of troops had four years to think and what did they decide? They'd die for their country," the major said. "They wouldn't die for a load of Tory toffs."

Next day Zoë registered as the independent candidate for Lincolnshire (South). She had a strong political base: she had run Salute For Stalin Week (socks for Red soldiers), followed by Wings Over Berlin Week (the county gave the R.A.F. a Lancaster) and Build Our Destroyer Week (a shilling bought a rivet). She knew every club and society in the constituency and they knew her. "Good start," Silk said. "Who are you up against?"

Zoë had four opponents but only two that mattered.

The sitting M.P. was 62, unmarried, a Tory backbencher for half his life. His fat majority convinced him that Lincoln (South) liked a steady hand on the tiller. His campaign slogan was *Business As Usual*. Nothing exciting. The country had had enough excitement.

The Labour candidate – also a local man – was an ex-soldier. France, Egypt, Italy. Invalided out in 1943; ran the family farm.

"He'll slaughter you," Silk said.

"He's got a beard, he shouts a lot, he's teetotal and he wants to nationalize the pubs."

"All the pubs?"

"And the breweries."

"Extraordinary . . . Who else?"

"A vegetarian and a nudist."

"Too much for me." Silk warmed his hands on the teapot. "I can't take the hectic pace of English politics."

"But you must. I need you to stand behind me at my rallies, Silko. In uniform. Don't say a word. Just look staunch."

He did his best. Her next rally was that same evening, on a piece of waste land in Lincoln. A couple of hundred turned up. Zoë stood on a barrel and used a megaphone. "Why are your pubs shut on a Saturday afternoon?" she asked. "Exactly when you want a drink? I'll tell you why. 1916! Scandalous lack of shells! Drunken munition workers! Lies – but that's who the government blamed and they shut the pubs! When the real blame lay with incompetent bosses! And *that*, my friends, is why, forty years on, you can't enjoy a drink after two o'clock! What hypocrisy! What humbuggery!" It went down well. They cheered lustily.

Zoë struck left and right. She demanded that, for every new law which Parliament passed, it must abolish an old one ("Muck out the stables of democracy!"); that everybody's wages should rise annually to compensate for inflation ("If you stand still, you fall back!"); that the Church of England must be separated from the State ("The prime minister – who might be an atheist – chooses the next Archbishop of Canterbury! Bishops pass laws in the House of Lords! Is that how we want to run the country today?").

She spoke for twenty minutes, answered three questions, moved on to a village hall, repeated the formula, and did it again at a tennis club.

Next day she made five speeches, all in farming areas. After her last, and biggest, meeting of the day, she stayed to talk with voters. Silk's calves ached from so much standing. His face was stiff with staunchness. He wanted to go home, he wanted a large drink, followed by another. Farmers kept talking to him about the warble fly. Silk didn't give a flying fuck about the warble fly.

At last Zoë said goodbye. The night was moonless, and it was a bad road. Silk drove slowly, snaking around potholes. "That went rather well," Zoë said.

"Okay. It's not real politics, is it? Where's your big election manifesto? Zoë Silk's ten-point plan to save Britain. Everyone else has got one."

"Not my style, darling. These people have just put in a hard day's work. They don't want to be lectured. They deserve some fun."

"I see. What does that make me? The clown?"

The potholes ended. He got the Frazer-Nash up into second gear. With peace, all the dimmers had come off the headlights: now you could see oncoming traffic a mile away. There was no oncoming traffic. She tied a scarf around her hair. Thirty miles an hour. Silk thought he was just stooging along, not much above a stall. He turned onto a main road and let the car off the leash. It swept through fifty and hit sixty. He held the wheel lightly. He enjoyed feeling the vibrations, it was how he'd held the control column of the Lanc, at one with the machine yet totally in command of it. At seventy the car was no longer working hard, it was following its headlights as they swept the road clear. Eighty wasn't too fast. The road was doing all the rushing. The car was untroubled, a rock in a torrent. Ninety would be nice. Ninety was take-off speed, when everything was roses. The engine died.

He groped for the ignition key and found nothing.

No headlights. Black night everywhere. The car slowed, and slowed more. Now the only sound was the wind, and it too was fading to a soft whistle. He put the gearstick into neutral. The wheels started to shudder on the grass verge. He used the brakes. The car stopped.

Silence, except for the faraway ping of the cooling engine.

"That was bloody silly," he said. "No lights, we could have hit . . . hit anything."

"Isn't that what you wanted?" She sounded very quiet, very calm. "The way you were driving, we were bound to hit something. Tree, telephone pole, low-flying aircraft. Quick death. Lots of strawberry jam. Laura inherits everything, and her only two."

"Give me the damn keys."

"You're a selfish bastard, Silko. Kill yourself, if you wish, that's your privilege. You're not going to kill me."

"That wasn't fast, for Christ's sake. We were just cruising along."

"Call it what you like. I'm driving now."

He thought about it. "You're a lousy driver. Slow as cold treacle."

"And you're ten years old."

He got out, and she climbed over the gearstick and the handbrake and settled into his seat. He slammed the door.

"Kick the wheels," she said. "Spit on the bonnet. Then get in and we'll go home."

"I'd sooner walk."

"Five years old." She started the car and he watched her drive away.

The R.A.F. did not do much marching. Bomber crews rarely marched at all. Silk had been standing all evening. By the time he walked a mile his feet were beginning to ache. There was very little traffic on this road and none was willing to stop for him. After two miles his calves were weary. After three miles he felt crippled. The Frazer-Nash was parked on the grass and Zoë was asleep at the wheel. He woke her up. They drove home.

2

They slept late.

The sun was up, the day was warm enough for breakfast in the garden. There was little conversation until Silk felt stronger now that he had some grub inside him and he said, "Sorry about last night."

"No, you're not. You're not a bit sorry." She wasn't laughing at him, but she was definitely enjoying herself. "The only thing you're sorry about is the fact that you got caught out. You got rumbled, Silko."

"Nonsense."

"You're a terrible cheat. You couldn't fool a flea."

"Wrong. I've fooled dozens of fleas. Hundreds."

"Oh yeah? Name three."

"Hank. All called Hank. American fleas. Big, muscular specimens, very hard to fool." He cleared his throat. "Foolhardy, in fact."

She rested her elbow on the table and her head on her hand, and looked at him with some affection. "One person you *can* fool, and that's you. You're really sorry the war's over, aren't you?"

"Of course not. That's ridiculous." He ate some toast. "Maybe a little bit. It's all I've ever done." He put marmalade on the toast. "I suppose I miss the flying. Ops were a hell of a kick, can't deny that." He licked marmalade off his finger. "Provided you survived."

"And you'd do it again," she said. "In a flash."

"Funny you should say that. Barney Knox wants me to join him." He got up and strolled around the lawn. "He reckons there's a big future in the airline business."

"Then go, Silko. I'll miss you. What I shan't miss is you standing about, pretending to be a civilian. I didn't marry a civilian."

Silk was inspecting a rose bush. "Busy bees," he said. "California has the most amazing hummingbirds. They hover and poke and—"

"I know. Seen them. Now let's go back to bed and you can demonstrate your hummingbird technique."

"Wizard prang," he said. "Whatever that means." It turned out to mean a lot of steamy, squeaky sex. So that was all right. In the afternoon he cabled Barney and took the job.

3

The end of the world war released tensions that set off small wars. There was already civil war in Greece. The Dutch were losing a colonial war in what would soon be Indonesia. There were uprisings in Poland, Palestine, Algeria and the Philippines. The French were determined to keep their possessions everywhere, and soon they were fighting in Syria, Lebanon, North Africa, and in what was then known as Indo-China. France bombarded Haiphong in 1946 and the Vietnam war began. Korea had civil war. India divided itself in a frenzy of killing. Malaya had civil war. China's internal battles went on and bloody on. Latin America wasn't at war, but nobody could say it was at peace. In the past fifteen years, governments had been overthrown by military coups in Argentina, Brazil, Chile, Nicaragua, Guatemala, El Salvador, Honduras, Cuba and a few more. The world war had ceased, but local violence kept breaking out like forest fires. Barney Knox had considerable experience of war and of flying, and he told Silk that he saw a large business opportunity in servicing impromptu and irregular military requirements by air, in an informal global context.

"Gunrunning to civil wars," Silk said.

"That's about it, yes."

"Why the bullshit?"

Knox massaged his eyes. "I've been up too late, talking to my backers, the guys putting money into the outfit. They like bullshit, it makes them feel smarter. More corporate."

"But it still boils down to gunrunning."

"Guns or medicine or radios or whatever's in demand."

"What happened to the airline business? Coast to coast in seven hours?"

"Couldn't raise the big bucks. Couldn't compete with Pan Am, T.W.A., the rest. Besides . . . who wants to fly scheduled routes? Might as well drive a Greyhound bus."

Knox's outfit was called The Outfit, Inc. That was only in the United States. The company had different names in different regions. In the Orient it operated as Total Transit Ltd., in the Middle East as Complete Couriers Ltd., in South America as Rapid Action Consolidated. Knox bought some surplus transports from the Air Force and hired veteran crews. He ran The Outfit, made the deals, planned the flights. Silk did what he was told: flew here and picked up the goods, flew there and delivered them, usually at an isolated airstrip left over from World War Two. He had an Australian navigator and an American radio op. They never got excited if the aircraft got shot at from the ground or buzzed by fighters. Silk enjoyed the work. He travelled the world and earned ten times his R.A.F. pay. Occasionally he flew home for a spell of leave.

The first time he returned, he met Zoë at the House of Commons.

"I can't tell you how proud I am," he said, as they embraced. "I honestly thought you were completely useless, and now look! I'm married to the next Prime Minister but three."

"You're very jolly, Silko." She took his arm and steered him towards the bar. "I haven't seen you so happy since you bombed Mozart's grave. What have you been up to?"

"Oh . . . stooging around, making myself useful. Tell me about you. How did you get in here?"

She ordered drinks, and told him. First, the Tory M.P. had revealed that the Labour candidate spent the war in the Pay Corps, far from the fighting line, until invalided out with piles. Useful, yes. Gallant, no. Retaliation was fast. A Labour supporter who was a printer rushed out five hundred posters showing the familiar face of a Tory peer who had recently been found at night in Hyde Park, behind some bushes, with a corporal of the Coldstream Guards, both naked. The caption was: *I'm buggered if I'll vote Tory!* The Tory M.P. was white with fury. The posters got ripped down, too late: the joke was all over Lincoln (South). The Labour–Tory fight turned ugly. At a Labour rally, a farmer asked a simple question about subsidies. The candidate stumbled, blustered and thoroughly cocked-up his answer. The farmer said, "You can't fertilize a field by farting through a hole in the fence." The candidate's name was Carter. Now he was Farter Carter throughout Lincoln (South). Thereafter, Labour and Tory were so hellbent on savaging each other that they ignored Zoë. She went about her independent campaign, talking sense, entertaining the crowd, looking lovely, and winning with a majority of over four thousand votes. "Piece of cake," she said.

The division bell rang. M.P.s hurried out of the bar. "Shouldn't you be doing something?" Silk asked.

"No. It's a debate about oil. Why bother? Shell and BP and Esso have got Iran and Iraq and Persia all sewn up, anyway."

"Iran *is* Persia, darling."

"Well, that's their problem. Isn't it lucky that I kept the apartment at Albany? So handy for the Commons. Shall we go there now?"

"Tempt me," he said. "Has it got hot and cold running sex?"

As they left the building, the policemen saluted her. Years of habit made his saluting arm twitch. Peace still felt odd.

HOLY DEADLOCK

1

That was the shape of their lives for the next twelve years.

Zoë kept getting re-elected. One of her constituents suffered at the hands of an arrogant civil servant. She led a vigorous campaign which forced the government to hold a public inquiry. Her constituent got justice, and she had found her place in politics: she defended lost causes. She won more than she lost.

Silk too did what he was good at, but quietly. In '48 and '49, The Outfit sent crews to help the Berlin Airlift. Russia was trying to starve the Western Powers out of the city. Silk flew Lancasters converted to carry cargoes of fuel. Berlin was easy meat for him; he just looked for the same old landmarks and made the same old turning points. After a year Moscow gave up, and Silk rejoined The Outfit, which was soon absorbed by something called Air America.

"You might not like it," Barney Knox told him. "It has absolutely no connection with any department of the U.S. government."

"I see. Which particular department is it absolutely not connected with?"

"The C.I.A. No link whatsoever. The pay's good."

"Will I have to kill anyone?"

"Only if they insult the queen. Hell, what do I know? They're paying top dollar, so it's not going to be a milk run. You want out, I wouldn't blame you."

Silk wanted in. Air America suited him. It had a large stable of aircraft, from single-engined air taxis to four-engined airliners.

Every task was different. He flew sacks of rice (or something labelled rice) into Burma, and he flew body bags (or bags of something) out of Nicaragua. The years passed; when he flicked through his log-book he was surprised how quickly they had passed, and how many types he had flown: Constellations, Globemasters, a Ford Trimotor, a Catalina, various Piper Cubs, Mustangs, freighters converted from Marylands, Baltimores and Bostons. And many more. Occasionally his flight plan sent him to a U.S. Air Force base. He was always made welcome: Barney Knox's influence. Sometimes they offered him a flight in a military aircraft, just for the experience. He flew as co-pilot in a Lockheed Hercules, a gentle giant of a plane. He flew in the two-seat trainer type of some astonishing jets: the Sabre fighter, the twin-engined Canberra bomber, the U.S. Navy's Phantom. He even flew an Air Force version of the Boeing 707. Once he got accustomed to their kick-in-the-back acceleration, he liked jets better than anything. After a jet, Air America's freighters felt like wheelbarrows.

2

Silk always took his leave during the Parliamentary summer recess, when Zoë would be free. That arrangement failed in 1957.

She wasn't at the apartment or the cottage. Her office said she was part of a Unesco team investigating illiteracy in the Third World. Where, exactly? Right now, in Singapore. "I've just come from bloody Singapore," Silk said. The office was sympathetic. It had tried to contact him via Air America but apparently the airline's number was unlisted. Very unusual.

1958 was worse. Zoë's diary was so full that he gave up any hope of a normal reunion. Instead he found out where she was going and he tagged along. Big mistake.

He was sitting in a lecture theatre at Birmingham University, not listening to her speech about secondary education, when he knew they were in trouble. She wasn't the woman he had married, she wasn't skittish, slightly crackers, lithe as a kitten, totally unpredictable, huge fun. She was Zoë Silk, M.P., in a tailored navy blue suit, the skirt two inches longer than he liked, and wearing the permanently interested expression of the politician. She'd changed in twelve years – well, of course she'd changed, everybody changes. That meant he'd changed too, and not for the better. Laura – growing up fast and usually away at boarding school – seemed to treat him like an uncle. A distant uncle.

He left the lecture theatre, went to the lavatory and stared in the mirror. He looked like his father. Especially the eyes. He was looking at his father looking back at him, a bit critical, a bit dissatisfied. The old man had been a pain in the ass. Christ Almighty. He washed his face. Made no difference. Same eyes.

On the train back to London, Zoë said, "Please don't take this the wrong way, Silko darling, but would you mind awfully having the guest bedroom tonight? It's just that I've got an early start tomorrow, and you can be so enormously *restless* when you sleep."

"Can I?" he said. "Bloody hell."

"And I suppose I'm accustomed to sleeping alone."

He was glad when he could go back to Air America, but not for long. After a week or two he began resenting the work because it kept him away from Zoë. Yet he knew that if he went back to London he would be bored and boring, and she would be as remote when she was in the House of Commons as she was when he was flying to Chile or to Portuguese Angola.

He got to know Angola quite well. Portugal had clung on to its empire in Africa by never changing the simple formula of total white supremacy and brutal black repression. Then Lisbon had declared that its African colonies were now in fact overseas provinces of Portugal, so any prospect of freedom for the black population was stone dead. Action and reaction were equal and opposite: the first attacks came from the M.P.L.A., the *Movimento Popular de Libertação de Angola*. The Soviet Union sent aid and advisers to the M.P.L.A. The Pentagon couldn't be seen to support colonialism, but something had to be done, and Air America supplied much of it.

In the spring of 1961, Silk flew a Douglas DC-3 to Angola and landed at a military air base near Nova Lisboa. He was wearing what he always wore: leather flying jacket, cavalry twill slacks, calf-length boots: all stained and battered. He went up into the control tower and watched men unloading crates marked *Refrigerator – Handle With Care*. Heavy mortar shells began marching their explosions along the runway until they hit the aircraft. It blew up with a ferocity that no refrigerator could provide. That took care of his return trip. The next problem was how to get out of Angola.

It took him five days, travelling by taxi, bus and train all across Africa, to reach Tanganyika. He flew first class to London, a scruff surrounded by suits. At least he managed to shave on the plane. He used up the little bottle of aftershave by splashing it on the grimier, grubbier parts of his body. At Heathrow he phoned Zoë's office. They said she was at her house in Scotland.

"You mean in Lincoln," Silk said.

"No, in Scotland. She has a small hunting lodge, in the Trossachs."

"Where, exactly? What's the phone number?"

Short pause. "I'm afraid we can't give out those details."

"I'm her bloody husband, for Christ's sake."

"I see. Well, we could telephone Mrs Silk, and she could telephone you, if you'd like to give us your number."

It was a public callbox. He was still staring at its number, arguing with himself whether he should do what they said, wait here for Zoë's call and maybe fly to Scotland, or should he find a hotel, or go to the apartment, or buy a gun and shoot himself, when his call ran out of time and the line went dead. He had no more small change.

He came out of the callbox. A man was waiting to use it. He had a face like a rabbit with a tired, shaggy moustache. "Cheer up, chum," the man said. "It might never happen." Silk's fist made the decision, not Silk, his fist tightened and it was very ready to smash the man's teeth, when somebody gripped Silk's arm. "You don't want to do that, sir," a policeman said.

They kept him in an interrogation room for half an hour. They looked at his passport, checked the dollars in his wallet, gave him cups of tea and listened to his weary account of his travels and his faraway wife. Then they let him go.

"Bloody lucky for me you were there," he said to the policeman.

"We get all sorts arriving at Heathrow, sir. I could tell that you weren't having a very happy day."

Silk found a bar where they were willing to take his dollars and he got to work on a double Scotch.

"Just the chap I want to see," said a confident, Home Counties voice. Silk looked up. Bowler hat, club tie, pigskin gloves, walking cane. Total stranger. *Oh, fuck my old boots,* he thought in despair. Then the stranger took the bowler off, and grinned, and it was Freddy Redman, his navigator, his partner in the Lanc on so many dicey ops. "You look like shit, Silko," Freddy said, "but apart from that you haven't changed. I expect you'd like another."

"First intelligent thing I've heard all week," Silk said.

The barman did his stuff, and they moved to a booth. "Have you got a problem, Silko?" Freddy asked. "Apart from needing a bath, that is."

"Bath." Silk pulled open his shirt and took a sniff. "Bit ripe. That's Africa for you. Took a DC-3 to Angola, the buggers blew it up. Hell of a bang."

"So I heard. Occupational hazard in Air America, isn't it? They won't dock your pay."

"You know about . . ." Silk did more damage to his Scotch. "How do you . . ."

Freddy waved it away. "Not important. So what's your big problem?"

"Zoë. Marriage is on the blink, Freddy. We never meet. I'm always . . ." He gestured, feebly, with his left hand. "And when I get here, she's always . . ." An equally weak gesture with his right hand. "See? We're income . . ." He yawned, hugely. "We're income . . ." He thought hard. "Patible. That's the problem."

"I may have a solution, Silko."

"No, no, no. Can't be done. I'm no good unless I fly, and if I fly we never meet. It's holy deadlock."

"No such thing," Freddy said. "I have the answer." Silk stared. As Freddy watched, he saw Silk's eyes go out of focus. "Drink up, old chap. I'll drive you home. We'll sort it all out tomorrow."

KICK LIKE AN EARTHQUAKE

1

They met again at the Reform Club.

Silk had slept at the Albany apartment. He'd taken a long bath and had a haircut, and now for the first time in years he was wearing a dark suit, a white shirt with a cutaway collar and a dull tie, polished black shoes. He'd never been to the Reform Club and he was taking no chances. "I feel like a Harley Street pox doctor," he said.

"Wrong club." Freddy looked at the crowd of members near the bar. "Try the R.A.C. Now then: we haven't much time, I should have been in Bonn half an hour ago . . ." He checked his watch. "They'll just have to start without me. Here's my idea. You rejoin Bomber Command." Freddy had a confident smile. "Solves all your problems."

Silk scratched the back of his neck; barbers never got rid of all the bits. "Rejoin," he said. "You're the one with the problem. Your bowler must be five sizes too small. I'm thirty-eight, Freddy. Bomber Command doesn't want me. Never did. They tolerated my funny ways, that's all. Rejoin now? I wouldn't get past the commissionaire. He'd chuck me in the gutter along with the rest of the garbage."

"So you say. But I think I'm in a better position to judge."

Silk stared at him. Freddy had put on a few pounds and his hair was silvering gently at the temples, but there was something more than that. He had a calm and steady gaze that Silk always associated with ranks of group captain and above. "Better position? What's your racket?"

"Air Ministry. I'm the tenth assistant deputy director as you enter on the right. Bomber Command's changed, Silko. Even you must have heard—"

"Yeah. Big jets. Doesn't change me. I'm still thirty-eight."

"So what? We've got bomber captains who are over forty."

It took a few seconds for Silk to take in that information. "Thank God for a navy, is all I can say."

Freddy took a photograph from an inside pocket and gave it to Silk. It was a close-up of a four-engined jet bomber taking off. "Vulcan," he said. "I don't know how many Lancasters we made for the price of one of these, forty or fifty, certainly. This is a very valuable aeroplane. Air Ministry isn't going to give it to some slap-happy twenty-two-year-old so he can hedge-hop across the Cotswolds and fly under the Clifton Suspension Bridge."

"Nobody's that crazy."

"Aren't they? You were. I can remember looking out of the navigator's window and seeing the church steeples go by."

Silk was silent. His shoulders were hunched and his mouth was compressed. Painful memories. Painful because he could remember the happiness of living a blink away from death.

"Forget it, Silko. That was then and now is now," Freddy said. "Air Ministry is looking for serious, mature aircrew with big flying hours, counted by the thousand. We want great experience, proven flying skills, self-discipline, balance, solidity. Good health, obviously."

"All right," Silk said cautiously. "Suppose I did a tour. I see more of Zoë, but when the tour's over you post me to Hong Kong. She won't live in Hong Kong."

"It's a five-year tour. All part of the policy. We keep the same crew together, on the same base, for five years. Think of it. Bags of flying, and Zoë nearby, for five long years."

Silk studied the photograph. "Big beast, isn't she?"

"Handles like a Spitfire with twice the speed, and one sortie can do more damage than the whole of Bomber Command managed in the entire war . . . Now I really must go."

"What are those engines?"

"Bristol Olympus jet turbines. Twenty thousand pounds of thrust each. Noise like a volcano. Kick like an earthquake. Don't get up. The Vulcan leads the world, Silko. Think of that. And Zoë, of course."

"Tell me one thing." Silk said. "If it's so damn special, how come you need new crews so badly?"

"A couple of bad prangs," Freddy said. "And the odd suicide. We'll talk tomorrow, shall we?" He strode away.

2

It was a long and strenuous medical. First he met the Chief Medical Officer, a wing commander. "I don't smoke, I drink the occasional beer, and I swim half a mile every day if I can find a pool," Silk told him. "No venereal disease, and no insanity in the family."

"All pilots are slightly mad," the C.M.O. said.

"Not this one."

"Well, that's what you said once. It's down here, in your records." He held up a typed page. "Must be true. Take your clothes off."

All day, men in white coats tested his health and strength, his stamina and resilience. They made him toil at a series of machines until his legs cramped and his lungs burned and sparks raced across his eyeballs. They measured his reactions. They looked deep into his eyes and ears and throat. They seemed obsessed with his blood pressure and his pulse. Finally they said he could get dressed. "Thank God that's over," he said.

"It's only just begun."

They strapped him to the end of a centrifuge forty feet long, and spun it at increasing speeds until his eyes greyed out and finally blacked out.

"G forces," he said. "Tremendous fun." They said nothing.

Next day began with sea survival training: several hours, dressed in flying kit, with or without a lifejacket, in an indoor pool where artificial waves fought to keep him out of a rubber dinghy. Then – wet, cold and hungry – he was put in a flight simulator. Nobody told him that the controls and the instruments were all reversed. To bank right, you had to steer left. The altimeter revolved the wrong way. Green meant red. Ten years with Air America's mongrel fleet helped Silk here. He adjusted rapidly, even when some hidden bastard pressed a switch and reversed the reverse. It was a game. They tired of it before he did, and sent him to the decompression chamber to see how his heart and lungs liked going up to and coming down from great height. That was definitely not fun; but he came through it, went back to the white coats, gave blood and urine samples, even had a cup of tea and a biscuit. "What did I score?" he asked.

"Score? There is no score." Which made him think.

Next day was very relaxed. A few x-rays, some hearing and eyesight tests, a good lunch, a long wait in a room where the armchairs were comfortable. An army officer came in: a colonel, fiftyish, red moustache, three rows of medal ribbons, clipboard. "Milk?" he barked. "Flying Officer Milk?"

"No, sir. Silk. Flight Lieutenant."

"Damn." The colonel took a pencil from behind his ear and altered the sheet on the clipboard. "Bloody admin orderlies . . . Makes no difference. You've got the chop, Silk. Blown it. Flunked, as the Yanks say. Down the pan." He rapped the clipboard with his knuckles. "If this is the best you can do, you're not fit to drive a Naafi van."

"That's . . . disappointing, sir."

"*What*? It's bloody unpatriotic." He advanced on Silk and poked him in the chest with the pencil. "You thought you could bullshit your way into Bomber Command! Look at these fucking pathetic scores! What? What have you got to say?"

"Nothing, sir."

"A gentleman would apologize!" The pencil-prodding got harder. "Damned insolence! Damned arrogance! Don't try to deny it. To think we fought two wars for the shoddy, shabby likes of you." Spots of saliva were reaching Silk's tunic.

"Three wars, sir." Silk pointed at one of the colonel's medal ribbons. "Isn't that the Boer War medal? Sixty years ago. You must have been jolly young."

The colonel's face turned red. He began to shout. He damned and insulted Silk, cursed him for a sponger and a wastrel and a fraud, and stamped out.

Ten minutes later an orderly arrived and escorted Silk to the Chief Medical Officer. "Boer War gong," he said. "How did you know?"

"My uncle won it. Used to wear it every Armistice Day. Anyway, what's a pongo colonel doing in Bomber Command?"

"Testing your self-control, see if you would crack. It's a bloody silly idea, but just occasionally it draws blood . . . Anyway, you're medically fit to fly Vulcans." He signed a form. "You have the heart and stomach of a sixteen-year-old boy. Pass it on to me when you've done with it."

"You'll have to lose thirty pounds first."

The C.M.O. added the date to the form. A five looked slightly unstable, so he straightened it. "You've been out of the Service for a long time, flight lieutenant. You have forgotten the courtesy due to senior rank." He looked up, his eyes wide open; and Silk's toes curled.

"Yes, sir."

"Group Captain Evans is in Room 800. Do not joke with Group Captain Evans."

"Thank you, sir."

Silk found Room 800. Evans told him to take a seat. He was a big man, almost completely bald, with a permanent frown. Silk suddenly worried about his taxes. He'd left all that stuff to Barney Knox.

Evans leafed through a thick file. He closed it, and said: "You're a bloody mercenary, flight lieutenant." It was true. Silk stayed silent. "A whore of the skies, that's you," Evans said. "What?" Silk frowned, as if thinking. "Scum rises to the top, flight lieutenant. That's your story too, isn't it?" Evans whacked the file. "What?" No reply.

Evans went back into the file. He found a tattered page that briefly made him hold his breath. "Christ Almighty," he muttered. "You could go to jail for this." He read it again. "Didn't anybody . . .? No, of course not. They gave you the saw and sent you up the tree, and watched you cut off the branch you were sitting on. Now look at you: stark bollock naked. What?"

Silk chewed his lip and studied the group captain's face. Large wart on the left cheek. Must make shaving tricky.

"Air America," Evans said. "Cowboys paid by crooks. C.I.A. pulls the strings, Mafia makes a killing." He tossed a reporter's notebook at Silk, then a ballpen. "Come clean, flight lieutenant. Full confessions, and I mean *full*. It's your only hope." He went out. A key turned in the lock.

Evans came back five hours later. It was dusk; a lamp burned on the desk. Silk gave him the notebook.

"1835 hours," Evans read aloud. "Urinated in waste-paper bin. Appears to be watertight. 1907 hours: telephoned Officers Mess, spoke to Duty Officer. 1920 hours: airman opened door with master key. 1930 hours: Mess servant delivered dinner on tray with half-bottle of claret. 2015–2050 hours: took a nap. 2100 hours: discussed football with office cleaner."

"He emptied your waste-paper bin," Silk said. "I gave him ten shillings."

Evans grunted. "Extravagant. Five bob would have done. And I'm not paying for your wine." He sat at his desk. "You've read your file?" Silk nodded. "Anything to add?" Silk shook his head. "Thank God," Evans said. "You've been okayed by M.I.5, Special Branch, the F.B.I. and the Dagenham Girl Pipers. Also, it didn't hurt that President Eisenhower invited your titled wife to dinner at the White House."

"Did he really, sir?" *Zoë's not titled,* Silk thought: "She never told me," he said.

"Amazing. Why on earth d'you want to join Bomber Command again?"

The honest answer was *To be near Zoë.* Silk briefly considered *To help defend the West.* He said, "To fly the Vulcan, sir. Finest aircraft in the world."

"It's a nuclear weapon with wings. Killing a quarter of a million Russians doesn't bother you?"

Silk thought of all the Germans he must have killed in two tours. "Not if it doesn't bother you, sir."

Evans got up and walked to the window. "Britain's not a bad country, you know. I'd certainly kill to save it. When you think of the

79

Hitler war, of the huge pressures we put bomber crews under . . . They wouldn't have been human if they hadn't gone on the razzle, got drunk, got laid, got into fights . . ."

"It helped, sir."

"Not now, Silk. Not in the Cold War. Too dangerous. A Vulcan crew is the closest thing to God hurling down thunderbolts. The crew can never relax. On duty, all day every day, for five years. Hell of a burden. If you've got a weakness, flight lieutenant, it will find you out, it will break you and you will crack, you will fall apart, collapse, kill someone, probably yourself, anything to escape the nightmare of being God, not the God who allegedly created the world but the God who exists to destroy it. If you find that weakness, come and tell me."

"Yes, sir." Silk relaxed. He was in. He was flying. He had no weakness. "Thank you, sir."

POOR RUMPTY AND TUMPTY

1

By the time he rejoined Bomber Command, Silk had flown more than sixty types of aircraft; and the more he flew, the more he admired birds. Gulls especially. He marvelled at the way they did so much, so easily. Gulls could soar and wheel, and search and hunt, and call or scream, and all with such grace. He watched, and sometimes daydreamed about flying an aircraft with a performance better than any bird. When this came true it resembled a fish. The Vulcan looked like a sting ray.

He had joined an Operational Conversion Unit, and an instructor was showing him around the bomber. "Not quite a perfect triangle," the instructor said. "Slight kink in the leading edges. Helps airflow, which makes the boffins happy. Big fin, keeps her nice and stable. No tailplane, of course, because the wings do that job. In fact the wings do just about everything. The Vulcan's a flying wing, with a nose up front for the crew to sit in."

They walked underneath. Silk raised an arm and could not reach the wings. The undercarriage struts were massive. Each unit had eight wheels. "What does she weigh?" Silk asked.

"Depends on the fuel load. All tanks full, something like a hundred and twenty tons."

Silk tried to remember what a Lanc with a full bombload had weighed. Twenty-something tons came to mind. "I'm glad to see we've got runways to match."

"Yes." The instructor was ten years younger than Silk and he had respect for a double D.F.C., so he didn't smile. "Actually, we need less than half the runway for take-off. The Vulcan doesn't hang about. She rather likes the direction of up."

They climbed the ladder in front of the nose wheel and squeezed into the cockpit: side-by-side seats for the pilot and co-pilot, each with duplicated controls. Silk fingered the stubby joystick. "Very sporty," he said.

"It suits the Vulcan's style. This is a bomber that thinks it's a fighter. You'll see."

Silk's first flight was on a sunny day. The instructor made a low-level pass over the airfield. Silk glanced to his right and saw their shadow ghosting below: a giant sting ray skimming the ocean bed. All his previous flying had been a preparation for this. Silk and the Vulcan were made for each other. "Now see how she climbs," the instructor said. He stood the Vulcan on its tail and they went up as if somebody up there was hauling them in, hand over fist.

2

The Frazer-Nash two-seater was long gone; now he had a rakish Citroën with running boards, as seen in all the worst French cop movies. During leave from Air America, he taught Laura how to drive. She liked that, and liked him for it; they became friends. Then she went to America, to Radcliffe. Ivy League: nothing but the best. He was surprised how much he missed her.

Weekends were free. Zoë's office told him where she expected to be – the Albany apartment, the Lincolnshire cottage, or the lodge in Scotland – and he drove there on Friday evening. This weekend it was the cottage, only a quick seventy miles from the Operational Conversion Unit. He was there by six.

He opened the door and called her name. No answer. He went

in and she was sitting at a table, asleep, her head resting on a scattering of typed papers and open books. She had been holding a fountain pen and it was still touching a letter. A pool of blue ink had spread.

"Wake up, fathead," he said. He took the pen from her fingers. "That is, assuming you're not dead."

She groaned, and sat up, slowly, feeling her neck where it ached. Her hair was tangled and one side of her face was creased. Her eyes flickered, hating the light. "Not dead," she said. "Bit shattered."

"All this bumf-shuffling will kill you."

She yawned and stretched. "We've been here for days. Arguing over . . ." Another yawn seized her.

"Is it politics?"

"Obviously."

"Then I'm not interested. And who's we?"

"John and Debby. They're upstairs."

Silk went upstairs two at a time. Within ten seconds he came clattering down again. "No they're not," he said.

"What?" She stopped brushing her hair. "Oh. Sorry. Forgot. They went back to London."

"Good for them. You need a hot bath. Brush your teeth while you're at it, and I might consider giving you a kiss."

He strolled around the garden, pulling weeds, talking to the birds, while steam drifted out of the bathroom window. Half an hour later Zoë came out with two large gin-and-tonics. She was transformed: new face, clean hair, black sweater and white slacks. "Give that lady a gong," he said.

"Darling Silko . . . Have you had a good week?"

"Steady progress."

"Good. Don't crash, will you, or the Chancellor will have to put twopence on income tax. Either that, or cancel a battleship. Let's go to the cinema."

They drove into Lincoln and saw a so-so Western. As they came away, Silk said: "The bad guys never shoot straight. Every time there's a gunfight, the bad guys always miss the good guys."

"That's because they wear such awful black hats."

"Russians wear black hats. Does that make them bad shots?"

"Who said Russians are the bad guys?"

His mental shutters crashed down. Change of subject. "Are you hungry? What d'you fancy?"

"Fish and chips. Just like during the war. Go to the flicks and then have fish and chips."

They ate as they strolled. "Only difference between now and then is no blackout," Silk said. "I must have walked into every lamp-post in Lincoln."

"I think I'll definitely sell the cottage."

After all these years, nothing Zoë said or did came as a total surprise. But the cottage was his only home, and he felt a small kick in the stomach. "Definitely?" he said. "I didn't know you were even thinking of it."

"Not enough space. There's a manor house coming on the market soon, not far away, good size." She talked about its rooms, its grounds, its suitability for holding seminars, what with all the catering and car parking. "It has a lake. You can swim."

He dumped the remains of his fish and chips in a litter bin. "Well, it's your money. You know best. I don't suppose you'd rent me the cottage?"

"Too late, darling. I've got a buyer."

They walked to the car. Now Silk didn't want to go back to the cottage that he couldn't call his home. A subversive memory slid into his mind. "Chap I met told me you got invited to the White House."

"Me and twenty others."

"This chap said you were titled."

Zoë groaned. "*That* again. It's all so boring. Mother married Lord Shapland, twenty years ago, fucked him to death. You met her, didn't you?"

"I did. Unforgettable cocktail party. She was drinking battery acid."

"Yes, she was tough, and that's about all. Eventually she married an American senator. Arizona, I think. He didn't last long. She died last year. Didn't I tell you? I thought I told you. Anyway, I got everything. The lawyers are still counting the money. Do I inherit the title or am I just a sad and pathetic Honourable? Frankly, sweetheart, I don't care a damn."

"Haven't you got a brother? In Rhodesia?"

"Dead too. Spencer Herrick-Herrick. He had fifty thousand acres of beef ranch. Tried to ride a steer, for a bet, and broke his neck. The only thing he didn't leave me was his hyphen." She screwed up her fish-and-chip wrapper and gave it to him. It was a greasy mess.

"Thanks awfully. That's all I am to you, isn't it? Just a rich woman's plaything."

"You're so good at it, darling."

"Well, you're not the only pebble on the beach, you know. Ginger Rogers wanted to marry me."

"Have you got her number? Ask her to stay. The manor house has a ballroom. You and Ginger could jitterbug the night away. Is she Democrat or Republican?"

"I've no idea. We didn't discuss politics."

"Oh dear. Deadly dull."

As they drove home, Silk wondered if he was dull. Just because he was training to fly a Vulcan didn't make him personally interesting. He had known plenty of pilots, hot stuff in the air, boring as old boots on the ground. Tommy Flynn: nothing ever went right for him. His bitching, gentle but endless, could empty a Mess like the smell of bad drains. So Flynn was dull. Not as bad as Bob Rossi, who thought he was funny, told tedious jokes, nobody laughed except Bob. "I've got a thousand like that," he said, and told another. And another. Imagine sharing a room with Bob. Imagine sharing a life. What a bore. And that fat navigator, Jenks or Tonks or something, did his sums with the speed of light in the kite, but off duty he couldn't decide anything in less than an hour and a half. Ask him if he felt like a drink and he'd think hard and say he wasn't sure. Amusing at first. Then boring. Bloody boring. "You think I'm a bit dull, don't you?" he asked Zoë.

"I didn't marry you for excitement, darling."

"That's not an answer."

"No, but it's the best you'll get." She spoke lightly. "I'm too tired to argue."

Half a mile later, he said, "Listen: if I don't create highpowered, high-falutin, highly polished bullshit, the kind that has Members of Parliament wetting themselves with joy . . ."

"Please no. Awful thought."

"Well, it's not because I've got my brain switched off and my thumb up my bum. I've got plenty to say that you'll never hear. The Official Secrets Act sees to that."

"I know, Silko. I've signed it too."

He was so surprised that his foot gave the accelerator a small stab. "You have? Why?"

She snuggled down in her seat. "If I told you, I'd be breaking the Act. Slow down, darling, before you get arrested."

3

There was a lot to learn. The Vulcan looked sleek and simple on the outside, but the cockpit was dense with dials, gauges, buttons, switches. There were 56 items of equipment for navigation, signalling and lighting, from the accelerometer to the second pilot's knee-pad lamp. There were 37 separate controls for the engines and fuel system, starting with the bomb-bay tanks control panel and ending with the throttle control levers (re-light press switch in handles). All this equipment fed vital, or at least valuable, information and assistance to the pilot and co-pilot. They also had to manoeuvre the aeroplane. 38 flying controls and instruments made that possible. Some were familiar: rudder pedals, auto-pilot, air speed indicator. Some were not: artificial feel failure, yaw damper, machmeter. Instruments and equipment overflowed onto side panels. Yet more items filled the elbow space between the pilots. The Vulcan's cockpit was small and intensely crowded. By contrast the Lanc had been as simple as a country bus.

Silk was quick learner. All those years flying all those types for Air America had kept his brain sharp.

As they were walking out to the bomber, his instructor said, "You know what makes her tick, but do you trust her?"

For one mad moment, Silk thought he meant Zoë. But Silk had never mentioned Zoë. "Trust her?" he said.

"Some people have a problem. The nose pokes out so far in front of the aeroplane, we can't even see the wingtips, let alone the tailplane, which of course doesn't exist. We have to take everything on faith."

87

"I've got faith. The Ascension into Heaven was good enough for the Almighty, so it's good enough for me."

"That's blind faith. Do you always trust the instruments? Don't you get a flicker of doubt sometimes? You're out in front, driving, all alone. Maybe the rest of the Vulcan *isn't* following."

"It wouldn't dare. No, I haven't got a problem that way. I'm beginning to worry about you, though."

The instructor laughed. "Oh, I trust her. Some kites are just heaps of hardware, but . . ." They reached the bomber and strolled around it. He touched the tailfin. He patted a jet pipe, and rapped its end-cap with his knuckles. "Purpose?" he said.

"Keep the dust out."

"And the rain. The Vulcan is packed full of electrics. Wet weather is bad for her vitals. You get all sorts of nasty little short circuits."

Silk looked at the huge sweep of the wings. Close to the fuselage they were thick enough to swallow the engines. At their extremes they tapered to thin, finely curved tips. You could play tennis on top of a Vulcan. Doubles tennis. "You're quite fond of her, aren't you?"

The instructor saw a thin streak of birdshit and picked it off. "More than fond. Flying the Vulcan is the greatest privilege imaginable. It makes sex look like gardening."

Silk had done a lot of gardening at weekends. Zoë was always busy: writing, phoning, meeting V.I.P.s whose names he'd never heard of. Silk didn't want to think about sex. "Not that I'm complaining," he said to the instructor, "but isn't it odd that Air Ministry should recruit an elderly gent to fly such a beautiful beast? Why me?"

"You've been flying everything for twenty years. You haven't crashed and burned. I suppose they trust you."

"Big mistake," Silk said. "I never paid my last mess bill, in 1944. It was a whopper, too."

Later, the instructor put him in the left-hand seat, the captain's position, while he took the second pilot's place. At twelve thousand feet they found a sheet of cirrus cloud, thin as lace curtains. "You've shown me you can fly fast and high," the instructor said. "Piece of cake, in a Vulcan. Now show me you know how to fly slow. Assume the cloud is ground level. Perform a little display for the crowd."

Silk flew wide circles, letting the speed decay to 180 knots. "Too fast," the instructor said. Silk eased the throttles a hint more. "Trust me," the instructor said. "She's a lady. She won't stall." Silk banked. He was two hundred feet above the cirrus. The Vulcan seemed to be hanging in the sky, yet it flew beautifully. Cautiously, he reversed the bank. The Vulcan swung comfortably from one wingtip to the other. He turned through a slow half-circle and came back. "I could open the bomb-bay doors," he suggested. "The crowd would like that."

"You're the captain."

Silk did it. The Vulcan revealed what she was made of.

When they landed, the instructor said, "That went okay. But don't try anything flashy. Every aeroplane has its limits. A couple of years ago someone displayed a Vulcan at low level, flew too fast, exceeded the 'g' limits, and the entire starboard wing disintegrated, *bang*. Ass over tit, straight into the deck. God knows what anyone found to bury."

"Sandbags, probably." Silk looked at the bomber. "Doesn't seem possible," he said.

"That's what they thought, right up to the bang. After that it was too late to think."

* * *

The course lasted ten weeks. Silk studied every aspect of the Vulcan:

airframe limitations, engine controls, fuel economy, emergency procedures, ejection seat, oxygen system, ditching drill, airbrakes, and a hundred others. He worked hard on everything except the ditching drill. He feared the sea. If 120 tons of Vulcan stopped flying over the ocean, it would make an almighty splash, as if God had dropped anchor. There would be no paddling away in a life raft. Silk was convinced of this. Ditching drill was irrelevant.

He spent many sweaty hours in the flight simulator, where every part of the Vulcan was fallible. Single engine failed on take-off. Double engines failed. The take-off was aborted, or he got airborne only to hit severe buffeting. He had to land crosswind. Or with only one undercarriage leg down. Or in thick rain with no windscreen wipers. He had engine flame-outs and relighting at altitude. Instruments failed. Cabin pressure failed. Heating failed. He enjoyed it all. Air America had had cock-ups, but nothing like this.

4

Silk completed the course, qualified, got his posting, packed his bags and drove to the cottage. A man with a shaggy grey beard was painting the window frames. A fat spaniel sprawled on the grass and watched. "It's not for sale," the man said. "We just bought it."

"Damn." Silk felt cheated: he hadn't even had a chance to say goodbye to the old place. "I . . . uh . . ." He didn't know how to define himself. "Used to live here," he said.

The man stopped painting. "Are you the husband? Good. I found something in the attic you can take away." He went inside. Silk squatted on his haunches and stroked the spaniel. It growled and tried to bite, but it was too fat and slow. "Well, sod you, then, you miserable bitch," he said. The man came out with a leather suitcase. "Locked," he said. "No key."

Silk took it. "I suppose all our stuff is now at the manor?"

"Manor? Don't know anything about a manor. Forwarding address I got given is Rich something. Goodrich? Goodrich House . . ." He squinted at Silk. "Didn't she tell you?"

"Don't bother. It's not far away." He heaved the suitcase into the car and left fast. He was low on petrol, he didn't have a map, but someone must be able to tell him how to find the bloody silly house.

He drove around this part of Lincolnshire for forty minutes until he was grim with failure and sick of repeating the same question to people whose eyes immediately went as blank as old pennies. The needle on his fuel gauge was tapping empty. And then, finally, he met a policeman on a bicycle who said he knew for certain there was no Goodrich House in the county. On the other hand there was a Richards Court, big house, just bought by a lady M.P., not far off.

"I may have to walk," Silk said. "I'm running on fumes."

The policeman mounted his bike and led the way to a petrol station, which was shut, but he got the owner to leave his TV and unlock his pumps.

"You're a prince," Silk said. The policeman aimed a finger at Silk's medal ribbons. "You did your bit, too," he said.

* * *

Richards Court sat in its own grounds, half a mile from the road, hidden by woodland, an early Victorian country house with a stable block and a dairy, plus a few smaller buildings which stood in the background, minding their manners.

The east side of the house was flanked by a broad terrace. A pair of peacocks was in residence. "Good evening," Silk said. "You must be Abbot and Costello." One bird slowly displayed its tail feathers. "I stand corrected. Rodgers and Hammerstein."

French windows opened, and a man in black trousers and a dove-grey waistcoat appeared. "May I help you, sir?"

"That depends. Who are you?"

"I am Stevens, sir. The under-butler."

"Well, I'm Silk, the under-husband. Is my wife here?"

"Her ladyship is in conference, sir. In the library."

"In conference? Who with? Never mind. Tell her I'm here. Tell her I've brought Rumpty and Tumpty with me and we'd all like the pleasure of her company."

"Rumpty and Tumpty." Stevens didn't even blink. "Very good, sir. Drinks are in the Music Room, if you would like to wait there."

Silk was on his second Scotch-and-water when Zoë hurried in, kissed him, hugged him, and awoke long-forgotten tremors in his loins. "Darling, how gorgeous to see you, and looking so well, you should have telephoned, we're frantically busy here, isn't it a dreadful dump? But big."

"I've been trying to find Something Court. I've driven all over—"

"Damn, damn. I meant to tell you. *Frantically* busy, you've no idea. The thing is, I knew a man called Richards, centuries ago, complete shit, I couldn't live anywhere called Richards Court, so I changed it to The Grange . . . Anyway, you're here. We'll put you in the Red Room. Lovely views."

"The only view I want is you, starkers."

She kissed him again and backed away, towards the door. "Poor Rumpty and Tumpty . . . This thing I'm chairing will go on all night . . ."

"I can wait. Tell you what: I'll stand behind you and look staunch. That'll speed things up."

Zoë shuddered, purely for effect. "Blow things up, more likely."

"Really? What's it all about?"

"Can't say, Silko. Politics. You know."

"All I know is I've been flying all week and driving all evening, and . . ." He heard the grate of bitterness in his voice and let that sentence die. "How about tomorrow?"

"No, tomorrow's hopeless. Hordes of people coming, absolute hordes." She wrinkled her brow. "Perhaps Tuesday?"

"I'll be flying. I've been posted to Kindrick. Remember? My last base, in '44. Twenty miles away."

"Kindrick, how nice for you. You'll meet all your chums again." She blew a kiss and was gone.

"All my fucking chums from fucking Kindrick are fucking dead," Silk said. He opened the lid of a grand piano and ran his forefinger down the keys. "Not Freddy Redman. He's in the Air Ministry, but that's a living death, isn't it?"

He left the piano and stood in the middle of the room, sipping his whisky and thinking about dead aircrew, something he had managed to avoid doing for ten, fifteen years. Then a tall, lithe young man came in and introduced himself as Charles Ferris, Zoë's personal assistant. "I look after her appointments book," he said. "She thought we might liaise."

"I don't want to bloody liaise. Liaise about what?"

"Mutually convenient dates," Ferris said. Silk stared, frowning as if the light hurt his eyes. "Oh well," Ferris said. "Not such a good idea, after all."

"Here's a much better idea," Silk said. "Where's the nearest pub?"

When he opened the Citroën's door he saw the big leather suitcase on the back seat, and on impulse he dragged it out and flung it away. He got in and started the car and knew how childish he'd been, so he got out and carried the suitcase into the house and dumped it. Stevens, the under-butler, came in sight. "Not mine," Silk said. "Tell her ladyship it was found in the attic. Bloody heavy. Don't herniate yourself." Then he went to the pub. They had ham sandwiches two inches thick and best bitter that washed away the sins of the world. When he got back to The Grange only Stevens was still up.

5

He slept late. By the time he reached the breakfast room, all the guests had eaten and moved on. He had a kipper and bacon and eggs and read a copy of *The Times* that had coffee stains on the Parliamentary News.

It was a mild, sunny morning. He went for a stroll around The Grange. The place was even bigger than he thought: he identified an ice-house, a laundry and a sprawling garage, once a coach-house. Under a Scots pine he found a cemetery for pets. He scraped the moss from a small tombstone. *Tommy, a Good Pal*, in flowery letters. Another stone was for *Jessy, Gone But Not Forgotten.* "Not true," Silk said. "Jessy's gone and forgotten and so are you."

He looked around. It must take a platoon of servants to run The Grange. Obviously Zoë had more money than God. And she spent it hand over fist. Well, so what? He wasn't being asked to do any work. Then why did the sight of this place depress him?

At the back of the house was a walled garden. Inside it, dirty smoke was boiling up. He found a doorway. An elderly man in overalls was poking the fire with a spade. As Silk got closer he saw that what the man was burning was the leather suitcase.

"I guess you're the gardener," Silk said.

"I'm Ted, sir." He took off his cap.

"And that's a suitcase."

"Her ladyship's orders, sir."

Silk took Ted's spade and chopped at the locks until the suitcase sprang open. It was full of clothing. On top was an R.A.F. officer's uniform, neatly folded. The smoke made Silk cough, but he used the edge of the spade to lift out a tunic. "Pilot," he said. "See? Flight lieutenant." The smoke swirled and went for his eyes, so he let the tunic fall. "Damn. Damn."

"Someone you knew, sir?"

"Chap called Langham. Tony Langham. Good type." He gave back the spade. "Rather a long time ago. Keep up the good work, Ted."

Silk collected his things from the Red Room and drove to R.A.F. Kindrick. Tony had been her first husband, she owned his clothes, she had a perfect right to destroy them, nobody should live in the past. Still, it was a hell of a way for Tony's kit to end up. First he went down in flames, then his best uniform went up in flames. Silk put his foot to the floor and made the Citroën charge so hard that it left Tony in its slipstream. Speed cures all.

PART TWO

BAGS OF SWANK

OKAY IF I STRANGLE YOUR WIFE?

1

The R.A.F. Kindrick that Silk remembered from 1944 had been a windy prairie with a triangle of runways and a cluster of buildings and hangars whose camouflage paint was peeling like sunburn. Now the same wind blew; everything else was different. The new runways were twice as long and the whole station had grown until there were signposts at the road junctions. The corrugated black Nissen huts had disappeared. Today the buildings were brick, the windows glittered, the paintwork looked new. The grass was inch-perfect, as measured by the R.A.F. Service Policemen who patrolled the base with Alsatian dogs. In Silk's day, the S.P.s had passed their time in the back of the guardroom, making toast on the coke stove. Then, there had been numerous gaps in the perimeter fence, short cuts to the pubs used by groundcrew and aircrew. Now the perimeter was wired tight like East Berlin.

Another difference was the station commander. Silk remembered Group Captain Rafferty, the big man who always stayed up late to say, "Damned good show." Now Kindrick had two squadrons of Vulcans and a group captain named Pulvertaft.

He summoned the batch of newly arrived aircrew to his office and asked them to sit. *Bugger me*, Silk thought, *he's not much older than I am.* Station commanders were supposed to be grey-haired types who tore you off a strip for beating up the control tower. If a kite hit a stuffed cloud, the station commander carried the wreath from the Air Ministry. This bloke was as fresh as aftershave.

"Let's get Pulvertaft out of the way," the group captain said. "An odd name, but I didn't choose it. Not nearly as funny as, for instance, Mönchengladbach, a very amusing town in the Ruhr where the flak got my Lancaster in September 1944." Pulvertaft wasn't smiling. "I'll do a deal with you. I won't bore you with my memoirs if you won't sneer at my name."

That's smart, Silk thought. *That's clever. Now he's softened us up, here comes the sucker punch.*

"You have the best, and the worst, job in the world," Pulvertaft said. "You have the Vulcan, incomparably the finest bomber. That's the best bit. Your job is to fly to the Soviet Union and destroy cities. That's the worst bit. Why? Because, for the first time in Britain's history, the army can't save us and neither can the navy. If Moscow decides to go berserk, Soviet bombers can attack us with nuclear weapons. Say we destroy ninety per cent. Ten per cent will get through, enough to turn these islands into a smoking wasteland." He tugged his ear. *Routine speech,* Silk thought. *Given it a hundred times.*

"And of course there would be a hail of incoming nuclear missiles," Pulvertaft said. "Nothing could stop them. Only one thing can deter Moscow, and that is fear. If Moscow decides to obliterate Britain, it does so in the sure and certain knowledge that Britain will obliterate Moscow and simultaneously two dozen cities from Leningrad to Stalingrad. You will do that. And be in no doubt: you *will* do it. No turning back. Any doubt, any hesitation, is suicidal. The maniac in Moscow cannot be allowed to think we do not mean what we say." He let that sink in. "Any questions so far?"

Silk raised a hand. "So it's crucial that the Moscow maniac knows we exist, sir."

"We know he knows."

"But not everything, presumably."

"Just the bare facts. If he discovers anything more, it's a chink in our armour." Pulvertaft paused. "A metaphor from the medieval battlefield. Meaning?"

"A knife in the ribs?" a navigator said.

"Yes. For Bomber Command, security is ten-tenths of the battle. We keep the enemy guessing. *Outside* your squadron, say nothing. *Inside* your squadron, say no more than the other person needs to know. Never allow yourself to become vulnerable to outsiders. Last week I got rid of a highly competent sergeant armourer. All his pay went on dogs and horses. Compulsive gambling is a weakness, a vulnerability, a chink in the armour. He was groundcrew. Imagine how much higher your standards must be."

2

Silk had to show his pass three times before he found his pilot in a room in the sprawling Operations block. He was Squadron Leader Quinlan: D.S.O. and D.F.C., taller than average, thick black moustache, wide grey eyes. He was looking at a wall map of Eastern Europe and Russia. It covered the whole wall.

"Glad to see you," Quinlan said. "We've got a training exercise this afternoon, and I hate borrowing crew. I suppose you've had the station commander's standard speech?"

"Scare Moscow, and keep your nose clean."

"You're married, as are we all. So that removes one major problem. What's left? Drink, drugs, politics, religious mania? Nude leapfrog? Playing the ukulele? You've been cleared by Special Branch. Don't bend the aeroplane, and you should have five happy years here."

"That would make a nice change."

"And if at any time you get a funny feeling that someone's

watching you, don't panic, because somebody is. Always."

Silk wrinkled his nose and shuffled his feet. "I'm not supposed to tell you this, sir, but . . . I'm here to watch you."

Quinlan was only half-amused. "Jokes like that are in bad taste, Silko. We live in each other's pockets, week in, month out. A Vulcan crew can get twitchy. You play silly buggers with someone like Tom Tucker, my nav radar, and he'll deck you." Quinlan threw a punch that stopped an inch from Silk's nose. "And when you're lying there, stunned and bleeding all over the carpet, don't come running to me for sympathy."

"I withdraw my confession," Silk said. "Not watching anyone. Never even saw them. What should I know about this exercise?"

Quinlan turned to the map and found a town about 150 miles north of Moscow. "Jaroslavl. That's our target."

"Not very big, is it?"

"And considerably smaller by the time we've finished."

3

The whole point of having the Vulcan was being able to get your retaliation airborne before the Russian nuclear weapon hit the ground. Silk had learned all about this from lectures at his Operational Conversion Unit. Four minutes was the maximum warning time that Bomber Command could expect. "You haven't got four minutes," the lecturer had said. "You haven't got two minutes. If your bomber has not come unstuck and begun climbing like a rocket within two minutes of scramble, the blast from the nuclear explosion will get you and fling you far out over the Irish Sea, where you will descend in tiny burning fragments. You won't like the Irish Sea, gentlemen. It is cold and rough, like my first wife. Not recommended."

The R.A.F. had boiled the answer down to three words: Quick Reaction Alert, or Q.R.A. Quinlan's training exercise began with a practice Q.R.A. The crew moved into a caravan that was parked at the end of the runway near their aircraft.

Silk had already met the other three men, all flight lieutenants. "Nav plotter," Quinlan said. "Jack Hallett." He was short and stocky, with a round and happy face; he looked more like a farmer. "Jack drives the bus. We just sit in front and look brave."

"Damn right," Hallett said.

"Nav radar: Tom Tucker." This was the man with the short fuse. He shook hands and did not smile. Quinlan said: "If we ever drop the thunderflash, it'll be Tom's finger on the button." Tucker displayed the finger: right index. He said nothing.

"Air Electronics Officer, Nat Dando," Quinlan said. "A.E.O. stands for Any Old Excuse. They got the letters wrong, like everything else. I don't know what he does, but it smells of sulphur."

"I bamboozle Ivan's defences." Dando was as sleek as a band-leader. "I baffle him with wizardry. The navs couldn't baffle a pussy-cat with a kipper."

"A kipper," Silk said. "Heavens above. And here's me thinking you used a mackerel."

"I didn't understand any of that," Quinlan said, "and I'm grateful for my ignorance. Everyone been briefed? No questions? Good. Here's my briefing: It's a long flight, so empty your bladders."

"He always says that," Hallett told Silk.

"It's not a Lanc," Quinlan said. "You can't go for a stroll down the fuselage and pee in the Elsan, because there's no fuselage and no Elsan. And I don't like plastic bottles of piss in my aeroplane. Unprofessional."

*

103

They waited in the aircrew caravan, wearing flying kit, for almost an hour. "No room for ballroom dancing in a Vulcan," Quinlan told Silk, "so on word of command, we sprint to the kite in strict order of charm and ability. First me, then you – up the ladder and into the cockpit – followed by nav plotter, nav radar and A.E.O. Door shut, engines fire, wheels roll, goodbye Mother Earth in one minute fortyish."

"And be sure to take your lucky Cornish pixie," Dando said, "because he won't let you go back for it." He showed Silk a tiny coin. "George the Third farthing. Life insurance. Cheap at the price."

"I thought all that superstitious stuff went out with the war."

Hallett fished a tattered ace of spades from an inside pocket. "Trumps," he said. "It got me through a tour on Hampdens in 1940."

Silk looked at Tucker. "You too?" But Tucker yawned.

"Tom's not superstitious," Quinlan said. "All the same, he hasn't changed his underpants since his first op. February '42, wasn't it?"

"Hamburg," Tucker said. "Bloody dump."

"Somebody gave me a lucky greyhound once," Silk said. "Bequeathed it, actually. Nice dog, but not quick enough. Got flattened by the C.O.'s car."

"Luck ran out," Hallett said.

"Not necessarily," Dando said. "Dog's dead, Silko isn't."

A klaxon blared. "Into battle!" Quinlan was running for the door. "Go go go!" Silk was still tightening his straps when the Vulcan turned onto the runway and Quinlan opened the throttles. By now Silk was accustomed to the sudden charge, as if the bomber were racing down a slope. In a fully loaded Lancaster, the take-off run had been toil; and with the roar of engines alongside the cockpit, it had been deafening toil. Now the Vulcan accelerated with the zeal of a fighter, and its engines created their thunder far to the rear. Silk checked dials and gauges, and thought: *One hundred and twenty tons.* Quinlan eased the stick back and they were airborne. He touched the brakes to check the wheelspin, and then retracted the undercarriage. It took eight seconds for the bays to swallow the gear. Now smooth as a swallow, the Vulcan stood on its tail and climbed.

Quinlan levelled out at fifty-five thousand feet. There was nothing to see but blue sky so dazzling it was nearly white, and not much of that: the windscreen was narrow and it gave only a forward view. The cockpit roof was solid canopy. Small portholes to left and right added little.

"Not much to look at, is there?" Quinlan said.

"I had a sports car with a bigger windscreen," Silk said.

"There's nothing to see up here but thermonuclear explosions. See one, you've seen 'em all. Fix the blackout."

Silk closed the anti-flash screens on the windshield and the portholes. Quinlan flew blind to the Baltic and back again, on courses given by the navigators. Silk's main job was to make sure the fourteen fuel tanks were used in the correct sequence, and to stir the sugar in Quinlan's coffee. After four hours of sitting in near-darkness he opened the screen as Quinlan made his approach to Kindrick. It was dusk.

They taxied to a hardstanding and gave the bomber to the groundcrew. "Enjoy yourself?" Quinlan asked.

"I have a strange feeling that we went nowhere, and we did nothing." Silk said.

"Oh, we went somewhere. Not Jaroslavl. Not this time. Jaroslavl would have been the next stop on the line. But we got close enough to have Soviet radar breathing hard. I bet they scrambled a few MiGs, in case we pushed our luck too far."

"With their anti-flash screens closed?"

"Possibly."

"Like two blind boxers."

"It's a little more complex than that."

5

The crew went to debriefing. It was a sober business, far removed from the wartime sessions that Silk remembered, when some men were all noise and bad jokes while others couldn't speak of what they'd seen, and everyone was weary and hungry for bacon and eggs. This was different. This was experts discussing technical problems. Their talk was spiced with jargon; Silk half-understood about half of it. After a while he got up to stretch his legs and saw a face that made a fool of time and place and rushed him back to 409 Squadron, and Kindrick, and 1942.

Silk didn't think. The jolt of astonishment made the decision for him and he walked across the room. The man was talking to another officer. "Skull," Silk said.

"Not now, old boy," the man said, without even looking around, and went on talking. Silk backed away. He felt a rush of blood to his ears: he had been snubbed; put in his place like a thoughtless servant. By Skull, for Christ's sake. He looked again. Skull was a wing commander, talking to an air commodore. Some things never changed in Bomber Command and rank was one. In the R.A.F., a blunder was known as a "black". Silk had just put up a black. What rankled was that Skull had caused it. In the war, Skull had put up more blacks than God made little green apples. Never bothered him then. Now he couldn't bring himself to look around when he told Silk to push off. What a sod.

6

Skelton had been a young Cambridge don (Tudor history, with special reference to the northern Puritan sects) when he fell in love, disastrously, and joined the University Air Squadron on the rebound. It was a reckless act. Hitler was chucking his weight about, everyone said war was inevitable, Skelton thought that maybe he would die a glorious, sacrificial death, and then she'd be sorry. There was never any risk of this. By now she was in Kenya, happily married to a man who hadn't read a book since he left school; and the R.A.F. knew at once that, even in the direst national emergency, it could never make a pilot out of Skelton. They could straighten his academic stoop and teach him to salute; they could even cram his lanky body into a cockpit; but his spectacles were as thick as clamshells and without them he couldn't see worth a damn. Forget aircrew.

"My word, this is our lucky day," the University Air Squadron adjutant said to him. "We badly need an Intelligence Officer, and you're splendidly qualified."

War came. Skelton was posted to a Fighter Command, to a Hurricane squadron. On his first day he got his nickname. His forehead bulged, his cheeks narrowed, his nose was boney, he had to be Skull.

He learned his trade by on-the-job training. If he had a fault it was his brain. The Cambridge don in him could not ignore the truth, and sometimes he challenged the official view of the war. Commanding officers resented critical comment from a man who didn't fly and therefore couldn't know what he was talking about. At the height of the Battle of Britain he infuriated an air vice-marshal by pointing out an awkward truth. It was a black too many. Skull got sacked.

He was posted to a training airfield in a remote and drab corner of Scotland. "We make our own entertainment here," a flying instructor told him. "Ping-pong and funerals, mainly." Skull avoided the funerals. He did a lot of trout fishing, put up no blacks, and was quietly living out the war when he was suddenly ordered south, to join 409 Squadron of Bomber Command, which was flying Wellingtons. That was where he met Silk. They had little in common, but sometimes opposites attract. Two years of war, and war's cock-ups, had made sceptics of them both. Bomber Command claimed to be hammering Germany. Skull saw the intelligence reports and did not believe them. Silk saw the burning incendiaries and knew they had missed the target; often they had missed the city; sometimes they hit the wrong city. Nobody else agreed. Naturally, Skull and Silk formed a connection. It was not a friendship. All the friends Silk had known when war broke out were dead, and he didn't expect to live much longer. No point in manufacturing grief: that was Silk's opinion. He amused Skull. Few pilots were so candid about faults and failures when senior officers were listening. Skull felt encouraged to speak his mind, and he put up a fresh series of blacks. Silk was a valuable pilot; he became 409's joker in the pack, too good to lose. Skull was an intelligence officer, a penguin, a flightless bird, and he got the sack. Kicked out of Bomber Command and into the Desert Air Force.

"The bad news is there's nothing in Libya but sand and camel dung," he told Silk before he left. "The good news is you can have as much as you like." Silk made a gentle belch. "Not a funny joke," Skull said. "Not even a joke, actually." That was the last Silk heard of him. Until now.

7

An airman tapped on Silk's door, presented Wing Commander

Skelton's compliments, and asked if Flight Lieutenant Silk was free to dine tonight. If so, the car would be outside at 1930 hours.

It was a Lagonda. The tyres alone cost more than Silk's Citroën. The leather upholstery smelled like the tearoom of the House of Lords. The engine had a soft growl that belonged in the Brazilian jungle. "Load of junk," Silk said. "Piece of piss. You had this bloody tractor in 1942."

"Regular maintenance is the key," Skull said. "A sergeant in the M.T. section does it for me. Not illegal, of course. Well, maybe just a tiny bit illegal." As he drove out of the base he took the R.A.F. police sergeant's salute. "Sorry I had to treat you so boorishly, Silko, but when an air commodore is in full flow, you don't cut him off."

"Don't you? I wouldn't know." Silk stretched his legs: there was ample room. "Air commodores never speak to flunkeys like me." His backside slid on the leather as Skull accelerated into a long right-hand bend. "But I see you're still climbing the greasy pole, wing commander."

"The rank suits me. Civilians think I actually command a wing."

"Took you fifteen years."

"No, no. Much less. When the war ended, I went back to Cambridge. Not a wise move. Severe anticlimax. They thought modern history ended with Queen Victoria's death. Any unpleasantness after that was unfit for discussion. So I left and learned Russian instead."

"Cunning bugger."

"I rather enjoyed it."

"Who paid?"

"Uncle Henry. What a sport he was. On his eighty-third birthday he hooked a twelve-pound salmon, had a heart attack, and left me everything. Perfect timing. It financed two years at Cambridge, one at Harvard, one in Berlin. By 1950 the Cold War was big business and the R.A.F. was quite keen to welcome back a slightly shop-soiled intelligence officer who was fluent in Russian."

"What's the Russian for bullshit?"

"Almost everything," Skull said. "Alas."

Ten minutes later they stopped at a small manor house, steeply gabled and half-timbered. "Private dining club," Skull said. "There's a vast U.S. Air Force base just down the road. This is where the higher-ranking officers can escape and think the unthinkable over a good claret. I'm a member."

"So you're an honorary Yank."

"Not as honorary as you were. Don't argue, don't get into any fights, smile if you can, and *listen*."

"God help us," Silk said. "It's a Baptist outing."

The dining room was large. All the curtains were closed. The tables were widely spaced and dimly lit. Somewhere the Modern Jazz Quartet was playing "Misty", maybe in the minstrel gallery, more likely on L.P., and with great restraint.

"I was wrong," Silk said. "It's a Baptist speakeasy."

A middle-aged man in a steel-grey suit came to greet them. He had rimless spectacles and a square face. He reminded Silk of a geologist he'd known in Venezuela. That man looked like Harry Truman's kid brother but he found great gushers of oil, so what did a face tell you? Skull introduced Silk to Brigadier Karl Leppard.

"I flew with Barney Knox in the Hitler war," Leppard said.

"Awfully nice chap. He got me into Air America."

"Which doesn't exist," Skull said.

"Just like Communist China," Silk said. "And the far side of the moon."

Dinner was simple. Everyone ordered steak. "They hang the beef in a meathouse out back," Leppard told Silk, "until it starts to rot around the edges. Called creative waste."

"We did that in Lancasters. Called area bombing."

"No nostalgia, Silko," Skull warned him. "Six years of war was enough, without your tedious reminiscences." Chilled bottled beer arrived. "What's new from the Pentagon?"

"Well, Kennedy says we'll do anything, go anywhere to protect liberty," Leppard said. "The Pentagon seriously doubts that, but not out loud."

"Damn good beer," Silk said.

"So Tibet is fairly safe," Skull said. "The West is not going to fight Red tyranny in Tibet."

Leppard spread his hands. "No votes in it."

"Hungary?"

"No oil in it."

"Saudi Arabia?"

"Be serious, Skull."

"Well, that leaves Germany," Skull said. "We think the Kremlin thinks it's the jewel in their crown. We think they think we think it's not worth shedding Anglo-Saxon blood over. They fought Hitler, they won, they deserve it. All of it."

"I agree," Silk said. "Take sauerkraut, for instance."

Leppard waited briefly, but that was all Silk had to say.

"We don't think they think they can get away with a smash-and-grab attack on Germany," Leppard said. "Not with armed B-52s on patrol 24 hours a day."

"That scenario assumes rational, reasonable behaviour," Skull said. "War isn't rational. It's a dance of death."

"Sure. But this isn't about war, is it? It's about non-war. And we think the Kremlin respects logic too much to invite nuclear reprisal."

"Logic?" Skull said. "I knew a professor of logic who strangled his wife."

"She was a miserable cow," Silk said. "She had it coming."

Soon the steaks arrived and the conversation lost him. It was dotted with too many technicalities: talk of Blue Danubes and Yellow Suns, Red Shrimps and Blue Divers, and much more. Later they got around to discussing Micky Finns and Lone Rangers. Silk half-remembered some of the terms from O.T.U. lectures; right now there were more interesting things in his life. He ate his steak. It was thick as his wrist and so tender, you could cut it with a spoon.

Coffee on the terrace. They had it to themselves.

"Shall we examine the broader aspect?" Skull suggested. "Hail to the Chief! Everyone here seems to think he's a good egg. What do your people think?"

"We think that Kruschev thinks that Kennedy's just a pretty face," Leppard said.

"Fur coat and no knickers," Silk said.

Skull almost winced. "And you think that Kennedy thinks that Kruschev . . .?"

"Is a loose cannon."

"All mouth and no trousers," Silk said.

Leppard polished his glasses with a handkerchief and peered at Silk. "Is your family in the garment trade?" he asked.

"I hear voices. Nasty prang in '43." Silk tapped his forehead. "Solid silver. Grateful nation."

"Do shut up, Silko . . . What are the world's hot spots, Karl? I mean, leaving aside Berlin, where would you say Kruschev and Kennedy are most likely to lock horns?"

"The Congo first. Unbelievably rich: copper, uranium, cobalt, diamonds, gold. We can't just leave it to the Soviets to take their pick. Persia second. The Shah's getting old. Russia's itching to get the oil he's sold to us. Thirdly: Cuba, which is more of a nuisance than a problem. Hell, if Moscow wants to buy Castro's sugar, let 'em."

"Well, I say we bomb Cuba," Silk declared. Skull closed his eyes. Leppard poured more coffee. "Congo's got uranium, Persia's got oil," Silk said. "It's absurd to bomb the stuff we want. What's Cuba got? Bloody awful rum, nobody wants *that*. So the obvious answer is: bomb Cuba. No Cuba, no problem."

"Crushing logic," Leppard said. "Okay if I strangle your wife?"

"Time for bed," Skull said. "Any word on the great cricket–baseball occasion?"

"I'll have news tomorrow," Leppard said.

* * *

Skull was silent for the first five minutes of the drive back to base. Then he said: "Is there anything that isn't a joke to you?"

"Drowning. Definitely not funny, especially in the ocean. And dentists. Never heard a dentist joke that worked. And dogshit. Drowning, dentists and dogshit. Anything beginning with a D is bad news, unless of course it's dentists drowning in dogshit."

"Was that a joke?" Skull didn't wait for an answer. "How about death?"

Silk yawned. "I never saw much fun in death. Dying, yes, plenty of jokes there. New Yorker cartoon. Two old ladies looking at a tombstone. One says: I told him it wouldn't kill him to be nice once in a while, but it seems I was wrong." Silk laughed freely.

Skull changed gear. "Mildly facetious."

"Bloody funny. Your trouble, Skull, is you've got too many rings on your sleeve. Mental handcuffs, that's what they are."

"Not a problem you're ever likely to have."

"I liked you better in the war. You didn't believe anybody, you put up lots of blacks, you got the chop. Now you're too damn serious."

"We do a serious job."

"Cobblers. We don't do anything. We fly nowhere and bomb nothing and come home, and none of it makes a blind bit of difference."

Skull allowed a long pause before he answered. "If that's what you genuinely believe," he said, "you made a large mistake in rejoining Bomber Command. You've joined a suicide club, my friend, and we play for the highest stakes, nothing less than the survival of civilization itself and—"

"I've heard that speech," Silk said. "It was all balls then and it's all balls now."

End of conversation.

TONS OF MAGIC BOXES

1

The crew had breakfast together. For the first time, Silk looked around the Mess and got a sense of the size of the two Vulcan squadrons stationed at Kindrick. About a hundred men were present. Others would be abroad or on leave. Enough to crew twenty Vulcans, and scattered across England were another dozen V-bomber squadrons, Vulcans and Valiants and Victors. Each bomber could knock out a Soviet city. Silk knew that all war was brutal, but this struck him as a very casual kind of organized slaughter. You might kill the entire Moscow Philharmonic in the middle of a nice bit of Tchaikowsky. Or annihilate all the girls in the Bolshoi ballet. There were some real corkers in the Bolshoi, he'd seen a film, what amazing legs! Put him in bed and wrap a pair of legs like that around him and he'd join the Red air force . . . "Oh, thanks," he said. A plate of bacon and eggs had appeared in front of him.

"I hear Skull took you to the Bum Steer last night," Jack Hallett said.

"Is that what it's called? Very clever."

"Rumour has it the steaks are beyond compare," Nat Dando said.

"I've had worse. There was a price to pay: Skull's conversation. Deadly dull. Not like the old days."

"Everything's funny when you're young," Hallett said. "Remember how we laughed during those ops on Berlin in winter? Hilarious."

"I saw two Jerry nightfighters collide," Tom Tucker said flatly.

They looked at him, expecting more. "With each other," he explained.

"I'm sure it brightened up the night," Dando said.

"No doubt you met Brigadier Leppard," Quinlan said to Silk. "That's why Skull goes there: to broaden his mind. What did they talk about?"

"Generalities." Silk could see that this wasn't good enough. "Intelligence gossip. Who's up, who's down."

Quinlan leaned forward, and tapped on the table with the butt of his knife. "See here: we are one jump ahead of the enemy or we're dead. You spent last evening with a senior U.S. intelligence officer and you heard *gossip*?" The knife had left dents in the tablecloth.

"He gave us his forecast of the most likely hot spots in the Cold War," Silk said rapidly. "He reckoned the hottest is the Congo, all that mineral wealth. Next is Persia, for the oil. Last is Cuba, because of Castro."

"Next time, listen harder." Quinlan swigged his coffee and got up and walked away.

Tom Tucker looked at his watch. "A man of very regular habits," he told Silk.

"And if the Russians attack us now?"

"They'll be told to wait," Dando said. "If they want a proper war, they have to behave properly."

2

The crew was scheduled to train on flight simulators. There were three of these. The pilots' simulator replicated their cockpit. The two navigators' simulator was set up in another building; all their systems, including radar, operated as if in flight. The Air Electronics Officer was at a third location. His equipment worked with the same total realism. The three simulators were linked. "Take a Mars bar with you," Tucker advised Silk. "I always do. These exercises are bloody exhausting."

First they were briefed on the strategic importance of the operation. Skull did this.

"Today's exercise calls for a different tactical approach. Tula is your target, a city about 150 miles south of Moscow. Instead of making your orthodox insertion, via the North Sea and Baltic, you will take a more direct route across West and East Germany and into the U.S.S.R. Navs and A.E.O. will get their full separate briefings, as usual. You'll penetrate Soviet airspace at height, so no weather problems. No doubt Soviet countermeasures will pull out all the stops, but you have ways of ducking and dodging."

"Why the southerly route?" Quinlan asked. "Why make life easy for their early warning system?"

"We're testing a new battle plan," Skull said. "We use the tactical bombers stationed in Germany and England – Canberras and Super Sabres – to make nuclear strikes on the battlefield. This cleans out the entire Warsaw Pact front. By then our Thor missiles are deleting the first air-defence bases and communication centres in western Russia. You'll carry a Blue Steel stand-off missile. You should have a clear run-in and be able to launch your Blue Steel one hundred miles from target."

"What's so special about Tula?" Silk asked.

"Special?" Skull bared his teeth and narrowed his eyes in a display of concentration. "Nothing *special*. It's a city, a population centre, a communications hub."

"You forgot the cathedral," Dando said.

"Yes, of course it's got a cathedral. St Basil's. Quite exquisite."

"Skull is fond of Russian cathedrals," Dando told Silk. "He knows where to find all the best ones."

"Enough chat." Quinlan was on his feet, impatient to go. "Are we done here?"

"One last word," Skull said. "The flight plan is designed for your survival. Stray from it, and you may stray into the nuclear contribution of another bomber."

"He says that every time," Dando told Silk.

"Come on, damn it!" Quinlan said. He urged the crew out, rotating his arm as if winding them up. Silk was last. "What's the rush?" he asked. "It's only a session in the simulator. It's not the end of the world."

"One day it might be," Quinlan said, "and I don't intend to be late."

* * *

Three hours later they were all back in the same room. "Shambles," Quinlan said. "What went wrong?"

"What do you think went wrong?" Skull said.

"East Germany was like an air display," Hallett said. "Our inward route was filthy with stuff."

"But surely you flew above it? Sixty thousand feet?"

"We weren't alone up there," Dando said. "Somebody locked-on and took a pot at us."

"You told us tactical nuclear strikes would clean out the Warsaw Pact area," Silk said. "Well, they didn't."

"That was the *plan*," Skull said. "Our Canberras and the Americans' Super Sabres took heavy losses. Those who succeeded had to return and rearm and make a second attack."

"Second *attempt*, you mean," Tucker said heavily.

"Return and rearm *where*?" Silk asked. No answer.

"Tom reckons somebody hit the wrong town," Quinlan told Skull.

"My radar picture doesn't lie," Tucker said. "We got routed smack over some other bastard's mistake."

"Which buggered up my lovely black boxes," Dando said, "on account of they got a bath in electro-magnetic radiation."

"The fog of war," Skull murmured.

"Nothing foggy about it," Quinlan said. "The Soviet missile defences saw us coming, clear as day."

"Remind me of the plan," Silk said.

"Our Thors should have cleared the way," Skull said. "Maybe the Soviets moved their missile sites . . . Still, you got through and launched your Blue Steel?"

"Tula is no longer answering the phone," Quinlan said. "And I'm completely knackered."

"Yes, we thought you would be."

"All those cock-ups were deliberate?" Silk said. "The plan was meant to be crap? What the hell does that prove?"

"All plans go wrong," Skull said. "What matters is that you pressed on, at all costs. You scored highly there."

"God speed the plough," Hallett said wearily.

"And now, lunch." As they left, Skull signalled to Silk. "Freddy Redman is here. You'll find him in the Mess."

3

It was a brief meeting. Freddy, on his way to a conference, just stopped to grab a sandwich and a beer. He wanted to know if Silk had settled in okay: any problems? Silk said he hadn't expected to crew with a bunch of suicidal geriatrics, but the food was good. Freddy laughed. "Geriatrics I understand. Actually, when you joined that crew, its average age came down *below* forty. But suicidal? Surely not."

"All our briefings are about outward trips. Nobody ever talks about coming back."

Freddy took a deep breath and puffed out his cheeks. "Not my department, Silko. Try Skull, he was always good at crossword puzzles . . . How's your lovely wife? You see much more of her now, I hope."

Silk said Zoë was fine, always busy but that's how she liked it. Some women had bridge, some had astrology, Zoë had politics. All a total mystery to him. They had an understanding: he didn't ask what she got up to, and she didn't talk about it. One politician in the home was plenty.

"Absolutely right," Freddy said. "Bang on target. Stay out of trouble, Silko. Politics is always trouble. Always."

His gravity surprised Silk. "Well, you should know, Freddy. You're a lot closer to it than me."

"What I meant was . . . Well, talking shop is the death of many a marriage. You're lucky you can't talk to Zoë about . . . you know . . . any of this." Freddy's gesture covered all R.A.F. Kindrick. "*Especially* to Zoë. I mean to say, security here—"

"I've had the lecture. Several times."

"Of course you have. I must dash. You and Zoë have an open invitation. Sunday lunch, for instance."

"Sounds good," Silk said. But he knew Zoë wouldn't come. She'd be busy. As usual.

4

Nat Dando and Silk walked slowly around their Vulcan. "There it is," Dando said, pointing.

"I can't see anything," Silk said.

"That's the beauty of it. Point zero one per cent is actually visible. All the rest is hidden inside the fuselage, especially in that bulge behind the tail. Tons and tons of magic boxes. The Vulcan's a flying power station, with us out in front, twiddling the knobs."

"So where does your Technicolor zoo fit in? Yellow Prawn and so on."

Silk had spent part of the afternoon going through the notes he'd made during lectures on air electronic warfare at the O.C.U. He wasn't good at electronics. His notes were heavy with acronyms and clumps of alphabet that now meant nothing at all. In the end he went looking for Dando and asked for a Cook's tour of the A.E.O.'s kingdom. Nothing too technical. Fifteen minutes, say. Twenty minutes, max.

"Yellow Prawn," Dando said. "Sounds most unhealthy. You're thinking of Red Shrimp . . . I'd better start at the beginning. The Soviets know we're coming, right? Their early warning radars are looking for us. We blind them with jamming. Blue Diver is our jammer. Two Blue Divers, one on each wing tip, swamp their radar receivers with white noise. Their screens look like a really bad migraine."

"Isn't that a bit crude?" Silk said. "We sneak into Russia, shouting our heads off."

"It's a big country. They can't defend it all. Anyway, it's not just us. With a whole fleet of Blue Divers going full blast, they won't know where to look."

"Blue Diver. Strange name." Silk went to the nearest wing tip. "Damned if I can see anything."

"Trust me. Moving on: Blue Divers are hotly pursued by Red Shrimps. Russian flak uses gun-laying radar, which is very clever, so we can't allow that, and we jam it with our Red Shrimps." Dando led him to the jet pipes of numbers 1 and 2 engines, and pointed to a small flat plate between them. "See? Red Shrimp. There's another on the other side."

"Looks like a tea-tray."

"Yes? I could brain you with a tea-tray if I hit you hard enough. Red Shrimp radiates outwards at forty-five degrees. From fifty thousand feet that makes a huge footprint. Or two."

"Fifty thousand feet is a hell of a height to send a shell. What makes you think the Soviets can do it?"

"What makes you think they can't?" There was an acid sting in his voice that silenced Silk. "They also have missiles. Red Shrimp transmits on their frequencies too. Baffles their radars."

"No flak, no missiles," Silk said. "That leaves the field clear for their fighters, doesn't it?"

"So we carry Blue Saga and Red Steer. One is a radar warning receiver that picks up the fighter's signal, the other's a tail warning radar transmitter that scans in search of the fighter. Your twenty minutes are up. I've got a squash court booked."

Silk watched Dando stride away.

"Red Shrimp," he whispered. "Blue Saga." Joke names for deadly serious boxes of electronic counter-measures. Against which Russian boffins would have figured out equally deadly counter-counter-measures. Probably not called Green Caviare or Pink Vodka. No, definitely not Pink Vodka. Iron Gauntlets, maybe. Notoriously humourless, Russians. Especially when foreigners tried to kill them. Take Napoleon. Take Hitler.

THE HENS WOULD LAY OMELETTES

1

He found Zoë on the terrace. She was wearing a white silk blouse and grey linen slacks with blood-red slippers and she was feeding the peacocks. The scene looked like a bad cover for *Vogue*. "Had a good week?" he asked.

"Perfectly frightful. Yours?"

"Frightfully perfect. Right now the Vulcan's in the hangar with a sick whatsit and so the crew's been stood down. I'm completely at your mercy for the next forty-eight hours. As the actress said to the bishop: 'Scream your loudest, my pretty one, nobody can hear you here.' Or I hope not."

"Let's go to Cambridge," Zoë said. "I want to punt on the river."

"Punt. Well, it's not what I was thinking of. But if you really want to . . ."

"I've been dreaming of it all week. It'll be heavenly."

They stopped halfway for lunch and reached Cambridge early in the afternoon. Silk found the boatyard. There was a long queue of undergraduates. The sun was hot and the queue was not moving. "This won't be heavenly," he said. "This looks hellish. Bloody students. Why aren't they at work?"

"I'll go and investigate. You park the car, darling."

When he came back, she was at the boathouse jetty, talking to a man whose foot was hooked over the side of a punt to stop it drifting away. "Such a pleasure," she said, and flashed a smile as she tipped him. She stepped into the punt. The man handed Silk a pole, and glanced at the tip: a pound note: half a day's pay. "Pleasure's all mine, sir," he said. "Remember, give it a twist so it don't stick in the mud."

As Silk poled away, there were angry mutterings from the queue, some whistling and stamping. He concentrated on his punting. It was not like flying a Vulcan. The boat yawed horribly until he learned to trail the pole and use it as a rudder. They reached King's College backs before he felt confident enough to let the punt drift alongside the bank and come to rest. "You bribed them," he said.

"Certainly not. I told them we'd driven all the way from Lincoln, and you were a double D.F.C., and they were awfully decent about it."

"What bollocks. How much?"

"Twenty quid."

"Bloody hell, Zoë. You could *buy* a punt for that."

"Actually, I think I did." The punt had plenty of cushions, and she was stretched out on them. Her straw hat was tilted forward to keep the sun out of her eyes. Her hands were linked behind her head, and this lifted her breasts in a way that made him breathe deeply and blink hard. "Hullo," she said. "You want sex."

"Christ . . . Am I so obvious?"

"Not your fault, Silko. I'm definitely not complaining. Come on, let's do it. Here and now."

Silk looked up and down the river. "I can count a dozen punts, and a hundred people walking by."

"All of them English. They'll be more embarrassed than we will. They'll look the other way and talk loudly. Come and join me, Silko. Let's make whoopee."

The straw hat shadowed her eyes, but her mouth was smiling. "You're serious," he said.

"Well, sex is a serious business. The future of mankind depends on it. Not to mention the fate of nations."

He sat down. "You'd risk your reputation for the sake of a quick shag in a punt."

"It needn't be quick. Take a chance, old sport. Live dangerously for once."

He leaned back, resting on his arms. He looked at the sky and tried to picture the scene. Both stark naked? No. But their clothing would be dishevelled, at the very least. The punt would rock, perhaps rather a lot, and make waves. Passing students would applaud. Someone would have a camera . . . "I live dangerously seven days a week," he said.

"No, you don't. You're up at sixty thousand feet, with your enormous bomb. *We're* the ones living dangerously, down below."

"That's the fate of nations." His words sounded cheap. "Anyway, outdoor intercourse would certainly get me kicked out of Bomber Command, and you wouldn't like that. I'd end up lord of the manor, pissed as a fart by breakfast, rogering the chambermaids, shooting the poachers from the clock tower. Might upset your guests."

"No poachers to shoot. Nothing on the estate to poach."

"Then I'll hire some bloody poachers." Silk stood up and eased the punt away from the bank. "I'll hire dozens of the buggers, all poaching like fury around the clock, and all paid top whack with a Christmas bonus to boot. We can afford it, can't we?"

"Heavens, yes." Zoë sounded sleepy. "I think I must have married you for your bum, Silko. When you bend your knees like that, and tense your buttocks, they're so *shapely* . . ."

"Really? The group captain said exactly the same thing, just the other day. So it must be true."

Briefly, he considered adding something nice about Zoë. Whatever he said, it might cause sex to raise its foolish head, again, in this punt. Zoë was thinking too: thinking of mentioning other reasons why she married him. They were complicated. In the end, they both said nothing. Eventually they saw an undergraduate fall off his punt, still grasping his pole, stuck firmly in the riverbed. He made a large splash. "Crashed in flames," Zoë said. "Damned poor show." That made Silk laugh. From then on, the afternoon went happily. When it finished, Zoë donated the punt to a young couple. "Gosh, thanks," they said.

2

They drove home at no great speed. The evening sky put on a five-star performance. "Look," Zoë said. "Old gold, baby blue and shocking pink. God must be holding a clearance sale. Turn left here, Silko."

He slowed. "It's just a lane."

"It'll take us to a nice old pub. You'll like it."

The lane was flanked by thick hedges; they made a green tunnel. The car hit a pothole. "What a shocker," he said. "Take a letter to my M.P., Miss Smith. No, hang on, you *are* my M.P. Can't you do something to—"

"No, I can't. Look out: horses."

He stopped to let the riders go by. A girl smiled down. "Good God," he said. "She looks just like Laura."

"Rubbish. Laura's a brunette."

"Really? I remember her as sort of blondeish."

"You're a man, Silko. You don't know mauve from mashed potato." He grunted a denial. "Okay: tell me what I'm wearing," she said. "Don't look. Speak up. What colours?"

The riders had passed. "You can't expect me to drive *and* think," he said. "Besides, I haven't seen Laura for years. I bet she was blonde once." They argued amiably for a while: familiar phrases, comfortable attitudes. "Why doesn't she come over and see you?" Silk asked.

"If she wants to, she will."

"I could see *her*. The squadron sends a Vulcan to the States now and then. I could easily pop over to Radcliffe."

"No. Lousy idea."

"Why? We could—"

"She's in love, Silko. We talk on the phone, Laura and I. She's thoroughly, happily, totally in love with some lucky fellah. Think back: when you were her age, would you sooner spend a day with someone young and wonderful, or with someone twice as old and half as funny?"

The sun was setting behind clouds and the lane became suddenly dark. Silk switched on his sidelights. "I can be funny," he said. "I can—"

Zoë screamed. A man on a bicycle sailed across the lane and just missed the Citroën. Silk swore, stamped on the brake, wrenched the wheel. The Citroën clipped a tree, bounced back into the lane and skidded to a stop. He swore some more, and looked back. The bicycle had vanished. Zoë's nose was bleeding. He gave her his handkerchief. "I hit the dash," she said thickly. "Nothing broken."

They got out and went back to where it had happened. Or, thank God, hadn't happened. "Crossroads," Silk said. He walked a few yards up a side-road. "He came down here. Look: there's a halt sign. He didn't halt. Never even saw us. Miles away by now."

"One second earlier," Zoë said. She looked at the handkerchief. "Half a second. We'd have killed him."

"Killed *them*. He had a little boy sitting on that thing behind his saddle. That seat-thing."

"Little boy?" Zoë sniffed hard. "Didn't see a . . ." Blood ran again. "Oh, sod it."

"Very small boy." The image was vivid in Silk's mind: a tall man, in black clothes, sitting upright on a tall bicycle, looking dead ahead, going fast, with a small boy sitting behind him. Such speed! Crossed the lane in a flash. "I suppose the idiot took a chance."

The Citroën had a bashed mudguard. Silk used the jack handle to lever it clear of the wheel. "Pillion," he said. "That's the word. Kid was on the pillion."

"Does it matter?"

"Not in the slightest."

They drove home, not talking. All the way, Silk kept thinking of cricket-bat oil, another name he hadn't been able to remember, long ago. And that didn't matter either, not in the slightest. So why think of it?

* * *

Hot bath. Food and drink. Bed.

"We get there half a second earlier, and he's dead," Silk said. "His problems are over, but we live with the consequences for ever and a day. His fault, and we pay."

"I don't care about him. Let him kill himself. But not the boy. He has no right to kill the boy, does he?"

"Of course not. Nobody does."

"Except you," Zoë said. "Tens of thousands of children. Cities full of children." She wasn't starting a fight; just making a point.

"I can't think about that." Silk turned a switch in his mind.

"I can," she said.

No more talk. Silk lay in the dark and wondered if they could ever be permanently happy. She'd been hot in a punt, for Christ's sake! And now, when you'd think the best answer to that suicidal maniac on a bike would be a long, strong roll in the hay, she was very, very un-hot. Marriage guidance books always said: *Be sensitive to her needs*. Silk was sensitive, damn sensitive. So what was going wrong? He drifted off to sleep and dreamt that he was a trapeze artist in a circus, swinging by his hands, letting go, reaching for another pair of hands that was never quite there. He woke up, heart pounding. *Not very subtle*, he told himself. *You can do better than that, you fool.*

3

Silk was alone in the crew room, studying a town plan of Leningrad, when Quinlan came in. He was very jovial. He looked over Silk's shoulder and flicked a finger at the centre of the plan. "There," he said. "That's where our warhead will hit."

"Railway station."

"No. Too vague. Platform seven. Under the clock. Next to the girl selling coffee."

Silk looked at the plan. He imagined rings of shock-waves speeding outwards from the station, as shown in the training films on nuclear attack. As shown in the wartime newsreels, too, when a blockbuster hit an ammunition dump. Which, of course, was a popped balloon compared with a nuclear explosion. "That's how you see it?" he said. "Aim at the girl selling coffee?"

"World War Two was a slaphappy affair, Silko. We thought we were shit-hot, didn't we? All we were doing was chucking out dozens of iron bombs in the hope that a lucky one might clip the target. Now we've got a true precision weapon. We use it precisely. If platform seven is our aiming point, I shall be highly displeased if we hit platform eight. But not today. Tell me, which bit of Britain is the most surplus to requirements?"

"Slough? Betjeman said—"

"Bugger Betjeman. The Isle of Lewis, top left-hand corner of Scotland, is totally superfluous, especially a spot called Benbecula, and that's where we're off to. Dando gets a chance to test his electronic countermeasures on the sheep, all stops pulled out and loud pedal down."

"You're very chipper today, Skip. Have I missed something?"

"The crew's back in business. When my idiot second pilot got hurt we lost our Combat Status. Went down to Non-Operational. If all hell broke loose, we'd be spectators. Now we're Combat again. Evidently the C.O. thinks you're competent."

"Well, we conned him there, didn't we?" Silk said. Quinlan almost smiled.

The rest of the crew arrived. As they went out to the station wagon, Silk found himself next to Dando. "Benbecula," he said. "Seems a long way to go just to play with your Pink Shrimps."

"You don't know the first thing about E.C.M., do you?" Dando said. "I've got toys in the back of the bomber as big as your mum's dustbins. They draw down enough power to drive a destroyer. Only one way to supply that kind of juice: from the engines. Are you ready to sit on the deck, throttles wide open, for half an hour?"

"Not for half a minute."

"So we're flying. Stooge around here at six, seven thousand? While I test my jammers? Full blast? Okay by you?"

"Uh . . ."

"We'd fry every T.V. set in the county. The hens would lay omelettes and the clocks would run backwards and every mirror would split with a noise like the crack of doom."

"I say. Extreme bad luck."

"Which is why we go to Benbecula, where there's nothing but No. 81 Signals Unit, and nobody cares a shit about them."

"Well, that's a relief," Silk said.

The car pulled up near the bomber and they got out. "Kick the tyres and light the fires!" Quinlan cried.

"He always says that," Tom Tucker said bleakly.

4

The station commander had the best office on the base, high in the Ops Block with a fine view of the airfield. All the blinds were closed. This was because Pulvertaft knew that pilots couldn't resist looking at aircraft taking off or landing, and he wanted the full attention of 409's C.O., Innes Allen, and his Operations Officer, Joe Renouf. Skull, the Chief Intelligence Officer, was there too. They settled into their seats.

"I've been handed a hot potato which could turn into a banana skin," Pulvertaft said. They smiled. That was good. Stress levels in a Vulcan squadron climbed with rank. He liked to keep everyone de-stressed.

"So far, there's nothing on paper," he said. "All I've had is a very informal phone call from someone at Group H.Q. He'd received a similar call from Command H.Q. They'd like to know what we think about a pilot on 409 who has links at the highest level with the Campaign for Nuclear Disarmament."

"Kick him out," Joe Renouf said. He had a face like a divorce lawyer: nothing surprised him. "Get rid of him, pronto."

"I hope you don't mean instant discharge from the Service," Innes Allen said. He was a Scot from the Western Highlands: every word rang crisp and clear. "That's both unwise and illegal."

"There's no precedent," Pulvertaft said. "That's the trouble."

"We can't have Ban-The-Bombers infiltrating 409," Renouf said. "At the very least it's corrosive of morale."

"Have you seen any sign of corrosion?" Allen asked. "I certainly haven't. Morale is superb."

"Then why take a risk?" Renouf said. His tone suggested he'd played his ace.

"It's Flight Lieutenant Silk, isn't it?" Skull said.

Pulvertaft breathed deeply. "What on earth makes you say that?"

"My low threshold of boredom, sir. Also, I worked it out from what I read in *The Guardian*." Skull turned to the others. "Intelligence starts at breakfast. You can pick up quite a lot in the political columns."

"Silk's wife's an M.P.," Pulvertaft said. "She supports C.N.D., in fact she's one of the brains behind it. She's their liaison with similar bodies abroad, France, Germany, Italy, Greece. Organizes conferences and so on."

"Organized subversion," Renouf muttered.

"I haven't got time for *The Guardian*," Allen said. "It puts a slant on everything."

"Not its racing tips," Skull said sharply. "I'm a hundred pounds to the good this season already."

"What does that prove?" Allen asked.

"Proves sometimes the papers get something right," Skull said. "Roman Warrior romped home at Kempton Park yesterday. Six to one."

"Enough." Pulvertaft rapped his desk. "Silk. What's to be done?"

Nobody spoke. Everyone was thinking the same thing. What if some grubby journalist stumbled on the truth? Irresistible story. *V-bomber pilot shares a bed with top anti-nuke campaigner.* The Press would milk it. *She bans, he bombs.*

"Blame M.I.5," Renouf said. "It's their job to check out Silk."

"They did," Pulvertaft said. "He was clean when he rejoined the Command. She wasn't active in C.N.D. then."

"Even if she had been, it's not a criminal offence." Skull linked his hands behind his head and stretched his legs. "If you get rid of Silk now, it amounts to accusing him of being a security risk. On what evidence?"

"This is absurd." Renouf was too restless to stay in his chair. "Don't tell me there's no risk. What if the silly bugger talks in his sleep? He could recite the entire squadron targeting plan! And never know it!"

"I can't see Zoë Silk making shorthand notes in bed at four in the morning," Skull said. "Her mother was Lady Shapland. *Very* rich. The Tatler made Zoë deb of the year."

"And dope of the century," Renouf said. "If she had her way we'd be dropping C.N.D. leaflets on the Kremlin." He saw a crease in the carpet and stamped on it.

"This is getting us nowhere," Pulvertaft said. "Skull, you know him best. Suppose he got posted somewhere safe. Transport Command, say. In Singapore. Would he go quietly?"

"He'd raise merry hell," Skull said. "He'd appeal to C-in-C Bomber Command and Zoë would ask questions in the House. They'd allege victimization."

"Which it is," Allen said.

"It would look as if we're sniping at C.N.D.," Pulvertaft said. "Punishing the wife through the husband."

"Which we are," Allen said.

"I'd snipe at C.N.D. with an elephant gun, if I could," Renouf muttered.

"I can think of six wives of aircrew in 409 who belong to underground Nazi organizations," Skull declared. "They all want pre-emptive nuclear strikes on Soviet cities *now*."

"Good God. How did you discover that?" Pulvertaft asked.

"I didn't. I made it up, in the interests of balance. But suppose we discover an A.E.O. whose wife is a Quaker. Maybe she's brain-washing him. Quakers will stoop to anything in order to thwart the nuclear holocaust: honesty, decency, even prayer. Pacifist subversion may be twisting that A.E.O.'s brain. The humanitarian weevil may be boring into his soul. Or not. Dare we risk it? Should we sack him? Just in case?"

"Sweet Jesus," Allen said unhappily. "I can't start an inquisition into aircrew wives. Morale would fall through the floor."

"And what about C.N.D. in bed with a Vulcan pilot?" Renouf said. "Will that be good for morale?"

"Whatever we do is wrong," Skull said. "The question is, how wrong are we willing to be?"

Pulvertaft wasn't listening. "I'd better see him," he said. "Where is he?"

"Over Benbecula," Allen said. "Jamming the seagulls."

5

The Benbecula task was routine: cruise the 400 miles to the Isle of Lewis, arrive at forty thousand feet, fly straight and level towards the Signals Unit while Nick Dando switched his electronic gear on and off at various strengths, then do it again and again on different bearings.

Silk flew the Vulcan. Quinlan kept the blinds up and got an occasional glimpse of the Western Isles. They looked like emeralds scattered over blue velvet, which meant they were no place to make an emergency landing. Very few places were. You couldn't put a hundred tons of Vulcan down on a field of sheep and walk away from it.

Their route home was clockwise around Britain. Ten minutes after they left Benbecula, Tucker told Quinlan that the aeroplane was being illuminated by somebody's radar.

"From below? We're nowhere near land."

"So it's a ship. Strong signal."

"Cheeky devil." To Silk he said, "Russian trawler. No fish, of course. Stuffed with electronic gubbins. They're snooping on us. Okay, I've got control. We'll go down and see."

Tucker guided Quinlan down the radar signal. The Vulcan fell easily in the thin air. The signal vanished but by then Tucker had found the ship on his own radar, and soon Quinlan saw it: a black blob trailing a short white wake. He circled, shedding speed, creeping closer. "They've got antennae like my dog has fleas," he said.

"Now they're transmitting on a VHF channel," Dando said. "Sounds familiar." Quinlan told him to put it on the intercom. The crew listened to the lazy strut of a jazz trumpet. Its volume rose and fell as the trawler climbed and dipped in the Atlantic swells. "That's Kenny Ball," Silk said. "'Midnight in Moscow'. Unmistakeable."

Quinlan banked and flew directly at the ship. The Vulcan was three hundred feet above the sea. "Full throttle," he said, "*now*." The bomber stood on its tail and went up as near to vertically as made no different. The trawler got the deafening blast of its roar, and the hammering backlash of its power. He took it up to ten thousand and levelled out.

"All transmissions have ceased," Dando said.

"Maybe they were just trying to be friendly," Silk said.

"I don't like friends," Quinlan said. "Never have."

*

135

6

The crew walked into debriefing and Skull told Silk the station commander wanted to see him. Now. The others turned and looked. "He probably needs my advice," Silk explained. "I saved his life several times in 1943, over Berlin. Or was it Bremen?" Tucker raised his right leg and broke wind, loud and long. "He always says that," Hallett remarked.

Silk got shown straight into the station commander's office. Pulvertaft told him to take a seat. "Why didn't you inform us that your wife is up to her neck in the Campaign for Nuclear Disarmament?"

Silk's head recoiled as if he had been punched between the eyes. "Christ Almighty," he said. "Why didn't *you* inform *me*?" Pulvertaft glared. "Sir," Silk added. Short silence. Then: "Crikey. It's a bugger, isn't it? Sir." Which wasn't what Pulvertaft wanted to hear but he couldn't disagree. So he started talking about the implications, the consequences, the risks.

Silk was only half-listening. He felt as if a shutter in his mind had been thrown open and the light was dazzling. Now he understood what Zoë had been saying to him, and also not saying, in recent weeks. He realized how much he had contributed to his own ignorance: nothing mattered more than flying, so nothing mattered *except* flying. Not true: being with Zoë mattered. But each of them had somehow made a tacit agreement: your business is your business, not mine. Until now. Suddenly, her business *was* his business, and vice versa. He was looking at a head-on collision. No escape, no survivors . . . Pulvertaft was talking about the indivisibility of peace and security. "Shit and corruption," Silk said. "I'm for the chop, aren't I? Sir."

"It's one solution. Fortunately for you, there are arguments against it."

All the colours in the room brightened. It was a strangely exhilarating phenomenon. Silk had experienced it only a few times in his life. He relaxed and enjoyed listening to Pulvertaft. He had dodged the head-on collision. Survival was pure happiness. "Talk to your wife," Pulvertaft said, urgently. "You know what to say." He walked with Silk to the door, shook hands, watched him go. "At least, I bloody well hope you do," he said softly. He went around the room, opening the blinds.

BREAK A LEG

1

The prospect of public speaking frightened Zoë. Not the reality, but the prospect. When she first went into politics she had revelled in talking to crowds; but now she knew how dangerous it was. As the time approached for her to walk onto a stage, her heart pounded, even though she knew she was good at this because she'd done it a thousand times before. So the hour before the event was something of an ordeal, whether it was in a village hall or the Albert Hall. You could make an idiot of yourself in front of two dozen people as easily as five thousand or five million.

Tonight it looked like two thousand had come to a rally at the Central Hall in Bristol. They were standing at the back and all down the side aisles. Not to see Zoë – Bristol was a long way from Lincoln South – but to hear Bertrand Russell. Some came because he was a great humanist philosopher, most because he was so old that he had known Robert Browning and Lord Tennyson and had met Gladstone and Lenin, and because he had gone to prison as a pacifist in the First World War. They came because he'd been hired, fired, and hired again by American universities; and because he held the Order of Merit and had won the Nobel Prize for Literature and inherited a peerage but discarded the title; and because he denounced both Kennedy and Kruschev as nuclear villains; and not least because he'd divorced three wives and married four. Plus other reasons. Russell was a hell of an act to follow, and Zoë was glad to be the opening speaker. Her job was to warm up the audience. After that Canon

Collins, chairman of C.N.D., would introduce the big man. By then Zoë would be in the wings, listening, with a large and well-earned gin-and-tonic.

The house lights dimmed. The P.A. system announced her name. She took three deep breaths and walked from the wings. *Smile, for God's sake,* she told herself. Applause surprised her. Her reputation had reached Bristol. Now to kick-start the evening.

"Welcome," she said. "I should warn you, the last time I came to the West of England to speak, the local paper wrote that I made a Rolls-Royce of a speech: old-fashioned, inaudible, and it went on for ever and ever."

Several people laughed. That's what she wanted. This was a C.N.D. rally but there was still room for enjoyment. "Now, I have another confession to make. I don't know much about Bristol. Or about Bath, your near neighbour, which I'm told is different. In Bath they walk down the street as if they own it." A couple of shouts from the balcony, blurred by distance. "Whereas in Bristol they walk down the street as if they don't give a damn *who* owns it."

Not the greatest joke in the world, but it scored, it made her one of them. Laughter surged like surf. Then applause. She was off and running.

"Another thing I knew little of until yesterday was Tory illness. Tory influenza, Tory bronchitis, maybe even Tory boils on the backside, because there exists such a thing as a Conservative Medical Association. You're a diehard Tory, you don't want to take your Tory kidney stones to a doctor who votes Labour, you never know what he might find. I hear you say: So what? Who cares? Well, the Conservative Medical Association – the C.M.A. – has a Conservative Medical answer to the bomb. A C.M.A. report, just out, calls for an end to defeatist attitudes, an end to disarmament because, they say, it's possible to reduce casualties and curb disease from a nuclear explosion, by simple and inexpensive remedies. How simple? Well, if you have a basement or a central room in your house, you turn it into a survival shelter. How cheap? The C.M.A. reckons about £100 per house. And if you don't think your sad and miserable life is worth a hundred quid, stay away from the C.M.A. Join the Liberal Medical Association, maybe they can save you from nuclear annihilation for only fifty pounds. Maybe the Fabian Society Medical Association will do it for twenty-five. No. Wait. I've just thought of something . . ."

Zoë took a moment to stare into space.

"Central room. What is that? A room in the centre of a house, yes? With no external walls. So . . . how many people here have a central room?" A few hands went up. "And how many have a basement?" Perhaps two hundred hands. "Thank you . . . That means . . . Well, it means the rest of us are dead, aren't we? Should we feel badly about that? Certainly not. Because all our friends here, cosy and snug in their basements and their central rooms – they're dead too! The C.M.A. report is junk. *Junk.* It focuses on radiation hazard. You and I know better. You and I know that, by the time radiation kills you, you're long since dead from heat and blast. Ask any nurse! The Royal College of Nursing has calculated what would happen to us here in Bristol when a one-megaton bomb explodes half a mile away, at Bristol Bridge. Heat and blast immediately kill a quarter of a million people and injure countless others. Did I say countless? Apologies. Nobody's left to do the counting. And even if someone could count the injured, nearly all nurses and doctors are dead too. Hospitals? Blasted flat. Police? Fire services? No help there. As far as eight miles from ground zero, Bristol is finished, blown flat, burned to a crisp. Government talk of planning for mass casualties is lies.

140

No help would come. How could it? No transport, in or out. Anyone who survives in a shelter and emerges after two or three weeks is exposed to infection, dehydration, starvation and hypothermia, with the very real risk of leukaemia, other cancers, and blindness to follow. And all that from a single, solitary, one-megaton bomb. Why drop only one? Why not ten? Twenty? Fifty?"

Zoë let that thought sink in. She took out a booklet and opened it. "We British are said to be very level-headed. Calm in a crisis. Phlegmatic: isn't that the word? By God, we shall need to be. This is the official Home Office booklet on surviving nuclear attack. It ends with these words: 'The All-Clear signal means that there is no longer an immediate danger and . . .'" She spread her arms wide. Now she gave each word the same punishing emphasis: "'*and you may resume normal activities.*' How I would like to meet the civil servant who wrote that! What a comfort he is in time of trouble!"

Fifteen minutes later, Zoë wound up, damning the suicidal stupidity of nuclear powers, in contrast to the shining sanity of ordinary men and women, and she won thunderous applause. As she left the stage, Canon Collins came on. He paused to shake her hand. "Excellent. Truly excellent," he said. "Bertrand Russell's train has broken down somewhere in the Midlands. You'll have to go on again and fill in for him. Truly, truly excellent."

* * *

Delegate. When the burden is too great, delegate. Share the load.

Zoë couldn't go back onstage alone. "Get me three actors *now*," she told the local C.N.D. organizer. "Men." He said he knew no actors. "Ask the audience, for Christ's sake!" she shouted. "There must be a dozen actors out there! Go, go, go!" He ran. She switched on the P.A. microphone, named six people she knew were in the audience, and asked them to come backstage at once: two doctors, a military historian, a retired general, a university lecturer, a journalist. All were friends or acquaintances. By the time she'd washed her face and gargled with mouthwash (good for the voicebox) they had assembled. "Russell can't make it," she told them. "I need your help so I can do another hour. I want thirty nuclear questions – ten from Kruschev, ten from Kennedy, ten from Macmillan. Can you do it? In five minutes? My goodness," she said, turning and smiling at three men, "My most favourite actors." She cast them there and then: "Harold Macmillan, Nikita Kruschev, Jack Kennedy. Can you do it?"

"Is there a script?" one asked.

"Just notes. I'm relying on a certain amount of improvisation. In fact, a hell of a lot."

The questions were ready in eight minutes. Zoë dealt them out. "You three rule the world," she said. "Be tough. Be ruthless. Be creative."

"What's your role?" Jack Kennedy asked.

"I play God. We're on. Break a leg."

* * *

She hoped for forty-five minutes. They did an hour. There was passionate dialogue, accusation, interruption. Zoë chaired the fight. It was brilliant, ragged, angry, briefly chaotic, hilarious, and above all surprising. Nobody – not the audience, certainly not the actors – knew where they were going next, until it happened. The only thing Zoë had planned was the end. All three actors were bawling at each other, all shouting: "Mine's bigger than yours!" when she raised an arm and the stage went suddenly totally, black. Silence. Slowly the lights came up. "Thank you, everyone," Zoë said. "All the nuclear bombs have exploded. You are now officially free to resume normal activities." Tentative applause, swelling to hugeness.

She walked offstage, feeling both exhilarated and exhausted. Waiting in the wings was, of all people, Silk, wearing a foolish grin. "What a load of old crap," he said. She punched him in the eye and he went down with a crash that raised dust ten feet away.

2

Backstage at a C.N.D. rally is a good place to get decked. There was no lack of doctors in the building. "He's my husband," Zoë told them. "He walks into things. Poor judgement. Wanders about."

"She hit me," Silk said, thickly.

"Then he rambles. He wanders and he rambles."

By the time the doctors had decided he was fit to travel, the last London train had gone. That left a night in a hotel or a trip in the Citroën. "Sod hotels," he said. Zoë drove.

He angled his seat back to its maximum and stared at the roof. Someone had given him an eyepatch. Now his injured eye was manufacturing a sequence of big, soft hairy stars. They changed colour, mauve to green to pink, and drifted left. He tried to watch one move, but it didn't like being watched and it hid. Hid where? Whose eyeball was it, for God's sake? He felt cheated. It was easier to close both eyes. He slept.

They stopped near Leicester, at a 24-hour transport café. The night was black as treacle. He clung to her sleeve and stumbled over the broken asphalt. "I'm blind," he said. "The C.O. will kill me for this."

"Show him the eyepatch," she said. "It's the height of fashion in Vulcan squadrons. Everybody's got one."

"What d'you mean?" He trod in a deep puddle. "Explain." She said nothing. His foot squelched inside his shoe. He gave up.

Fluorescent lights were softened by a layer of blue-grey cigarette smoke. The jukebox was playing "Rock Around The Clock". Silk's nostrils twitched at the heavy aroma of fried onions. "Biological warfare," he said. "And I've got trench foot. Not that you care."

She ordered bacon sandwiches and mugs of tea. They sat at a wooden table. There was a catering-size flagon of brown sauce, loosely chained through the handle. "Here's a question," she said, and rattled the chain. "Is the bottle chained to the table, or is the table chained to the bottle?"

"Both. Neither. I'm not going to argue with an idiot like you. Why did you hit me? I only made a joke. Can't you take a joke?"

She sipped her tea and studied him over the rim of the mug. "I didn't hear a joke," she said. "I heard a load of old crap. Was that you?"

He couldn't think of an answer that would do him any good.

He ate only half his sandwich. She ate the other half, and steered him back to the Citroën. She drove without another break, all the way to The Grange. Freshly washed by the light of dawn, it was a welcome sight, even with one eye.

SEE ENGLAND AND DROWN

1

Silk got some sleep, had some breakfast, and felt just about fit to drive. He reached R.A.F. Kindrick at midday. The sun was out, he was ready to annihilate Chernyakhovsk, a Soviet bomber base south of the Baltic and Quinlan's allocated target of the week. Skull had said that Chernyakhovsk was like Kindrick with medals. Russian aircrew got awarded a lot of medals. Got taught a lot of Marxism, too. Medals and Marxism: an odd combination. Maybe they won a medal for listening to the Marxism. Silk wondered if there was a pilot at Chernyakhovsk right now, leaning over a map, tunic clinking with heroic medals, picking out his Aiming Point on Kindrick. The squash courts were pretty central. Don't bother, Ivan. By the time you get scrambled, the Vulcans won't be here. We'll be at one of the dispersal airfields, far far away.

Silk was wearing his eyepatch. He lifted it, to see what he could see, and saw double, so he put it back. He didn't want to go near the Mess or the Ops Block, where people would ask what had happened, so he walked onto the airfield and saw Group Captain Pulvertaft. Worse still, Pulvertaft saw him, and beckoned. Silk was still working on a reason for the black eye when Pulvertaft called: "Ever kept wicket, Silk? Innes Allen's team needs a wicket-keeper."

"Afraid not, sir." Beyond the station commander, Silk saw airmen preparing a cricket pitch.

"I'd keep wicket myself, but the knees, you know, the knees . . ." Pulvertaft saw the eyepatch, and took a pace back. "Now that's a bloody good idea. Why didn't I think of it? Harry . . ." He turned to 409's adjutant. "Why don't we put all our Vulcan aircrew in eye-patches, right now, make 'em distinctive, d'you see? Let our American allies see the stars in the show!" His enthusiasm grew. "*And* it sends a message – Kremlin or bust! Bit of a gimmick, I agree, but . . ." He clicked his fingers.

"Hell of a good gimmick, sir." The adjutant hurried off.

They stood and watched a small steamroller trundle back and forth, flattening the bumps between the stumps. "That reminds me," Pulvertaft said. "How is Mrs Silk, M.P.?"

"Um . . . fighting fit, sir. We had a chat. Laid down our cards. She understands the situation we're in. Nobody wants a scandal." Silk frowned, pursed his lips, nodded.

"Good, good." They strolled towards the steamroller. Smoke from the funnel, caught by the breeze, had a brisk tang of sulphur. "It lays low the mountains but it can't fill in the valleys, can it? The ball's going to fizz like a firecracker. Still, the Yanks know nothing about cricket, so they'll think it's quite normal. See if you can find a wicket-keeper, Silk. Someone fit and fearless."

Silk saluted and left, looking purposeful. In fact he headed for the Vulcans, a good place to avoid senior officers. The bombers were all immaculately lined up, their anti-flash white undersides gleaming, and looking so big and so sleek that he felt a small, unexpected kick of pride. Then a flicker of colour caught his eye. On the parade ground, alongside the R.A.F. ensign, flew the Stars and Stripes. People had been talking about an exchange visit from the nearby American air base. This must be it.

At Silk's Vulcan, the ground crew were in spotless white over-alls. The crew chief was watching one man hose down the wheels. Others polished the fuselage, got rid of oil streaks, picked off bits of birdshit. "Looks good, chiefy," Silk said.

"Bags of swank, Mr Silk. If it's wet it's clean, isn't that right? Etcetera."

2

Silk delayed his lunch until he knew the Mess would be half-empty. Even so, Quinlan and Tucker saw him and came over to his table. "The C.O.'s called off the eyepatch stunt," Quinlan said. "Too many accidents. One chap tripped and fell into a flowerbed. Prize petunias. Serious damage."

"You started it all, didn't you?" Tucker said. He had taken off his eyepatch and was wearing it like a knuckleduster.

"Not me," Silk said. "Blame Pulvertaft. It was his idea of a squadron badge. He's lost his marbles."

"On the contrary," Quinlan said. "The eyepatch represents this squadron at its gung-ho finest. Suppose your anti-flash blinds fail. You're looking at something so bright it makes the sun seem like a fifteen-watt bulb. What's the result?"

"I'm blind," Silk said. "We're all blind."

"No, we're *half*-blind. The eyepatch saves one eye. The op goes on. We hit the target."

"Crikey." Moments of amazement sent Silk back to the language of boyhood. "So we all attack Russia . . ."

"Wearing eyepatches. Unjammable. Kruschev can't touch us."

"Touch us? He can't even see us. Unless he's got an eyepatch—"

"It's no joking matter, Silk."

"Of course not. Does the army know about this? The Irish Guards could take Moscow looking like the Pirates of Penzance."

Tucker had listened with growing irritation. His shoulders were hunched, his knuckles flexed. "That's not a Service Issue eyepatch

147

you're wearing," he said. "That's some naff poncey girly piece of stuff." He hooked a finger into the elastic and stretched it. Silk expected pain and he flinched and half-turned and lost his eyepatch.

"Hullo," Tucker said. "That's not mascara."

Quinlan leaned forward and looked. "It's not Service Issue, either."

"My wife punched me," Silk said.

"No jokes," Tucker said. "What really happened?"

"It's true. She's tough. She used to box for Cheltenham Ladies' College. It was a sucker punch. You wait. I'll kill her next time."

"You're married to that M.P., aren't you?" Quinlan said. "Lady Shapland. One of the ban-the-bomb crowd. They're all maniacs. Can't you keep her under control?"

"She's not Lady Shapland. And neither am I." That made no sense, but Silk didn't care.

"Nobody mucks about with anyone in this crew," Tucker said. "Next time she belts you I'll break her arms." He strode away.

"The only thing he cares about is putting the bomb on the Aiming Point," Quinlan said. "He's very dedicated." He looked at his watch. "Bugger. I've got to go and keep wicket against the Yanks. Will your eye be okay tomorrow?"

"That depends," Silk said. "If I get burned to a crisp during the night by the Soviet nuclear juggernaut, then I'm afraid I can't make any promises." But Quinlan had gone.

* * *

The teams gathered on the airfield.

Pulvertaft wore a white coat: he had appointed himself umpire for the cricket match. He was chatting with Quinlan. "Hope you're wearing a box, old boy," he said.

"Certainly, sir." Quinlan flexed his knees and felt his crotch. "The crown jewels are safe."

"I've selected that tall red-headed armourer to open the bowling. He had a trial for Middlesex, once. I'm told his quick 'un reaches ninety miles an hour."

"Golly." Quinlan whacked his wicket-keeping gloves together. Thunderbolts, eh?"

Pulvertaft took the match ball from his coat pocket and tossed it from hand to hand. "I've told him to give the Yank openers a few rib-ticklers. Make 'em hop! They don't know the difference between cricket and croquet." He chuckled. "We'll educate them."

"Here comes their chief, sir."

Brigadier Leppard was strolling towards them, hands behind his back. "You guys ready to play ball?" he called. "We're willing to consider surrender terms instead."

"Awfully decent of you. Consider this instead." Pulvertaft threw the cricket ball at him, quite hard. Leppard swayed sideways and casually caught it in a glove the size of a saucepan. "What have you got there?" Pulvertaft said. "Heavens above. It's one of those baseball things, isn't it?"

"Correct." Leppard gave him the ball. "Baseball mitt. Essential equipment."

"Extraordinary. I hope you're not proposing to wear it in the match. Gloves are against the rules of cricket."

Leppard looked at Quinlan. "He's got *two* mitts."

"He's keeping wicket. That's an exception."

Leppard smiled. He had a good smile: modest, friendly, energy-efficient. "I'm all for exceptions. I'll buy your exception if you buy mine. My guys wear mitts and play with baseball bats. But you can use your ball."

"Awfully kind. You won't object if we keep the score?"

"Well, now." Leppard walked away, five paces, halted, stared at the sky, came back. "My guys aren't going to like that."

"Cricket is a complex game," Pulvertaft said. "Your guys won't know a square cut from a ham sandwich."

"A square cut is two pairs, jacks and queens," Leppard said. "At least, that's what it is in Detroit. Ever played poker in Detroit?" he asked Quinlan.

"A pleasure yet to come, sir."

"Okay. We keep the mitts, you keep the score." Leppard shook hands and went away.

"Baseball mitt," Pulvertaft said. "Looks more like a birth defect."

Quinlan laughed, briefly. He was thinking of the red-headed fast bowler. Ninety miles an hour. The slip fielders might feel glad of a catcher's mitt if one of those thunderbolts came their way.

* * *

The baseball teams had little to discuss before their game. The American captain, Major Jed Jakowski, met the British captain, Wing Commander Joe Renouf, to toss a coin. Renouf won and decided to bat first.

"Anything you need to know about baseball?" Jakowski asked. "Rules and stuff?"

"Nothing," Renouf said. He disliked sport. He hadn't wanted to play this stupid game, but Pulvertaft had made him captain without discussion.

"You sure? Cricket it's not."

"This country *invented* baseball centuries ago," Renouf told him. "Its true name is rounders, and it is played by small children at girls' schools all over England."

Jakowski looked for the joke but all he saw were Renouf's clenched jaws and bleak stare. "We take baseball a touch more seriously," he said. Leppard was approaching. "Okay, let's get the show on the road."

"Everyone happy?" Leppard asked.

"The R.A.F. want to use their cricket bats." Jakowski shrugged. "Suits me."

"Absolutely," Leppard said. "A bit of give-and-take is good for the soul. Sport unites nations, yes? I'll be watching from the balcony."

* * *

Quinlan won the toss and put the U.S.A.F. in to bat.

The redheaded bowler was a wiry six foot two. He used a long run-up and his final arm action was like a runaway cartwheel. His first delivery was pitched a little short and the ball fizzed past the batsman's startled head. Quinlan misjudged the catch and the ball sped to the boundary. "Four byes," Pulvertaft announced. "That's four runs to you," he explained to the non-striking batsman.

The man was impressed. "Keep swingin', pal!" he shouted to his team-mate. "We got four runs already. This game is in the bag!"

"Four runs is scarcely a winning score, old chap," Pulvertaft said mildly. "You should aim for a hundred, at least."

"Yeah, yeah." The American glanced sideways at the umpire. He'd heard about the famous British sense of humour. Also their famous love of understatement. How could a hundred runs be understatement? Babe Ruth never scored a hundred runs in a whole season. He gave up.

At the other end, the batsman assumed the classic baseball stance: knees well bent, bat held shoulder-high. He swung and missed. The ball thudded into his exposed ribcage and he collapsed onto his stumps. "Out, I'm afraid," Pulvertaft said. "Awfully bad luck." To the bowler he murmured: "You can take it easy now, I think." The man nodded. But a shark does not relax when it scents blood in the water.

The new batsman hit his first ball for six. The next ball ricocheted off a bump in the pitch and struck his left kneecap with a sound like a mallet hitting a tentpeg. A jeep was sent to collect him.

"They really shouldn't drive across the playing surface," Pulvertaft said. "It's very bad form."

The third American batsman had learned from his team-mates' experience. He stood well away from the stumps, too far away to hit or be hit. His first ball knocked all three stumps into a cocked hat. "No ball," Pulvertaft said.

"What was wrong with it, sir?" the bowler asked.

"The batsman wasn't ready. I'm sure there's a rule about that."

The bowler added a yard to his run-up, and again the stumps went flying. "No ball," Pulvertaft said.

The bowler didn't bother to ask why. He spent a little time polishing the ball. "Is everyone ready?" he asked. This time he bowled underarm and hit the stumps.

"Oh dear," Pulvertaft said. "I had the sun in my eyes." But the batsman was already walking away.

After three overs, the Americans had scored seventeen runs and lost nine wickets, five of them Retired Hurt. "We'll take tea soon, I expect," Pulvertaft said.

* * *

Word of the carnage in the cricket match reached the baseball game just as the home team was due to bat. Jakowski called his men together. "Change of plan," he said.

The R.A.F. players knew something of baseball. They had seen it played in movies. They had watched their opponents warming up and had noticed how the pitcher, especially, made the ball fly as straight as a bullet. So the first man at bat was surprised to receive slow and harmless lobs. He even managed to mis-hit the third offering. "Run, you feckless idiot!" Renouf shouted.

He ran, stumbling over his bat until he remembered to drop it. By then a fielder had scooped up the ball. His bullet-straight throw smacked into the runner's legs, and he fell. "Don't bloody stop!" Renouf bawled. The man got up, lurched forward, and another fielder hit him again, this time on the ass. But he stumbled into first base. Jakowski was fielding there. "Fearfully sorry about that," he said. "The ball must have slipped, or something."

After that the Americans allowed every batter to run, while the ball raced between fielders like tracer, bouncing off the runners, who fell, and rose, only to fall again. Nobody was tagged out. Eventually the bases were loaded. All the runners were bruised and limping. One man, who had been trapped by lethal switch-hitting between second base and third, was bleeding from the head.

Renouf had seen enough. "Match abandoned," he told Jakowski. "I don't know what your damned game is, but it's over."

"According to you, it was rounders," Jakowski said. "Or was that all balls?"

3

There was no flying, so the control tower was empty apart from the duty officer. Skull took Karl Leppard and a bottle of dry white wine onto the roof. They settled into canvas chairs. The sounds of sport down below were faint.

"I took part in a fairly highpowered seminar on our fragile world, recently," Skull said. "Without mentioning your name, I suggested the hot spots most likely to ignite: the Congo, Persia, and Cuba. Nobody agreed."

"I'm surprised. Persia. Full of gung-ho Arabs? Sitting on a sea of oil? Russia next door?"

"The Shah is a staunch ally of the West."

"Sure," Leppard said. "And a bloody tyrant in his spare time. He won't last. Oil means trouble. Russia likes trouble."

"Perhaps. But the Congo is different. Black Africans don't want blue-eyed white men from Omsk telling them how to live. As for Cuba . . . it's a backwater."

"Castro pissed off the Kennedys."

"You mean the Bay of Pigs?" Skull topped up their glasses. "More of a brawl than an invasion. A monumental cock-up by a mob of over-excited Cuban exiles. Why should Kennedy care? He wasn't involved."

"Wasn't he?"

"Well, that's what your man at the U.N. said. I saw him on television. Nothing to do with the U.S., he said."

"He lied. Kennedy inherited the plan from the Eisenhower administration. Could of killed it, didn't. Cheap way to lose Castro, Kennedy thought. Bay of Pigs was pure C.I.A. Money, arms, training, ships – all C.I.A. Exiles supplied blood. Blood and bullshit. Castro knew they were coming. So now the Kennedys hate him."

"Dear me." A pigeon landed on the parapet. Skull threw the wine cork at it and missed. The bird was unmoved. "Why Cuba?"

he asked. "It's nothing. Drop it in the middle of Texas and nobody would even notice."

"It's Communist."

"The Cubans like it that way. What happened to freedom?"

Leppard was amused. "Old man Kennedy didn't spend fifty million dollars buying the Presidency for Jack so that Castro could spoil the view."

"Well, he can't buy Cuba. And surely Jack's not going to send in the Marines. They'd end up sitting in foxholes for ever, while the natives sold them exploding cigars. The Kremlin would love that."

"Uh-huh."

Skull got up and strolled to the parapet. The pigeon shuffled away from him but did not fly. It knew its rights. Sunlight warmed the baseball game and the cricket match, but it was against a backdrop of dark cloud. Skull raised his head and sniffed, and smelt rain on the way. "Drink up," he said. "We're about to get drenched. Cricket has that effect on weather."

4

Silk ambled along the taxiway, walking not quite straight because he was one-eyed. Didn't matter. Plenty of room. The track was wide enough for a Vulcan. It led him away from everyone. *Good*, he thought, *let the rest of the squadron be nice to the Americans, not me, I'm fresh out of niceness . . . Sod it, now I'm even thinking like a Yank . . .*

"Women." He was surprised by the sound of his voice, but why the hell not? Hearing the word helped him focus on his problem. "Devious," he said. "Greedy." Was that going too far? "Look," he said, "she knows I got this Vulcan job so as to be near her, to give the marriage a second chance. I get the damn job, stroke of luck, and she can't wait to bugger it up with her rant-and-rave politics! *Then* I drive all the way to bloody Bristol, just to make sure she knows the score, and *bang*, she clobbers me. If that's love, you can . . ."

He stopped talking. A vehicle was coming up behind him. He didn't look back, kept walking. "Pacifism strikes again," he said. "Thank you very much, madam."

It was a jeep, open-top, and it stopped beside him. The driver wore pilot's wings. He was too young to drive, let alone fly. He had the reddest hair that Silk had seen since Ginger Rogers, and a smile so wide and generous that Silk found it disturbing. Nobody on 409 smiled like that. It was a large candle in a dirty world. "Goin' somewhere?" the driver asked. Midwest, probably.

"Nowhere special," Silk said.

"Me too. Coincidence." They took a long look at each other. "I'm lost. You want to show me the best road to nowhere, I'd be happy to take you along."

Silk got in, said he was Silko, they shook hands. The other man was a captain called, inevitably, Red. Full name, Red Black. "I wasn't born, they won me at roulette," he said. Silk chuckled. Just one chuckle. That's all it was worth.

They drove past the Vulcans, lined up immaculately as a guard of honour but with nobody to admire them except a tattered crowd of crows that couldn't keep formation if they were tied together with black silk ribbon. Silk took the salutes of Service policemen with Alsatian dogs. "Keep going," he said. They drove on, to the most remote corner of the airfield. "This is it," he said. "Best mushrooms in Lincolnshire."

The grass was longer here. A breeze chased through it, searching left and right, giving up, then trying again. "Never saw such greenery as you folks got," Red remarked. They flushed a hare, and stood watching it bound away.

"Beautiful beast," Silk said.

Red smiled his wide and wonderful smile. "Reckon that hare ate all your mushrooms."

"Could be." As Red turned away, Silk noticed how quickly his smile faded. It simply fell off his face. Now he looked, not sad, but stony, almost bleak. The contrast was startling. Yet the smile had been so true, so generous. How could it vanish so fast? After that, Silk watched for this change of face. It kept happening.

"The mushrooms are around here somewhere," he said. "I remember a day in ... must have been 1942. Pug Duff came by in his car and picked me up, just like you did, and we drove out here."

It was a slim fragment of memory, quickly told. Pug Duff, short but tough, got his wings same time as Silk but went up the promotion ladder twice as fast, so by '42 he commanded 409. That evening Pug had brought grub – bacon, sausages – and a Primus stove and frying pan. Add mushrooms and it made a decent meal, very decent. Silk searched his mind for more exciting detail and found none.

"You guys do a lot of that?" Red asked. "Hot sausages around the fire?"

"That was the only time. I think Pug needed a break. Had to get away from the war for an hour. We were losing too many aircraft. Good crews getting the chop. Bad for morale. Poor old Pug worried but of course he couldn't do anything except press on."

"Poor old Pug?" Red said. "Should I ask what happened to him?"

Silk thought about it. "Better not," he said. Did Pug get the chop? Must have done. This was turning into a gloomy chat. "Where are you from?"

"Manhattan, Kansas. New York City gets our mail, we get theirs." The smile was back. The American was pleased to find an

Englishman who knew so much of his country, and for a while they talked easily. Red was getting nostalgic about the great taste of American ice cream when the first raindrops smacked them in the face. They ran.

It was a cloudburst. The wipers flung water left and right and still the windscreen was swamped. Red put his head outside the jeep, and the rain hammered at his eyes: the faster he drove, the less he saw. Then Silk shouted and pointed, grabbed the wheel. They turned onto the concrete hardstandings where the Vulcans stood, and drifted gratefully under the vast delta wings of the nearest bomber. Red dragged a handkerchief from his pants pocket and mopped water from his eyes and ears. Now he could hear the steady bass thunder of rain. "See England and drown," he said. Big smile.

"It's what makes our greenery so green," Silk told him. A policeman arrived. "Hullo, corporal. We are orphans of the storm." He checked their identity documents and went away. "Airfields are all alike," Silk said. "Vast areas of nothing much. Not even mushrooms." He sneezed. "Damn. I've been talking garbage. Wrong place. I wasn't here with Pug Duff in '42. We were based at Coney Garth, in Suffolk. Well, that explains everything."

"You lost me there."

"Bags of mushrooms at Coney Garth. Famous for it."

Captain Black dried the wheel with his handkerchief. Now he had a dry wheel and a soggy handkerchief. He hung it on the gear lever. "I came out here to kill myself." He took a small automatic from his tunic pocket. "You'd better have this. I don't like guns."

"Very un-American." Silk examined it: compact, tidy, loaded. He removed the magazine. "Why carry it if you don't like it?"

"Standard issue," Red said wearily. "We all get one. Self-protection in case we get shot down."

Silk thought about it as they sat watching the rain bounce knee-high off the taxiway. The banging of the little gun might amuse Russian infantry in the few seconds before they shot Red Black dead; but it would be unkind to say so now. "None of my business," he said, "but going nowhere with a gun you dislike is an odd way to end your life."

"Oh, hell." He was thoroughly miserable. "It's not easy. Nothing's easy."

"Take some leave. Go to Scotland. Jump off a mountain. Lots of mountains in Scotland, highly dangerous. People fall off them without even trying. And the scenery—"

"You married?" Red asked. "You talk like a guy who's married."

"Many years. You, on the other hand . . ."

"She wanted to. I said, wait till I'm out the Service. She didn't wait. Found some other guy."

Silk exercised his arms. Wet clothes, gusting wind: cold was eating into him. "You volunteered for aircrew," he said. "And you must be damn good to make pilot in an elite squadron. Why blow it all?"

"It's a waste. Total waste." Now his head was trembling, whether from cold or rage or fatigue, Silk couldn't tell. "Look: everybody gets allocated a target, right? What's yours?"

"Um . . . it varies. Here and there." Dangerous question. Safe answer.

"Mine is East Berlin,"

"Ah. Not a friendly place."

"We're a tactical nuclear strike outfit. We take out the enemy air defence command centres. Clear the way so the big boys can go in and whack the Soviet cities."

"Jolly sporting of you." Silk wished he hadn't said that. The American hadn't heard. Apparently.

"The F-100 is a fighter-bomber. Carries a bomb big enough to leave East Berlin looking like Nagasaki times ten, maybe times twenty. Times fifty, who's counting? Not me, because a couple minutes *before* I get there, one of your Thor missiles, also tactical nuclear, is scheduled to take out the same target also. And a couple minutes *after* I get there, another Thor is scheduled to do likewise. That means if I arrive early or late, I get fried. Or if one of those Thors is early or late, I get fried. Slice it where you like, I'm fried, just so East Berlin gets taken out three times over."

"Dismal prospect, old chap. Still, buck up." *Christ Almighty*, Silk thought, *I sound like my father, and he's dead.* "Look on the bright side. East Berlin did its best to take me out, more than three times, so the wretched place deserves all it gets."

A ghost of the smile returned. "I'll try to remember that," Black said.

"Forgive my curiosity . . .." *Now I'm my grandfather, and he's extremely dead.* "How old are you?"

"Twenty-eight."

Got that wrong, then. Mind you, I only saw him through one eye. Only half-wrong. "You should meet my wife, Zoë," Silk said. "She's an M.P. Lady Shapland." He was in the grip of a paternal friendliness, searching for something to give a young American far from home. "I'm sure she'd love it. Does the notion appeal?"

"Sure. Is she here?"

"No, but we have a country house nearby. Not exactly a castle, although I think there's an arrow-slit somewhere . . ." *Stop!* Silk told himself. *Can the bullshit.* "Why not spend a weekend?"

Captain Black said he'd like that very much. "We have a small ballroom," Silk said. "You two could jitterbug. Or is that completely *passé* now?"

The storm blew over and they drove back to the base. Silk returned the automatic. "Keep it in your underwear drawer," he said, and got another blinding smile. The man was wired for light.

5

Stevens, the under-butler, said that he believed her ladyship was walking in the estate.

"You know she never inherited that title," Silk said. "She never uses it in her work."

"Yes sir. But the staff like to think of her as Lady Shapland. Life is quiet here. We make our own entertainment."

"I see." Silk turned away, then stopped. "What do they call me? The Unknown Warrior?"

"Nothing so disrespectful, sir, I can assure you."

"Pity. Ask them what they think of 'Sir Jasper'. Tell them I'll carry a horsewhip, if it helps."

Silk went out into the sunshine. It was early afternoon, Friday; the crew had been stood down after a week of hard training, in the simulators and in the air. He had a free weekend. The lawns had been mown in a precise diagonal stripe that flared and dipped where the ground ran into bumps and hollows. "Bloody clever," he said aloud. "Like a flag in the breeze." Fifty yards away a gardener stopped doing something to a rose bush and took his cap off. "Talking to myself," Silk told him and walked in the other direction. The Grange was as bad as R.A.F. Kindrick. You couldn't pick your nose without hiding in the bog.

The lawns ended with a ha-ha. Beyond it sheep grazed, or stopped grazing as he walked near. "Relax," he said. "I haven't rogered a sheep since the day the old king died." They bolted. "Lots of girls would jump at the chance," he called. "Double D.F.C. and all that." He went through a plantation of tall conifers, cool as a church, and out into the heat again, and looked down at a lake. In the lake was a punt and in the punt was Zoë, wearing so little it seemed pointless to make the effort.

"My stars," she said. "A handsome stranger. Have you come to give me the thrill of a lifetime?"

"I don't know." He sat on a log. "What if your husband turns up?"

"Oh . . . You needn't worry about him. He's at sixty thousand feet, obliterating Olenegorsk."

Silk was startled and tried not to show it. Olenegorsk was a Soviet strategic bomber base, on the Kola peninsula, near Finland. How did she know? "Not even close," he said, carelessly. "Olenegorsk got obliterated on Tuesday. I know it was Tuesday, because the Mess always serves spotted dick for lunch on Tuesdays. Wednesday we annihilated Murmansk Northeast. Thursday we took care of Lvov. But you know all that, don't you?"

She turned onto her side and propped her head on her hand. She tipped her straw hat over her ear. She smiled sweetly.

"You're shag-happy again, aren't you?" he said. "I don't understand it. Why punts?"

"It's a mystery, Silko. Don't just sit there. Use your initiative."

"It won't reach." He stood up. "I'm hung like a horse, but look: it's thirty feet at least."

"We're drifting apart." It was true; a breeze had caught the punt. "Dive. Swim."

He undressed, and waded into the lake. The cold made him gasp. "If I get castrated by a sodding great pike, you'll be sorry," he said. He swam, kicking up a lot of foam, and heaved himself over the end of the punt. "You're a cold, cruel woman," he said, "and when my balls come out of hiding I demand satisfaction. Where's the towel?"

There was no towel. They lay together and she gave him the warmth of her body. She could feel the heavy thump of his heartbeat gradually slow to normal. "This is special," she whispered. "This is our first time in a punt, on a Friday, near Lincoln, in July."

"It's June, Zoë. June thirtieth."

"Well . . . restrain yourself, Silko. Take it very, very slowly. Try to last until midnight."

"Send for beer and beef sandwiches, my sweet, and I can guarantee you a thrill a minute until three in the morning."

She moved her head. "Would you like mustard on the beef?" she asked. "Because I think I see Stevens waving to us."

Silk cursed and sat up. Stevens was waving a large handkerchief. "Telephone message, Mr Silk," he shouted. "From your squadron. A Mr Renouf, he said it was extremely urgent. He said it's a Micky Finn, sir."

"Renouf's the Ops Officer," Silk told her. "Micky Finn means—"

"I know what it means," Zoë said.

He stood, dived, swam. Stevens turned his back while Silk dressed. Underwear clung. Feet resisted socks. His hair dripped into his shirt. He looked towards Zoë and offered a shrug. She gave back the smallest wave.

"The Citroën is waiting in the drive, sir," Stevens said.

Silk jogged to the car, which turned out to be two cars. A jeep was parked next to it. Captain Red Black was waiting. *Damn damn damn,* Silk said to himself. *Nothing goes bloody right. Well, Stevens will have to sort it out.*

"I haven't come on the wrong day, have I?" Black asked.

"No, no. Glad to see you. Sheer bad luck, we've got a squadron panic, bloody nuisance but . . . Look, Stevens will take care of you, and Zoë's here, so . . . I'll be back soon as possible. Just . . . make yourself at home."

Black smiled. What else would he do? The Citroën started at once. Exit Silk.

6

Twenty minutes after Silk left, the breeze blew the punt to the bank. Zoë climbed out, put on her jeans and sweater and deck shoes, and looked up to see a man. One look was enough. Lust turned a switch and seemed to release a magnetic impulse. Nothing mattered except skin on skin. Her mother's dead voice warned: *You're acting like an animal.* And lust replied: *I bloody well hope so.*

"You must be Lady Shapland," Captain Black said.

"Must I? Yes, I suppose I must. Everyone says so, it must be true. And you are the promised kiss of springtime that makes the lonely winter seem long."

He laughed, which was a good start. The bank was steep. He gave her his hand, and she scrambled up. "Silko told me to expect you," she said. "And here you are. I suppose I ought to show you around the estate."

"I'm at your service."

"Yes? Well, that sounds like a very good arrangement."

They strolled across a meadow that was thick with buttercups. Behind them, Stevens was invisible in the gloom of the plantation. He got his binoculars in focus. Zoë had taken Captain Black's arm. Stevens made a note of that.

She said she hoped he could stay for dinner. He thanked her. He smiled, and the old earth took a couple of whirls. "Back home, people used to warn me. Said the English were, uh, reserved. But now look at us. And we just met."

"Well, sometimes friendship doesn't take a year. Sometimes it doesn't take two minutes. You're not married, are you?"

"Correct."

"Strewth. That's an aristocratic expression of surprise. Either the women of Kansas . . . I am right, Kansas? . . . are all dreadfully slow, or, well, to be frightfully crude, your wedding tackle is in less than full working order."

"Wedding tackle . . ." He found that amusing. "I wouldn't be an Air Force pilot if the medics had found any defects. And God knows they look hard."

"Splendid," Zoë said. "So reassuring. One doesn't want any disconcerting revelations, does one?"

"One sure as hell doesn't. And I guess two don't want them twice as much."

They reached a stile in a hedge. He went first, and then gave her his hand to help her over. They strolled on, fingers interlaced. Stevens put down his binoculars and made another note.

"That thing on a hillock, looking rather foolish, is our gazebo," Zoë said. "Not very high, but then Lincolnshire is fairly flat, isn't it? Let's go up, shall we?"

The gazebo was a six-sided room with a pointed roof, raised on iron stilts. They climbed the stairs. The air inside smelt faintly of varnish and turpentine. "The previous owner wanted to be an artist," Zoë said. "That divan was where his model posed."

"Peaceful. Quiet." He poked the divan. "Well sprung."

She removed a cotton sheet from a stack of canvases. They were all nudes. "He knew what he liked," she said.

"Yeah. I guess he did his best, but look: the bed is sexier than the girl. That's not a criticism."

"Certainly not." She was unbuttoning his tunic. "Somebody once said that the secret of a woman's success is to be born with a silver zipper in her hand." She unzipped his fly. "Can that be true?" She opened his belt buckle.

"The great thing about a railroad is the trains run both ways," he said, and unzipped her jeans. "And that's enough fancy talk for now."

Sitting comfortably in the branches of an oak tree, Stevens watched the movements inside the gazebo until the figures sank from view. He made a note. Twenty minutes passed. From his pocket he took two currant scones, wrapped in wax paper. Later he ate a slice of fruit cake and drank a small bottle of lemonade. There was nothing to record. He opened a paperback copy of *British Trout Flies* and was studying a colour plate of Greenwells Glory when the couple came out of the gazebo. They stood on the stairs, arm in arm. She spoke. He grinned. They went back inside. Stevens looked at his watch. An hour and seven minutes. Such stamina! He made a note.

ALL HOUSE-TRAINED MANIACS HERE

1

Some bloody fool had left a tractor parked beyond the end of the runway. It was the tractor that was used to mow the grass. Hooked up behind it was a triple gang-mower, capable of cutting a swathe twenty-five feet wide. Well, R.A.F. Kindrick was a big airfield.

Four Vulcans stood on the Operational Readiness Platforms, short strips of concrete that angled into the runway. At 1637 hours, Bomber Command Ops Room ordered a scramble. The crews spilled out of the Q.R.A. caravan. An umbilical cord linked each Vulcan to a massive trolley-load of batteries. As each captain reached his seat, the crew chief pressed a button that released a flood of electricity which simultaneously fired all four closely grouped jet turbines and thus released the makings of seventy tons of thrust. The cable fell away. Wheels rolled.

The first Vulcan to swing onto the runway, using far less than maximum effort, blasted the tractor and mowers off their wheels. The next Vulcan hurled them thirty yards back. Quinlan's Vulcan came third. He opened his throttles, and the wreckage smashed through the perimeter fence and killed three rabbits in the next field.

Pity about the rabbits. They'd grown accustomed to Vulcan take-offs. The air thundered, the ground shook, the rabbits flattened themselves until all faded and they went back to their dandelions, lightly flavoured with sweet kerosene. But a savage attack by a mad tractor was different. That was a hazard they were not prepared for.

The last Vulcan was airborne one minute forty-seven seconds

after the scramble order: satisfactory. Within half an hour they landed at their dispersal airfield, Yeovilton in Somerset; turned; taxied back up the runway; parked on the O.R.P. Nearby were operational caravans where the crews could rest, wash, get a hot meal. A supply of fresh underwear was available if needed. Nobody knew how long this exercise would last.

At midnight, Jack Hallett and Nick Dando were playing chess. Quinlan was reading a book on the Korean War. Tom Tucker was playing with his sliderule. Silk had just finished writing a long letter to Zoë. He reread it, and looked up. Tucker had found an answer on his sliderule. Or perhaps it was a question, because he was using his forefinger to write an invisible calculation on the armrest of his chair. He didn't like the result and he rubbed it out, although there was nothing visible to erase. He saw Silk watching. "Jack's fault," he said. "His threes look like eights."

"He always says that." Hallett said. He moved his bishop.

Silk flicked through his letter. He tore the pages in half, and in half again, and dropped the bits in a metal waste bin. Quinlan turned his book sideways to look at a photograph. Silk put his pen away.

Tucker said, "I bet Special Branch cleans these rooms when we go."

"It was nothing special," Silk said.

"Special Branch specializes in nothing special. They've got a file on you marked Nothing Special."

Silk took the waste bin outside and set fire to the bits. They made a fierce little blaze. When he came back, Tucker looked at the bin and said, "You've gone and blistered the paint."

"Tell you what," Silk said. "Stuff it in the bomb bay and tomorrow we'll drop it on Minsk and nobody need ever know."

Tucker cracked his knuckles and went back to his sliderule.

An hour later, an airman brought them sandwiches and coffee. "What's the score, laddy?" Quinlan asked. "When do we get out of here?"

"Don't know, sir."

"Poor show. In the war, cookhouse always had the gen on ops before anyone else." Quinlan peeled open a sandwich. "No mustard. How d'you expect us to biff the Russkis without mustard?" The airman left.

"Maybe this isn't an exercise," Silk said. The others chewed, and seemed not interested. "Oh well," he said. "I don't suppose it matters."

"What is it, if it's not an exercise?" Quinlan said. "This is your bog-standard Micky Finn."

"Very quiet."

"They'll call us when they need us," Tucker said.

"Relax, Silko," Hallett said. "It's a routine panic. A no-notice recall and dispersal. God knows, we've done it often enough."

"So we've dispersed to our wartime launch base," Silk said. "That's what this is."

"Obviously."

"If there's a threat of war, we'd follow the exact same procedure."

"It's a Micky Finn, my friend," Dando said. "That's what Micky Finns are all about. Who's got the sugar?"

Silk thought of giving up. Nobody cared. It was just a routine panic. But there was a long dull night ahead, probably, so he persisted. "For all we know, there really is a threat of war. Maybe they ordered a Micky Finn to get the squadrons onto their dispersal fields but they don't want the crews hanging about wondering if enemy missiles have already arrived, back at base."

That caused mild amusement. "If enemy missiles *had* arrived, you wouldn't be standing there, enjoying your ham sandwich," Quinlan said. "You'd be sitting next to me, twelve miles over Russia, making Mach point nine."

"That's assuming we had a basket of sunshine in the bomb bay," Tucker said. "Which we haven't. It's a dummy."

"You didn't see it loaded," Silk said. "None of us did. We could be carrying the real thing."

"Or it could be a barrel of tar," Quinlan said. "Your trouble, Silko, is you spent too long playing cowboys with that cloak-and-dagger Yank outfit. There are direct lines to all the dispersal fields. If an international situation boils over, Bomber Command and Group H.Q. will be on the blower giving us the gen, keeping us on our toes. Right?"

"Right, yes, absolutely." Silk reached for the coffee pot and then stopped, arm outstretched.

"Try again," Dando said. "Take a run at it."

"Suppose the situation boiled over while we were in the air," Silk said. He left the coffee pot. "Suppose the Kremlin wants to get it over with in a hurry, so they press the red button and in the time it takes to boil an egg, Soviet tactical nuclear missiles take out Command H.Q., Group H.Q., Air Ministry and while they're at it, R.A.F. Kindrick too. Leaving us in the lurch. Whatever that is."

"You're very generous with your supposing," Quinlan growled.

"Technically possible," Tucker said. "Landlines wouldn't survive missiles. But there's always radio."

"Well . . ." Dando began. He screwed up his face as if he'd found a bad smell. "Not always."

"I don't want to hear about the electromagnetic pulse," Quinlan said. "Nobody's done it. When somebody can show me EMP at work, I'll listen."

"That's the problem," Dando said. "Nobody can show it unless they do it. But I haven't the slightest doubt that if you detonate a hydrogen bomb at great height over, say, Paris, it will generate enough E.M.P. to turn every piece of electronics in Europe into fried spaghetti."

"The first time would be the last time," Tucker said.

"I know how to baffle E.M.P.," Hallett said. "Switch off all your gear two seconds before the big bang."

"Then what?" Dando asked.

"Put your fingers in your ears."

"This room smells of old socks," Quinlan said. "Let's get some fresh air."

They went outside and looked at the stars. "If worse comes to worst, I can always navigate by that lot," Hallett said.

"You're very quiet, Mr Silk," Quinlan said.

"I was thinking of the night I met Ginger Rogers," Silk said. "She had an electromagnetic pulse you could grill a steak on."

"That's nothing," Dando said. "I nearly got Hedy Lamarr's autograph, once."

They went back inside.

At 3 a.m. an order came from Command: all crews to cockpit readiness.

Quinlan and Silk went through the familiar pre-flight checks, a drill that was almost as familiar as shaving. No warning lights glowed except the ones that were meant to glow. Mist coated the narrow windscreen. Quinlan let it. There was nothing to see out there.

After twenty minutes' silence, he said quietly: "Those three

171

chaps in the back . . . they don't care. All that bullshit you were spreading about tactical missiles buggering-up our communications – it doesn't worry them. They know what Q.R.A. means. It means getting the hell out of Kindrick before Kindrick gets wiped out in one almighty flash. So what? They know we won't come back to family or friends. Who cares? The odds are we won't come back at all. Hullo Russia, goodbye England. Don't think they haven't got any imagination. The difference between them and you is they've learned how to keep their imagination in a bottle with the top screwed tight. So lay off. They're professionals. They know their job. If you want to have a fit of the scruples, go to Skull and weep on his shoulder. Better still, get out of 409 Squadron. We're all house-trained maniacs here. We don't need you crapping all over the asylum."

"I knew a maniac, once," Silk said. "The C.I.A. man in Macão. He dressed up as a ballet dancer and painted his hair green and hit the bishop of Hong Kong with a croquet mallet."

"Oh, shut up," Quinlan said.

"Do you play croquet?"

"No."

"I could teach you. We've got an international croquet court at The Grange. Lady Shapland and the under-butler would make up a foursome." Silk stopped. Quinlan was reading his book on the Korean War.

They were released from cockpit readiness at six: sooner than usual, Dando said. The Micky Finn ended at seven. The four Vulcans flew home. Twenty-four hours without sleep was enough. The crews stood down for the day.

172

PART THREE

SHOOT FIRST

A NICE OLD WIDOW-LADY

1

Silk slept until two, had a sandwich and a beer in the Mess, and drove to The Grange. Stevens told him that Captain Black wished him to know that he was very grateful for the wonderful hospitality he had been shown. Unfortunately, duty required him to return to his base. That was an hour ago. Her ladyship was taking a bath.

"I hope he tipped you well."

"Excessively, sir. I felt obliged to return half the amount."

Silk stared. "You're joking."

"Yes, sir. He failed to tip me. In compensation I took a bottle of claret from the cellar."

"Now I don't know whether you're joking."

"Not the good claret, sir. That would be impertinent. One of the more gullible years."

Silk went upstairs, thinking: Too bloody smooth. But it was the under-butler's job to be smooth, wasn't it? Yes. Maybe. Who cares? The hell with it.

Zoë's bath stood on castiron lion's paw feet and it was long enough to drown a Grenadier Guard. Her head looked very small in a sea of foam and bubbles. Silk sat on the edge and popped bubbles with the sharp end of a loofah. " I hope the Yank wasn't too much of a nuisance," he said.

"Quite charming. The ideal guest."

"I was afraid he'd get in the way of your work."

"Not a bit. We meshed perfectly." She let her head sink until her nose and ears were submerged and she blew bubbles as she looked at Silk. Her head rose and she said, "Such a shame you missed him. I asked if he could possibly come again. He seemed quite keen. How was your Micky Finn? Lots of innocent fun?"

"You know I can't talk about it."

"No? It was just a no-notice recall and dispersal. Routine panic, isn't that what you chaps call it? I assume your Vulcans got airborne in a lot less than four minutes, or Bomber Command would have been highly displeased and you'd still be getting a numb bum on the O.R.P. at your dispersal field."

"Now you're just showing off."

"Not half as much as your fat air marshals. They love to boast. Off the record."

"I wouldn't know. I'm just a flight lieutenant."

"I'm just an M.P., but I know where you went yesterday, and why, and what a complete farce it was. Vulcans are too big and noisy to hide, Silko. What makes you think the Russians haven't got Yeovilton on their maps?"

"I have a feeling you're going to tell me."

"The R.A.F. knows where all the Soviet nuclear bomber bases are, and Russia's *vast*. England's tiny. D'you honestly believe the Kremlin can't plant a missile on every R.A.F. bomber base? Main and dispersal? Twice over?"

"That's not my problem." Beside him, Zoë's right foot had appeared, pink and shiny. He fingered the toes. "All I know is the Kremlin won't survive an attack on Britain. Is Kruschev prepared to trade Moscow for, say, Kindrick? I don't think so." He tickled her foot. "None of which is secret, by the way."

"Stop. Stop! Or I'll splash you . . . the trains run both ways, don't they?" she said. "*We* don't dare attack *them* first, because . . ." Silk shrugged. "So nobody's going to drop the bomb," she said. "It's a useless weapon."

"Well, *mine* isn't. Mine's on standby, and fully operational. Bugger the Kremlin. How long are you going to soak in this tub?"

"Here's something else you ought to know. Your famous four-minute warning begs a very large question. D'you want to know what it is?"

"No." The foam was thinning; Silk could see more and more of her. Here and now. Why not here and now? "Yesterday, when I got called to the colours, we left unfinished business behind. Remember? Well, now I'm back, loaded for bear. So: shall we make whoopee?" *Four-minute warning? Damn right I want to know. But not now.*

Zoë raised her foot a little higher and wriggled the toes. She took a serious interest in the performance. Steam had turned her hair into black ringlets. She looked no more than twenty years old, which was what she was when Silk first met her. "Afraid not," she said.

"Look, I'll go and fetch the bloody punt," Silk said. "I'll carry it up the bloody stairs. I'll dump it in the bloody bedroom."

"I know you would, darling. But that wouldn't alter the bloody time, and the bloody time is what we haven't bloody got." She spoke sweetly. Silk found himself looking at her foot. If he grabbed it, jerked upwards, she'd go under. Hold tight, she'd stay under. And that would definitely solve . . . what? Nothing. So why was it such a tempting thought?

He reached out and, with one forefinger, pushed the foot down into the water.

"Let me guess," he said. "The end of the world is nigh. Your sources of intelligence have pinpointed . . ." He looked at his watch. "Sixteen hundred hours. Am I right?"

"You *are* clever, Silko. It's a cocktail party, at five. Go and have a bath, dear. You smell like the inside of a boxer's jockstrap."

"Well, you would know more about that than I," he said as he went out. It wasn't often that he got the last word, and it didn't make him feel any less dissatisfied.

2

The Old Rectory, just outside Lincoln, was big. It had been built in an age when parsons could afford large families and cheap servants. Now it was owned by a man who had inherited half a coalfield in Nottinghamshire. To express his appreciation of this good luck, he encouraged the arts in East Anglia by giving cocktail parties where the artists could meet people with taste and money. Like Zoë.

On their way to the party, Silk asked her if she'd noticed anything sort of, you know, morbid about Captain Black. She said he'd seemed remarkably well-balanced. Silk was frowning at the road, gripping the wheel so tightly that sinews showed up stiffly on the backs of his hands. "Still, what do I know?" she said. "I'm impressed by any man who can take his pants off without falling over."

He glanced at her, and went back to frowning.

"Joke," she said. "Well-balanced. Remember?" She squeezed his thigh. "Relax, Silko." He took his hand off the wheel and flexed his fingers. "Now smile," she said. He did his best. "Ghastly," she said. "Go back to looking miserable."

After a mile or so, he said, "It's just that I got the impression that Captain Black doesn't like his job. Prospects are deeply depressing. He's even thought of taking the easy way out."

"Suicide," Zoë said. "It's called suicide, Silko."

"Anyway, I did my best to change his mind. Buck him up."

"Did you? Why? He's flying an F-100 in a squadron that's tasked to make tactical nuclear strikes on population centres in Eastern Europe." She looked out of her window and waved to three children who were riding a fat old pony, bareback. They waved back. "If he's going to kill a couple of hundred thousand civilians, and himself, then the least we can do is let him kill himself first, don't you agree?"

Silk changed gear, unnecessarily, and changed back again. "I don't know anything about any of that," he said.

"Yes, you do, darling. You do now."

"Well, it's all balls. I want to ask you about Stevens. Don't you think he's got a funny attitude? And why is he only the under-butler when we haven't got a proper butler?"

"No particular reason. He came with the house, rather like the death-watch beetle."

"I never know what to say to him. All I know about is flying. How can I make conversation with ordinary people when . . . What's there to talk about? Cricket? I hate cricket. At school, I could never hit the damn ball. It hit me. I had scars on my scars. Maybe I should talk about that. Are you interested in my cricket scars?"

"You need a hobby," Zoë said. "Give your bored old brain a break. Find yourself a nice hobby, Silko."

"I could rob banks," he said. "That would be something to talk about."

"Do it. Do anything. Just get one foot in the real world."

* * *

Something artistic was happening everywhere at the Old Rectory: in the library, the music room, the drawingroom, the study; and activities overflowed onto the terrace, the lawns, the summerhouse. Poetry readings, pianists, displays of paintings, a string quartet, actors giving readings, pottery, prints, sculpture, weaving. Flower-arranging. Embroidery.

Silk toured the lot in fifteen minutes. Nothing was worth tuppence. Nobody mattered. He gave up. He noticed a small wrought-iron balcony, high up, so he went upstairs.

A man was leaning on the rail. Below, on the terrace, the string quartet was making short work of Mendelssohn. "Mind if I join you?" Silk said.

"Please do."

"I've taken all the culture I can stand. Wait a minute . . . This is your party, isn't it? Sorry."

"Not a bit. My contribution to the arts is writing a fat cheque for the booze." He pointed at a group of people. "If you're looking for sparkling conversation, I strongly recommend the lady in the green silk."

"Me too. She's my wife."

"Is that so? Lucky chap. Let me see . . . How about that one-armed man? Interesting fellow. Glass-blower. Can't be easy, can it? One arm."

"Quite a challenge." But Silk was looking at a slim woman in khaki trousers and a v-neck sweater. The trousers fitted her like skin. The sweater was blood-red and, from this distance, appeared to be v-necked down to somewhere just north of the navel. She had pulled up the sleeves until they bunched above her elbows. She turned her head, and Silk crashed and burned, right there. "Interesting face," he said.

"It's the glass-blowing," his host said. "Develops the cheek muscles."

"Really? Sounds fascinating."

Silk hurried downstairs, weaved through the crowd on the lawn, found the blood-red sweater listening to the glass-blower. "It all starts with the diaphragm," he was saying. He patted his stomach. "I can move a grand piano ten feet, just using my diaphragm."

"Excuse me," Silk said, "but there's a woman in the Music Room who wants to buy your glass. Lots of it." The man stared. "Didn't give her name," Silk said. "Plump, about fifty, big cheque book. Music Room."

They watched him go. "Thank Christ," Silk said. Beneath the sweater's deep cleavage she was wearing some kind of skin-coloured undergarment. He forgave her everything. "For a moment I didn't think he'd buy it," he said. No reply. Maybe she couldn't speak English. Swedish, maybe. Italian. Greek. "Who are you?" he asked. "Tell me you're not married." *Fool*, he told himself, and shut up.

She had half a glass of white wine. She drank a little, and looked at him curiously. Seriously. Then she drank the rest and gave him the glass. "Does that often work?" she asked. "Kicking down the door and throwing hand grenades?"

"Blame it on the sweater." What the hell.

"Why? Why not blame it on your balls?" She was calm. And slightly amused.

"Hey, hey. You're jumping several stages ahead."

"Hey, hey, no I'm not. I'm just stopping you from doing what every man does when he fails to score. He blames the woman."

Silk raised his hands. "Okay. I surrender."

She ran a finger along his jawline. "Cleancut. I like a man with a cleancut face. Come on, let's take a stroll."

He walked beside her. "Is this wise? You hardly know me."

"Oh, I know you. I should have married you, ten years ago, when you were still fairly sober."

"You're confusing me with . . ."

"Yes, I am. Anyway, he's dead. Drunk as a skunk, drove flat out, hit a bridge, end of story. Hullo, Millie." She waved to a friend. "Sings like an angel, cooks like a Borgia," she told Silk. "Avoid her dinners. They'll kill you." She led him behind the summerhouse and through a garden gate. "Where are we going?" he asked. He didn't care; it was just something to say. They turned right. "Deadman's Acre," she said. "Good view."

"Another fatality. You're dangerous to know, aren't you?"

She didn't laugh, or smile, or reply. *Got that wrong.* Silk said to himself. *This is not going well.*

They walked in silence. When she spoke, her voice was different: slack, easy, almost thinking aloud. "Thank God I'm out of there. I hate crowds, and crowds of artists are the worst, all those fragile egos, all that bullshit . . . I can't take the noise. I was ready to go and hide in the cellar when you turned up, bellowing like a wounded buffalo. Who are you, anyway?"

Silk explained.

"I've met Zoë," she said. "Ball of fire. Not like me. Slow burner, me. I used to be a model, fairly successful, I knew how to switch on and switch off. I could sparkle when I wanted. Still can, briefly. Brought you running, didn't I?"

"Did you? Can't remember. It was ages ago."

At last she smiled. "I know the signs. I'm thirty-two, Silko. Men have been falling in love with this face of mine since I was fifteen. Face and figure. Love at first sight, that's what they think, silly bastards. They don't know me. How can they? So it always ends in tears. Not my tears, hell no, don't blame me for my looks. You wouldn't enjoy it if women kept falling in love with you at first sight, would you?"

"I might."

"Twice a week? Year round?"

"That might be rather a strain."

They reached Deadman's Acre and admired the view. Blackbirds sang. Swallows stooged about the sky. One plunged and soared in something like a corkscrew. Hard work, and all to catch a few bugs. But beautiful.

They walked back. He found that her name was Tess Monk. She lived in an old farmhouse, alone. She taught music for a living and worked part-time in a shop for another living. "That's where the sweater came from," she said. "You want us to meet again. I can tell by the way you're chewing your lip."

"Well, I've always wanted to learn the saxophone."

"You're lying. And I don't teach the sax. I teach the cello."

"That was my second choice," he said.

* * *

On the way home, Zoë said. "I bought a painting of a tree, very ugly, but the artist's wife is pregnant again."

"Everyone needs a hobby," Silk said. "Talking of which, I took your advice. I'm going to learn to play the cello."

"Golly. Who's teaching you?"

"A nice old widow-lady. Tess Monk."

"Oh, *her*. She's batty. No, that's unfair. She lives in a world of her own. I asked her to join Artists Against The Bomb and she said she was against artists. In her experience, they had lousy judgement and bad breath and ninety per cent could be A-bombed and the world would be a better place."

"Damn right."

"Damn silly."

"What if you got Laurence Olivier on your soap box? Why should I do what he says? He's just an actor. Hasn't got a brain of his own. Why should anyone buy his opinions?"

"I'd have him in a flash, if I could."

"Just shows that Tess Monk was right."

"No, Silko. It just shows that your brain is away with the fairies, like hers. And you'll never learn the cello. I've heard you sing. You can't carry a tune in a bucket."

"It's only a hobby," he said. "Nothing serious. Like your hobby of dropping little hints about Vulcan operations. You said the four-minute warning begs a large question, but you never explained what that meant."

"Glaringly obvious. Look at the Vulcan. Look at Blue Steel. Now ask yourself why the Americans keep their B52s armed and flying around the clock, every day of the year. If you can't work it out, you don't deserve to know."

"Look," he said. "Cows eating grass. Isn't that amazing?"

They reached The Grange. She packed a briefcase and changed her clothes. The sun was setting as he drove her to Lincoln and saw her onto the London train. Then he drove to the farmhouse where Tess Monk lived. "You again," she said.

"I passed a pub. The Mason's Arms. Thought you might like to go for a drink. Maybe a pickled egg. Packet of nuts."

"You're full of wild ideas." She shut the door and took his arm.

ROCK THE PYRAMIDS

1

"Our information is that she has been an undesirable influence on him," Brigadier Leppard said. "Possibly subversive. Even seditious."

"All in twenty-four hours?" Skull said. "My God. It almost makes you feel proud to be British."

They were standing at the bar of the Bum Steer. It was lunchtime, and only a couple of tables were occupied. The place was, as always, dark.

"Twenty-four hours isn't enough?" Leppard said. "It's a day too long for the U.S. Air Force. Captain Black was shipped home last night."

"That's fast."

"You bet your sweet life. My God, it almost makes you feel proud to be American."

Skull ate some peanuts. "I've known her for years. She's an M.P., independent yes, but unpatriotic? Unthinkable."

"Our Intelligence guys are trained to think the unthinkable. Like thinking that your Mr Profumo, Harrow and Oxford, Secretary of State for War, might be bedding Miss Christine Keeler while she was bedding Captain Romanov, naval attaché at the Russian Embassy."

"Not simultaneously."

"You only have his word for that. And the man did lie to your House of Commons . . . Look, Skull: we have our own rotten apples, nobody denies that. So we don't want to make a big production out

185

of this. The Silks are your problem. We'll file it and forget – provided it doesn't happen again."

"What did happen, exactly?" Skull asked. "And who says?"

The barman was out of earshot, but still Leppard lowered his voice. "Your people. M.I.5. No details. They referred to Mrs Silk's links with C.N.D. and said her influence on Captain Black was . . . I can't remember the exact words."

"Contrary to good order and discipline, I expect. That's what we always say when we're on a slightly sticky wicket."

"Anyway, he's gone."

"What will happen to him?"

"There's always a need for good men in the Aleutians."

Skull shuddered. "Have you got time for another?" He signalled the barman. "How's Operation Ortsac coming along?"

Leppard pretended to look alarmed. "Never heard of it. Doesn't exist. Routine manoeuvres. Unimportant. Postponed. Cancelled. How did you know?"

"My dear Karl . . ." The drinks arrived. "You can't have a U.S. fleet, with a few infantry divisions and half the Marine Corps in landing craft, all charging around the Caribbean under an umbrella of warplanes, and expect to keep it secret. Everyone in Florida knows."

"It's probably over by now."

Skull asked: "Who came up with the name Ortsac, which even I worked out is Castro backwards?" Leppard swigged his drink, looked at his watch. "It was never meant to be secret, was it?" Skull said. "You're putting on a show, practising huge amphibious operations, all to frighten Castro. You're rattling your Yankee sabres."

"Well, I've got to get back to base. We must do lunch sometime."

"If Kennedy keeps threatening to go to war, somebody might start believing him," Skull said.

"Castro's flat broke," Leppard said, smiling. "And getting broker every day."

2

In 1956, Britain, France and Israel connived at a secret plan to invade Egypt. Israeli forces would advance towards the Suez Canal. Britain and France would then attack, claiming that they were separating the combatants and so safeguarding the Canal. In fact the whole bogus operation was an excuse for punishing the Egyptian President Nasser because he had nationalized the Canal. The British Prime Minister, Eden, said Nasser was a new Hitler of the Middle East.

Only those were fooled who wished to be fooled. America was not one. Eisenhower threatened to remove support from sterling. This would have sent the pound spiralling downwards. British troops pulled out and Eden resigned. The Suez Adventure had failed miserably.

But remnants of imperial power were still dotted about the globe. In 1962 the R.A.F. could still use bases in Malaya, Singapore, Hong Kong, Pakistan, Aden, Uganda, Iraq, Cyprus, Malta, Libya. For 409 Squadron, Libya was an invaluable training area. "We'll be taking our Blue Steel," Quinlan told Silk. "Not armed, of course. Just for show. Just for fun."

They were briefed to fly a dogleg route to Malta, supposedly avoiding enemy air defences, and then via Tripoli to the far south, where the Libyan border met Chad and Niger. From there they were to fly north-east and simulate a nuclear attack on Cairo.

"It's a sandpit," Silk said. "What's so wonderful about a sandpit?"

"It's flat, for a start," Tucker said. He pointed at the wall map of

Eastern Europe and Russia. "Like nearly all that. You can fly from Kindrick to Warsaw or Kiev or Smolensk or Leningrad at five hundred feet and you won't hit anything bigger than a goshawk."

"Tom knows his birds," Dando said. "You don't want to argue with Tom about birds."

"They like forests, do goshawks," Tucker said. "Russia's got forests. By Christ, do they have forests."

"Trees make a lousy radar picture," Hallett said. "That's why we're going to Libya. Sand is worse than trees. It's everywhere and it's nothing. You can cross Libya at five hundred feet and not hit anything bigger than a . . ."

"Long-legged buzzard," Tucker said. "Very rare."

"Libya is Russia with camelshit," Dando said. "And the sun beats down like a great brass gong."

"I hope you have a Plan B for when you get lost," Silk said.

"We shan't get lost," Quinlan told him. He spread a map of Libya. It was marked with red Chinagraph crosses. "See that? It's where three U.S. Fortresses got lost in 1942 and came down. Still there. Over here, an S.A.S. patrol got caught in the open by Beaufighters, mistook them for Jerries, left burnt-out vehicles everywhere. Here, this is where a flight of Me109s ran out of fuel, silly boys. Up here: small tank battle, lots of broken ironmongery. And so on. Heaps of metal give good radar echoes."

"The skipper was in the Desert Air Force," Dando explained.

"Wellingtons," Quinlan said. "Nice kite. Hot-air turbulence, made her shake her tail like a wet dog."

They went to the crew room and got into their flying kit. "If anyone has friends in Cairo, now's the time to call them and say goodbye," Quinlan said.

"He always tells us that," Hallett said.

3

The Blue Steel was a pilotless aircraft with a nuclear bomb in the nose, or a flying bomb with a Stentor rocket motor in the tail: they added up to the same thing. It was 35 feet long, with small delta planes at front and rear, and even smaller fins above and beneath. The Vulcan bomb-bay swallowed most of it; what showed was so sleek that it scarcely affected the aircraft's performance.

They were ten miles high and three hundred miles inside Egyptian air space, virtually invisible to anyone on the ground, when they made their mock attack on Cairo. If it had been a real attack, the Blue Steel would have detached and taken four seconds to drop three hundred feet and clear the Vulcan. Then its rocket motor would have fired and sent it soaring to seventy thousand feet, after which its inboard computer – stuffed with route data and constantly updating itself – would have navigated the weapon, perhaps taking an erratic course but always knowing precisely where it was. In thin air, at over twice the speed of sound, it would reach its target in four minutes. There could be no stopping it. Even in thicker air, Blue Steel would dive at a thousand miles an hour. Nobody would hear its arrival. In its nose a hydrogen bomb would be equivalent to over a million tons of T.N.T. The explosion would wipe out Cairo, rock the Pyramids, crack the Canal, shake all Egypt like a beaten carpet. By then, Quinlan and his crew would be far out over the Mediterranean, heading for R.A.F. Akrotiri in Cyprus, and tea. They did a jolly good tea at Akrotiri.

4

"Have you told Group Captain Pulvertaft about this?" Freddy Redman asked.

"I thought I'd wait until I got your reaction," Skull said.

They were lunching at the Reform Club. Beef and oyster pie, new potatoes, red cabbage. Half a bottle of Bordeaux.

"It's tricky," Freddy said. "Pulvertaft's brave as a lion, heart in the right place, but he's no man for the murky world of politics. Anyway, what can he do?"

"He can't sack Silko. Silko's done nothing wrong."

"I called a pal in M.I.5 this morning. No joy. He said the file had been Referred Upwards. Could mean anything." Freddy topped up their glasses with the last of the wine. "I daren't order a whole bottle nowadays. My doctor's an absolute bastard."

Skull put down his fork. "I'm a fool," he said. "I've been concerned about what Silko might let slip. That's not the problem. Silko's too smart, and he's heard all the lectures on secrecy. The real risk is what Zoë might do to his morale. We're asking him to commit an unspeakable act, and she may be making him *think*."

"Nobody's ever going to perform the unspeakable act," Freddy said.

"You try telling the Americans that. Not long ago they wanted to atom-bomb China. I've met a few U.S. Air Force generals who are ready to turn the Soviet Union into volcanic ash and make the world free for Coca-Cola."

"We won't let them."

"Certainly not. We'll send a few Vulcans to wipe out New York. That should restore common sense."

Freddy let his shoulders slump. "Now I'm thoroughly confused. Whose side are we on? I think I'd better have a chat with Silko."

"Don't believe a word he says," Skull advised. "He takes nothing seriously. Especially total global nuclear extermination."

SWEDISH FOR DRAGON

1

"Mind your head," Tess Monk said. "Everyone was five feet tall when they built places like this."

Silk ducked through the doorway. The kitchen ceiling was a little higher. Its beams were logs, and some sagged so that his hair brushed against them. The farmhouse was no bigger than a large cottage. It smelt strongly of dog. An old bull terrier got up and came over and sniffed his shoes, found nothing to eat, and padded back to the hearthrug. Silk looked around. The prevailing colour was clay, except for a dull cream baby grand. "Quaint," he said.

"It was a dump when we bought it. Looked as if a bomb had hit it."

"Hard to believe."

"Then it caught fire. That improved things a bit."

"You said that *we* bought it. Would that be . . ."

"The drunk who had a fight with a bridge, yes."

She showed him the rest. Small sitting room full of a big sofa and wallpaper dotted with tired roses that couldn't wait for winter to come and end it all. Stairs to a bedroom with, surprisingly, a four-poster. "Wedding present," she said. Bathroom, with no bath and no shower.

"Don't tell me you stand in the rain," he said.

"Nearly right. I run a hose from the kitchen to the garden."

"In the buff?"

"Stark naked. Sometimes the dog joins me."

"You should sell tickets."

"You can watch for a fiver." She didn't smile. "I need the cash. Reminds me: you said you want a cello."

They went downstairs, and she pulled an old, scarred cello from under the baby grand. "There's a case for it somewhere."

He looked it over. "This one's been around the block a few times, hasn't it?"

"Another wedding present. My father-in-law was a collector. You've heard of Stradivarius? He had a nephew called Cabrilloni, taught him all he knew. This cello is a Cabrilloni. Three hundred years old." She gave it to him.

Silk blew the dust off it and looked inside. "There's a label here," he said. "Joseph Parrish, Instrument Maker, Wolverhampton 1937."

"That's to keep it from getting stolen. Under the label it says Francisco Cabrilloni of Naples, 1667. In Italian, of course."

Silk took the bow and pulled it across the strings. "Christ Almighty," he said. The noise was like a bad cough. "Is it difficult to learn?"

"What do you care? You didn't come here to learn it in the first place." She took the cello and propped it against the piano. "Let us go and test the four-poster. It is by far the best thing in this house."

Silk paused on the stairs. "This is a good idea," he said, "as long as you know I'm not madly in love with you."

"That's a relief," she said. "For myself, I find you somewhat attractive. That's okay, isn't it? Or do you want to go for a long walk and think it over?"

"Definitely not."

He stayed for supper. When he left, he took the cello with him.

"Since you don't want to learn to play it, there are much smaller things you could learn not to play," she said. "I've got an old clarinet somewhere. Or a fiddle."

"I told Zoë I'm learning the cello. I'd better stick to what I said."

"Five pounds for the first lesson," she said. He paid.

2

Quinlan's crew, and two other Vulcan crews, were sitting in one of the briefing rooms in the Ops Block, when Skull came in.

"I have never been totally persuaded by the story of David and Goliath," he said. "It implies that bulk, because it is big, must be vulnerable. The ant beneath the elephant would not agree. And suppose Goliath, not David, had the slingshot? Or suppose David had a squint and he hit, not Goliath, but his own mother-in-law, watching from the side?"

"Moses supposes his toeses are roses," Dando said. "But Moses supposes erroneously."

"Which confirms my point," Skull said. "Trust nobody, check everything. Above all, know your enemy."

"France," a squadron leader said confidently. "That's our natural enemy. So my old dad used to say, anyway."

Mild amusement.

"May the good Saint Émilion forgive you both," Skull told him. "I see the enemy as a tall, fair-haired, athletic figure, cleanshaven, with a typically Slavic face. Married, two children. Brave – he flew Stormoviks and strafed German tanks in the Great Patriotic War, as they call it. Plays the flute. Not now, of course. Now he is a junior general in the Soviet air force, commanding a missile base at Dukhovskina Vyazma, which is near Smolensk. He has just pressed the red button to complete the firing sequence for an intercontinental nuclear missile. His job is done. So is his life, and that of his wife and their two children, whose names I can't pronounce, but it matters not because they will soon be pronounced dead, thanks to your pluck and courage. These remarks are in bad taste, but then so is nuclear annihilation. Any questions so far?"

"You're very chirpy today, Skull," Silk said.

"My back pay has come through. I hope I didn't offend you with that strictly factual recital of your duties."

"It was a bit stuffy," a flight lieutenant said.

"That was irony," Skull explained. "The mustard that excites the meat. It costs so little, yet it means so much."

"You're in a very pissy mood today, Skull," Quinlan said.

"The Lagonda's got a nasty cough. Probably the exhaust. Bang goes my back pay." A flight-sergeant came in with a bundle of files. "At last," Skull said. "Luncheon is served." They got down to the serious business. Each crew was given a Soviet strategic bomber base as their supposed target. Quinlan's crew got Tartu, easy meat because their Blue Steel could be released while they were still over the Baltic Sea. Silk noticed that Tartu was in Estonia. Rough luck on the poor bloody Estonians. First the East fucked you over, then the West blew you to buggery. But he said nothing.

3

The Vulcan climbed steadily across the North Sea. It reached the mouth of the Baltic at fifty thousand feet, still well below its operational ceiling, and going flat out, a little below the speed of sound. The plan was to make a dash towards the target, and get in and out while still over the Baltic.

The anti-flash blinds were up but there was nothing to see except a few thousand cubic miles of violet-tinged stratosphere.

Scandinavia was off to the left, lost under cloud. Even the cloud was out of sight.

Silk was making his routine check of instruments – altimeter, artificial horizon, air speed indicator, machmeter, compass – when Quinlan shouted: "Christ! What was that?" Silk looked and saw nothing. "What was what?" he said. Foolish question. He shut up. Quinlan was questioning Tucker about radar signals. Tucker said: "What signals? Nothing showed here." The others in the back agreed. Quinlan said, "We just got bounced. Some bastard just bounced us." His voice cracked slightly.

Silk leaned forward and searched. A speck of silver streaked, diving across the sky, almost faster than his eyes could follow, and was gone. "Delta fighter," he said. "I think."

"They're playing silly-buggers with us," Quinlan said. "Running rings round us. Look . . ." Before he could point, another tiny triangle shot past and soared and was lost in the sun.

"Mach two," Silk said. "At least Mach two."

After a couple of minutes, a formation of three delta-wing fighters dropped from considerably higher and escorted the Vulcan at what seemed a lazily sedate speed. "Swedes," Quinlan said. "We're being seen off the premises by a bunch of Swedes." He turned for home.

At debriefing, Silk made a sketch and Renouf, the Operations Officer, confirmed that it was a Saab 35 Draken. "That's Swedish for dragon," he said. "Very supersonic. Designed specifically to intercept blokes like you."

"They left us standing," Quinlan said. "They made us look like cold treacle."

"The Swedes are a bit touchy about maintaining their neutrality."

Skull said: "So would you be, with Russia just around the

corner. Theirs is not the only delta-wing fighter, of course. France claims their new Mirage can make twelve hundred knots at fifty thousand plus."

"The French always lie," Renouf said. "They add ten per cent. Like their rotten restaurants."

"Screw the frogs," Quinlan said. "What about the bear? Has he got a new delta?"

"Only the MiG-21," Skull said. "Probably a trifle faster than the others." Quinlan closed his eyes. "But it's also much smaller," Skull added. "So its range and firepower aren't as good."

"That's all right then," Hallett muttered.

"Hey, speed isn't everything," Renouf said sharply. "You can be too fast. I've seen fighters so keen, they went slap through the bomber formation, never fired a shot. If a MiG finds you, he'll be subsonic, and he'll be bouncing about in your wake, trying to get his guns lined up."

"He can't find us," Dando said, "because I've jammed his V.H.F. channels so bad that his ground controllers are weeping into their vodka."

Nobody cheered, but nobody disagreed. "Anything else to report?" Skull said.

"Has Tartu got a cathedral?" Quinlan asked.

"Yes. Rather a fine one."

"Not any longer, it hasn't. It evaporated, along with the orphanage, the infirmary, the old folks' home, and the tomb of St Bruno the Bastard." Quinlan was feeling better again.

"Precision bombing," Renouf said. "Name of the game." He was gazing out of the window.

"Game?" Silk said: "What . . ." He looked at Skull, but Skull just shook his head. Renouf's mind was elsewhere. Re-fighting the last war, probably.

4

Silk got the cello case out of his car and carried it to his room. Stupid bloody shape, too big to tuck under his arm. Why wasn't there a handle? Or a wheel on the end, like a golf trolley? He scraped the doorframe and flinched with guilt. The cello was probably worth twenty thousand. He opened the case. No damage done, thank God.

He tried using the bow. After a few minutes he got bored, so he plucked the strings instead. That was hard on the fingertips. Someone rapped on his door and before he could speak, Tucker came in. "Jack Hallett's up shit creek," he said. "Lend him a thousand, Silko." He looked grim.

"Bloody good idea," Silk said. "Only one reason why I can't." He plucked a few strings. "No, actually there's a thousand reasons."

"Don't give me that crap. Your old lady's rolling in the stuff."

"Rolling in it but not chucking it away."

"Then we're completely fucked." Tucker dropped into an arm-chair so hard that it groaned. "Nobody else has that sort of money."

"Okay." Silk rested the cello in a corner. "So Jack's up the creek. What creek?"

"Gambling. He owes his bookie a thousand. The bastard's threatening to go to the C.O. if Jack doesn't pay."

Silk made a face. Jack Hallett, the genial, steady, competent nav plotter? Not possible. "Gambling on what?"

"Dunno. Horses, dogs? Who cares what?" Tucker heaved him-self out of the chair. "If Jack gets found out, he's for the chop."

"Security."

"Of course bloody security."

They stood, not looking at each other. Tucker kept cracking his knuckles. "Can you play that thing?" he asked.

"Taking lessons. It's a hobby."

197

Tucker nodded. Silk noticed a vein throbbing on the right side of his neck. "Jack's bookie's waiting outside the Main Gate," Tucker said. "The S.P.s won't let him in, of course. Let's go and reason with him."

Hallett was in the corridor. "It's my idiot son," he told Silk, wretchedly. "Same name – Jack. He's been placing bets, using my telephone account, they thought he was me. He's twenty-one, it's legal. Isn't it?"

"It's brainless," Tucker growled.

They walked to the Main Gate. Jack's bookie was small, not young; an ordinary man in an ordinary blue suit. Only the brown shoes were wrong.

"You can't come on the base," Tucker told him. "Let's go for a walk."

"I didn't come here for exercise. I came for my money." He was calm. He'd done this a hundred times before.

"We'll talk as we walk," Tucker said.

They walked. The bookie explained that it was a simple business matter. People thought bookies were rich. In fact they worked on a very tight margin. A thousand pounds one way or the other made all the difference. "If you ran a garage and you serviced my car, I'd expect to pay you," he said. "Well, I serviced Mr Hallett's bets, and he should pay me."

"Can't we do some kind of deal?" Silk asked. "You know, pay off so much a week, or . . ."

"Tell that to my other clients, the people who placed bets and *won*. What would they say if I offered them a deal? So much a week?" He looked almost amused.

"Give us some time, at least. Maybe—"

"Time? This isn't the first time of asking. Is it, Mr Hallett?" But Jack Hallett was looking at the horizon.

"You haven't come to any old aerodrome, you know," Tucker said. "This is a Vulcan base. What are the odds against you being in business if Russia takes over?"

"I see," the bookie said. "This is your way of saving me from Communism, is it? Wiping the slate clean? You bet, you lose, you don't pay? That's your style in the Raff, is it?"

"Yeah," Tucker said. "And we're not in the Raff."

"I can probably find a couple of hundred soon," Silk said.

"Soon," the bookie said. "Probably. How often have I heard that before?"

They had turned a bend and were out of sight of the Main Gate. "I know how we can settle this here and now," Tucker said. "See that patch of nettles? I bet you one thousand pounds you'll lie in those nettles." The bookie laughed. Tucker punched him, a fast short right to the ribs, just below the heart. The man's legs folded and as he fell, Tucker's left fist swung and whacked his head sideways. He lay on the road in an untidy sprawl. Tucker picked him up and threw him in the nettles. "Now we're all square," he told him. The bookie crawled out. Tucker picked him up and threw him back. Then he put his foot on the bookie's head and rubbed it in the nettles. "That's a bloody silly thing to do," Silk said. Tucker had stepped away from the bookie. Now he turned back and seized a bunch of nettles. He ripped them up by the roots and lashed the bookie's face with them.

"Hey, enough, enough," Hallett said. His voice was thin. His face looked crumpled about the eyes.

"He wasn't going to change his tune," Tucker said. "So I stopped his clock. Now he knows not to bugger us about."

They walked back towards the Main Gate. Hallett said, "I think you bust his ribs."

"Next time, I'll bust yours. And any other manky bastard who calls me *Raff*."

"Your trouble is you think with your fists," Silk said.

"Shouldn't we . . ." Hallett began, but he couldn't finish. "Leaving him there, it's . . ." He gave up.

"Nettles are good for him," Tucker said. "My granny in Glasgow rubs her legs with nettles. Cures her rheumatism."

"That's bollocks. Suppose he goes to Pulvertaft," Silk said. "Then we're all in trouble. Assaulting a civilian—"

"I didn't touch him," Hallett said.

"You didn't stop it."

"Neither did you."

"And for why?" Tucker demanded. "Because deep down in your flabby hearts a spark of *esprit de* bloody *corps* was still burning! The crew always sticks together, right? That bookie had his knife into Jack, and if Jack got the chop we'd get a new nav plotter and bang goes our Combat status! And we start *all over again*. Bottom crew. Well, no poxy civilian is going to destroy our Combat status. If I can take out Murmansk East any day of the week, then God help any mouthy bloody bookie who gets in my way."

"You didn't hit him because he was in the way," Silk said. "You hit him because he was small."

"That's true. You're not very big yourself."

Hallett said, "If he was a small bookie, he shouldn't have taken such big bets." Nobody laughed.

"You break my ribs and I'll break your neck," Silk said to Tucker. "That's my Combat status." They stopped and stared at each other.

"Oh, come on," Hallett said miserably. "Today just keeps getting worse and worse."

*

Skull and Leppard sat at a rustic table on the lawn outside the Bum Steer and drank beer. Leppard said that his boss, a two-star general, wanted him to organize a War Game at the base. Nothing colossal: just a tactical exercise, something to keep the squadron staffs on their toes.

"Tactical," Skull said. "Define tactical."

"Kiloton weapons, maximum," Leppard said.

"Hiroshima, Nagasaki. Mere firecrackers."

"Look: I've got to begin somewhere." Leppard said his starting-point would be a Soviet seizure of West Berlin: small, vulnerable, isolated, a thorn in Kruschev's side. No warning. A swift grab. What then? Skull could join in, representing Bomber Command. Take a couple of hours. No big deal.

"That's what God said on Monday morning." But Skull agreed.

VIOLENCE BEGETS VIOLENCE

1

Silk was sitting on the farmhouse doorstep with a bunch of flowers wrapped in patterned cellophane and tied with a big red ribbon. When she arrived on her bicycle, he stood up. "What the hell have you got there?" she asked.

"Nothing. I found them in a graveyard. Quite fresh."

She saw the florist's name on the cellophane. "Robbers," she said. "Crooks."

They went inside and he gave her the flowers: tulips, carnations and some kind of silvery spray. "I look like I just won an ice-skating championship," she said.

"The under-butler gave them to me. He fancies me something rotten. You should have read the card."

"He fancied me, once." All she could find to put them in was the brass casing of a World War One artillery shell. She added tap water. "Weddings and funerals," she said. "That's what they smell of."

"We can't have a wedding. I suppose I could always go and kill someone for you."

She was holding bottles up to the light, searching for anything to drink. "I don't think you're capable," she said. "Not with your bare hands."

He looked at his hands, clenched them, stretched the fingers. "Maybe not. I thought about drowning Zoë, once. But then I didn't. So I'm no good at murdering women."

She yawned. "There you go again. Sweet-talking me into bed."

It was dusk when he left. "About the flowers," he said. "I haven't done that since I was eighteen."

"Next time, buy booze. Algerian red will do. Is that your cello in the car? I charge for lessons." Silk paid her.

2

Silk drove to The Grange, not because he wanted to spend the night there but because it was time for a fight. He was tired of being the silent partner, of having to listen while Zoë made her cheap points. He felt rebellious. Fine. Let's have a rebellion. Then he remembered: she was in London.

Stevens was waiting at the front door. Inevitably.

"Don't bother to put the car away," Silk said. "I'm going back to the base."

"It's no bother, sir. Her ladyship left instructions that no cars be left standing here."

"Why the hell not?"

Stevens gave the smallest of shrugs. "In order not to create the appearance of a used-car dealer's forecourt, sir. Her words, I should add."

"Yeah? Well, the Citroën stays. I'm here. She's in London. *My* words. Add them to hers, subtract the price of little green apples, and multiply by the speed of sound." He took the key from the ignition. "Got it?"

"Switzerland, sir. Her ladyship is in Geneva."

"Serve them right for being so goddam neutral. Where were you in the war, Stevens?"

"Utterly invisible, sir." He went ahead. "Shall I run a bath, sir?"

Silk tossed his car keys from hand to hand. "Do I stink so strongly?"

"I noticed your cello in the car, sir. A strenuous instrument. Some might say . . . exhausting."

Silk wanted a hot bath. Sex in the four-poster had been strenuous and squeaky and sweaty. Alternatively, he'd like to thump Stevens, but that could wait. He followed Stevens into the house.

After the bath, after some smoked salmon and an omelette and salad with a chilled lager, he went out. "Hullo," he said. "Fancy seeing you here. Anybody tried to buy my car?"

"Very droll, sir."

"Some might say hilarious. Listen: I'm spending the weekend with Freddy Redman and his wife. If Zoë turns up, tell her she's invited. She knows Freddy, he was my best man."

"Alas, her ladyship will be in Stockholm this weekend."

Silk got into his car and made a U-turn and stopped. "Look," he said, and pointed to a small oil stain on the drive. "See what my bloody car's done? Order ten tons of fresh gravel. Pay for it from the petty cash. And give yourself half a bottle of very humdrum claret from the cellar." He accelerated away. *Juvenile*, he thought. *Petty. But he started it.*

3

The War Game was a great success.

Senior staff officers at the base entered into the spirit of the conflict wholeheartedly. There was often heated argument. At first the older men proposed to give the Soviets an ultimatum: withdraw from West Berlin within twelve hours . . . But the scenario that Brigadier Leppard had prepared showed intelligence reports of Soviet armoured divisions heading for the West German border. In twelve hours the war might be lost. All Europe might be overrun. The players took a fast decision: B52 bombers should be ordered to saturate the vast plains of East Germany, Poland, Czechoslovakia and Hungary with nuclear weapons and so wipe out the armies of the Warsaw Pact. "Shoot first," somebody said. "That way, there's nobody to argue with later." The bombers got their orders.

Leppard then revealed that the seizure of Berlin had been the work of a handful of rebellious Soviet generals while Kruschev was on holiday in the Crimea. According to the Kremlin, the generals were all dead, shot by the K.G.B. What's more, the Kremlin had ordered all its armoured divisions back to barracks – but these orders might not have reached some commanders, because already nuclear explosions had badly damaged communications in the East.

Some players dismissed these claims as Soviet deception plans. However, it was decided to recall the B52s, or at least to have them hold off bombing until . . . But Leppard announced that some squadrons had already bombed parts of East Germany. So maybe the Kremlin had been right after all.

Now there was a big argument. Half the players said that if the East had been nuked, massive retaliation was inevitable and the only course was to keep on bombing and paralyse the U.S.S.R. The other half said the B52s must be recalled at once. Leppard intervened with a message from Kruschev: *You created this terrible crisis, you must end it. You caused a breakdown in communications, and so your American bombers are now out of control. Nato fighters must be sent to destroy the bombers before the crisis becomes a catastrophe . . .*

After that it got quite exciting.

Eventually the War Game ran out of time with no definite result, just at the point when the Soviet Pacific Fleet had begun to bombard Los Angeles. The officers went back to their duties. Leppard thanked Skull for taking part.

"I didn't do much, I'm afraid. Photo-reconnaissance missions, mainly."

"But your information was invaluable."

"Was it? I'm not sure your chaps trusted my chaps. Nothing goes as planned, does it? Violence begets violence which begets a nasty surprise all round. Rule one of war."

"Uh-huh. Still, it made the guys think."

"And a very painful experience it was," Skull said. "Thinking hurts. Bombing, on the other hand, is fun. Nuclear bombing is the most enormous fun."

"How about a drink?" Leppard said.

4

Freddy had been right: Sunday lunch at the Redmans' was good. It left Silk feeling relaxed, a little sleepy.

Freddy got out the deckchairs. "I'm sorry Zoë couldn't join us," he said.

"Yes. Bad luck. Sends her love, and all that."

"Very active, I see."

"Non-stop. I'm told she's good on television. I can't keep track of her. She racks up more flying time than I do, probably." He laughed, briefly, just to show it didn't matter.

"But you're still together," Freddy said. "That's the main thing."

"Thanks to you, pal. You got me posted to 409, didn't you?"

"It was an obvious move. No. I'll be honest. It was an obvious move *then*, before Zoë . . . well, you know."

"I know. I've dropped you in the clag, haven't I?"

"It's nothing you've done, old chap. Everyone's got absolute confidence in you. But . . ."

"But I'm an embarrassment. Life at Air Ministry would be easier if I quietly vanished. You don't want to lose a Vulcan, not at that price, but if I wrapped the Citroën around a tree, a sturdy English oak, that would solve a big problem." Silk waved away a wasp. "Remember Black Mac? Armaments Officer on 409 in, when was it, '41? Nasty piece of work. We used to say why doesn't Black Mac do us all a favour and kill himself."

"Yes. It was an accident during bombing-up, wasn't it?"

"Hell of a bang. He never felt a thing. Sandbags in the coffin."

"Nobody wants you to get killed, Silko, but we're in a very delicate situation. Suppose we found that another Vulcan pilot was regularly attending C.N.D. meetings. That's dodgy. That's something to worry about. See what I mean?"

"Zoë's brainwashing me. Is that it?"

"You tell me. Do you discuss nuclear war over the breakfast table?"

"She does. I stonewall." The wasp was back. "This little bastard's in love with me. Shoo! Go and sting Freddy." He flapped his handkerchief. "She's very well-informed."

"Westminster leaks secrets like a rusty bucket."

"I'll tell you what. If it's a matter of national survival, I'll kill Zoë for you."

"Not a funny joke, Silko."

"Who's joking? If it's a matter of national survival, you expect me to kill myself. When the battle begins, we just might hit our target. And then? No turning back. We shan't see England again. Nothing to see. All the Vulcans will go down, one way or another. And Zoë didn't tell me that. I worked it out."

"Disagree. Too pessimistic."

"Relax. It doesn't matter. I'd still make the trip, just for fun, just to see what a basket of sunshine really looks like when it takes out a city. We all owe God a death. Who said that? I don't care. It's true."

Freddy rolled up a newspaper, swung hard and missed. "People have been killed by a sting," he said. "Obviously this little bastard has been briefed to see you in hell."

5

Zoë's office phoned Freddy's office and between them they agreed on lunch at the House of Commons.

They swapped the usual smiles and chit-chat, and ordered food, and she said: "An American pilot spent twenty-four hours as my guest at The Grange and by the following day he'd been shunted back to the States. What's the game, Freddy?"

"I've no idea." He snapped a breadstick. "It's rather flattering, though, isn't it? I mean, if the U.S. Air Force thinks you're so dangerous?"

"You could find out." Just a suggestion. Not a challenge.

"They'll tell me it was a routine posting."

"And you know that's all balls. Are you planning on giving Silko a routine posting soon? Since I'm so dangerous, I mean."

"Ah, there's no escaping you, Zoë. I saw you on television last night. What was all that about Blue Steel's design problems? Made my flesh creep, you did."

She leaned forward, and so did he. "You know I've signed the Act, Freddy," she whispered. "I get my information on a need-to-know basis. If you don't know already, then I can't tell you, can I? That's how the system works."

He straightened up. "And where do you get your information?"

"I make it up, Freddy," she said. "And if you quote me on that I shall deny it." Waiters arrived.

"I seem to be in rather a hopeless position," Freddy said.

"That's what C.N.D. has been telling you for months," she said. With a smile.

BANG SEATS

1

409 trained hard, and Silk saw nothing of The Grange for a week; until Quinlan's crew got sent to bomb Rockall.

This was a lump of granite too small for anything bigger than a seagull to land on, and even a gull might get washed off by a sudden swell. It was about 180 miles west of the Outer Hebrides, which were the nearest landmark. Elsewhere was all Atlantic. Bombing Rockall was a test of navigation. The mock-attack was with a free-fall nuclear bomb, not a Blue Steel, so they would go all the way.

They flew to Land's End and then north-west around Ireland and north to the Hebrides. From top to bottom, the chain of islands diminished in size; it looked something like the skeleton of a dinosaur's tail. From fifty thousand feet, Tucker got excellent radar pictures. The Vulcan's navigation and bombing system was computerized. It led them to Rockall and opened the bomb bay door and, in theory, left an area of boiling sea and a million blind sea birds.

The rest of the exercise was routine. They flew around the north of Scotland and down into the North Sea, losing height to thirty-five thousand. Four Hunter jets intercepted them and Quinlan enjoyed twenty minutes of what was known as fighter affiliation: the Hunters failed to destroy the Vulcan because it could out-turn, out-run and out-climb them all. Then home to Kindrick. Quinlan gave Silk the controls. It was an almost perfect landing. The Vulcan floated down the runway, gradually losing the cushion of air under its vast wings, until the main wheels touched and ran, the nose wheel felt for the ground and found it and ran, and the aeroplane was slowing nicely when the nose-wheel tyre burst. Shredded rubber got flung aside like dung from a muckspreader. Briefly the wheel rim ran on concrete, spraying sparks. The cockpit vibrated so hard that the instrument panel was a blur. Then the wheel strut quit, folded, collapsed, and the Vulcan fell on its nose and skidded, spitting out bits of fuselage. It skidded a long way. When it stopped, the pilots were leaning forward into their straps, looking at the runway. Silk had killed the engines. Everything was very quiet.

"How are the boys in the back room?" Quinlan asked.

"All okay," Dando said.

"Nobody move."

"Too late, skip. I'm in the Mess," Tucker said. "Doing the crossword."

"Beware fire," Quinlan said. He and Silk were watching the fire-indicator lights for the fuselage, the wing tanks, the cabin. There was enough fuel in the tanks to burn a small village.

"We could jettison the canopy," Silk said.

"Possibly. Isn't the jettison gun linked to the seat-ejection gun?"

"Is it? I'm not sure."

"Neither am I. Are you willing to take the risk? A human cannon-ball at eighty feet per second, which might not chuck you high enough for the parachute to do its stuff? No, on the whole, I think we'll wait for the boys in asbestos to get us out. And here they are." Fire trucks arrived. Their sirens were still sinking to a moan as the firemen forced open the canopy.

An hour later, Silk and Hallett drove out to look at the cripple. Normally, a Vulcan on the ground had a balanced, predatory look. This one, tail high, seemed to be sniffing the runway. It looked a little foolish.

The ground crew stood aside to let them examine the damage. The entry/exit door, just ahead of the nose wheel, was crushed and buckled. "Nobody's coming out of there in a hurry," Hallett said.

"And that's your only exit."

"Seen enough? Let's go." They walked away from the ground crew. "It's the only exit for us back-room boys. Pilots have got bang seats. You know all that."

"Quinlan didn't want to blow the canopy," Silk said. "In case it fired the bang seats too. But suppose a fuel tank had ruptured ..."

"Look: we all know the score. In theory, if the bomber has a fit of the vapours, you two pull the trigger and the canopy departs, hotly pursued by the pilots. That's when we're upstairs. On the ground? It's too low. Eject, and chances are, you'll bust something. Hips, spine, skull, God knows what."

"How high is high enough?"

"Jesus, Silko. Didn't you learn anything at O.C.U.?"

"We played a little bridge."

They reached the car. Hallett stretched out on the back seat and looked at the clouds. "Minimum height two hundred feet, minimum speed ninety knots. That's common sense. If the kite's on fire, you don't want to eject and land in the flames."

"That's minimum." Silk started the car. "Maximum?"

"I forget. It's all in the aircrew manual. I think if you eject way up high, the parachute won't open until you reach ten thou. There's a speed limit too. For the rear crew it's 220 knots. We're not supposed to exit by the nose door if the bomber's doing more than 220. Too dangerous, it says. How we're supposed to depart if the kite's tumbling out of the sky like shit off a shovel, Christ alone knows, it's not in the manual. Who cares? It's all bullshit. I don't know anyone who's baled out. Wake up, Silko. Try engaging first gear. That's what makes it go."

"Ten thousand," Silk said thoughtfully.

"And use the clutch."

"We'll go into Russia at fifty or sixty thou. And quite fast." Silk switched off the engine.

"You're wondering what happens when something nasty climbs up and clobbers us," Hallett said.

"Hell, no. I know what happens to you blokes. You pass round the chocolate biscuits and you read a good book until you make a very deep hole in the Ukraine. But Quinlan and me, we're sitting pretty . . ."

"It's minus sixty up there, you daft bugger. There's no oxygen. No pressure. You'll have icicles on your testicles as big as barnacles."

"Barnacles aren't big," Silk said. "I've known some quite small barnacles."

2

Jack Hallett was playing darts when the adjutant told him a policeman wanted to see him. Not a Service policeman: a real cop, from Lincoln. Detective Sergeant Franklyn.

Tucker looked at Hallett's face. The left eyelid was flickering uncontrollably. "I'll come with you," he said. "Cops are bastards," he told the adjutant.

"This one seems decent enough."

They met Franklyn in an empty office. He was too tall for his weight, and his hair was too grey for his age, which was about forty; but his eyes were sharp and his nails were clean. He had questions to ask about a local man called Tommy Davis. "Your bookmaker, I believe, Mr Hallett."

"Turf accountant. I used to phone him once a year to put a couple of quid on the Grand National, that's all. I'm not a betting man."

"When did you last see him?"

Hallett screwed up his face. "I might have met him in a pub a year ago . . . No, sorry, that wasn't Davis, it was . . ." He gave up. "I'll have to think."

"If he's missing, you won't find him here," Tucker said brusquely.

"Tommy Davis is in hospital," Franklyn told them. "He suffers from an acute allergy to stinging nettles. At the moment he's in no condition to talk."

"A bookie who got stung," Tucker said. "That makes a change."

"His family are very worried," Franklyn said. "There's serious bruising. Maybe concussion."

"I expect he had a fall," Hallett said. "Chap I knew had an allergy, couldn't stand up to save his life."

Franklyn asked a few more questions, thanked them politely and left.

They went out and walked in the fresh air. "He didn't come all this way just to shake hands," Hallett said. "I bet he's looking for clues in the nettles. I bet he's got a sodding great magnifying glass."

"Which nettles?" Tucker said. "There's nettles everywhere. Lincolnshire's stiff with them. You can't throw a bookie without hitting a patch of nettles."

"Fancy having a stupid bloody allergy. Silly bastard's determined to drop me in the shit." Hallett picked up a pebble and hurled it at a bird. "I hate crows."

"Yon crow's a rook," Tucker growled, "and you're lucky you missed it or you'd have got a belt on the ear."

The adjutant saw them, and called from his office window. "What was all that about?"

"Nothing, Uncle. Just routine," Hallett said. "Mistaken identity."

"They're holding a Policeman's Ball," Tucker said. "Very painful. Asked if we could help."

Old joke. The adjutant didn't laugh. He went back to his desk. If they thought they weren't in trouble, he wasn't about to ask what sort of trouble it wasn't.

3

Silk lugged the cello case to his room and eased it through the door. He was beginning to hate the bloody thing. He should have taken Tess's advice and switched to a clarinet. But that would only solve half the problem. Weeks were going by, sometimes Zoë asked him to play something, and his excuses sounded weak.

He sat in an upright chair and put the cello between his legs. He'd learn a scale, that would be a start. Bowing was easy but pressing the strings hurt his fingertips. The noise was painful too. He tensed all the muscles in his legs, pointing his knees outwards. His groin hurt. Small panic: *Dear Tess, I practised so hard I ruptured myself . . .* He relaxed entirely. The cello sounded worse. It seemed to wheeze. He tried harder, played louder, and luckily someone knocked on his door.

It was Hallett and Tucker, come to tell him about Detective-Sergeant Franklyn's visit. "Davis is in hospital," Tucker said. "Speechless."

"He might recover," Hallett said. "Might wake up wanting our blood. You never know."

"He won't complain to the police," Silk said. "Bookies never do, it's bad for business. Davis has spent half his life dodging cops."

"They might find his accounts," Hallett said.

"Guys like him keep two sets of books. One for the taxman, one for real. Sometimes the real books are in code."

"You know a hell of a lot about it," Tucker said.

"I had a rear gunner used to be a bookie's runner. Got the chop coming back from Bremen. Good type."

"Rear gunners," Hallett said. "I never understood how anyone could volunteer . . ." He shook his head.

"You volunteered for Vulcans," Silk said. "No, forget I said that. Awfully bad form."

Tucker was fooling about with the cello. He plucked hard on the bass string, making it buzz as it boomed. "Hear that? I can play this fat fiddle better than Silko, and I'm piss-poor."

"Hands off," Silk said. He took the cello away, before Tucker broke it.

ASK THE REINDEER

1

That was in late August. September went by easily. Silk felt untroubled and complete in a way that he hadn't known since he'd stooged across America with Barney Knox in the Harvard. There was a boyish pleasure in being one of the gang. Two gangs, in fact: Quinlan's crew, and Tess Monk's friendship. Where Zoë fitted in, he wasn't sure and didn't care. She was away most of the time: C.N.D. conferences, rallies, seminars. Parliament was on its summer break but politics never stopped. Nor did television. "Saw your wife on the box last night," someone at Kindrick would say. "On top form, as usual."

Silk always gave the same reply: "Everyone needs a hobby." Neutral. Untroubled. Brief.

Zoë was fit and busy doing what she liked, and so was he. Whenever he could, he got off the base and drove to the farmhouse. If Tess wasn't there he knew where she hid the key. Sometimes he took the bull-terrier for a walk in the back garden. The dog was old and barrel-chested, and it wheezed as its paws left prints in the grass. At the end of the garden they both rested, and Silk told it jokes. Sometimes it dozed. Once he couldn't wake it and he had to load it in a wheelbarrow and trundle it up the garden. Tess came home as he was rubbing his side. "Pulled a muscle," he said. "Heavy dog."

"Leave him be. He'll come when he's hungry. I have just the stuff for your muscle."

He went inside and upstairs and undressed. She came in, carrying a quart bottle whose faded label said *Dr Sloane's Liniment.*

"That's for rugby players and dead horses," he said.

"I've jazzed it up. I cut it with rubbing alcohol and aftershave and dissolved some red ants in it." She cupped her hand and poured a little. "If this doesn't work, you deserve to die." She rubbed his side. His eyes widened; he stood on one leg and waved her away. "Enough!" he cried. "I'd sooner die. Jesus wept . . . That stuff's banned under the Geneva Convention." He walked in a circle. "Whooo."

She was looking at his loins. "Aphrodisiac, too."

"I'll strangle you first."

"Make a man of you."

"Ain't bust. Don't fix. And go scrub up. Those hands are lethal weapons."

She went out and washed. He climbed into the four-poster. His side was cooling to a pleasant glow. She came in, wearing nothing but elbow-length gloves of scarlet silk. As they began to enjoy the first, slowly accelerating ski-ride of sex, he wondered: *Was Zoë ever like this?* And rapidly lost interest in any answer.

Sometimes she cooked supper for him, usually sausage and mash or egg and chips. Once in a while they drove into Lincoln for a Chinese meal. The risk of their being seen together worried him a little. There was no reason why he shouldn't take his music teacher to dinner after his lesson. There was no lesson, although he carefully carried his cello into the farmhouse and carefully carried it away when he left. That meant he could truthfully say, if anyone asked, that he'd gone for a cello lesson. And he always paid, thinking *She needs the money.* Anyone who takes a bath under a hose in the back garden is hard up.

He never mentioned his work and she never asked. Otherwise, they talked freely. Silence bored her, so she filled it with information.

She said her father had been a racing driver called Fast Eddie. Also that women made the best barbers and she could shave him with a cutthroat razor in thirteen seconds. Also her late husband had three testicles and webbed feet. Also that Al Capone was not dead but hidden by Catholics in Mayfair. And so on, and on, anything to make Silk argue. She said her father was a blind jazz pianist until he got hit with a bottle and his sight returned.

"In time to become a racing driver, I take it."

"I never said he was a racing driver."

"Didn't you? I can't keep up with your phenomenal family."

"You're too slow. Listen faster, Silko. Dogs have better ears than men. Dogs hear earthquakes coming hours before they happen." She rubbed the bull-terrier's belly with her toes. It almost woke, and it drooled on the carpet.

"See? Tidal wave coming," Silk said. "We're all doomed." He thought: *Zoë would have that carpet cleaned instantly. The dog, too.* He smiled.

"What's funny?" she said.

"You are. We are. It is."

Something other than good sex and pinball-machine talk kept Silk coming back to the farmhouse. Tess Monk lived for the moment. She wasn't a prisoner of the past and the future didn't interest her. By contrast, everyone else – all the men on 409 Squadron, all of Zoë's friends and colleagues, Zoë herself – seemed to be trapped on an upward escalator. Silk liked meeting Tess Monk because there were no goals in her life, no targets, no scores. He was getting tired of targets. Especially targets that nobody was allowed to hit. It was about as much fun as coitus interruptus, and Silk had never been a fan of *that*.

*

The Vulcan got repaired. It went through a series of ground tests, and then a flying test, and was declared operational.

Skull briefed the crew for an unusually long-range training exercise. They would stand by for a scramble, fly to R.A.F. Akrotiri in Cyprus, refuel, and make a high-level approach over Turkey and Iran to the Black Sea in order to simulate a Blue Steel attack on Sevastopol, then reverse course and fly home.

"Crimea," Quinlan said.

"Indeed. We fought a war there once, nobody knows why. Nearby is the town of Balaclava, named after the famous British woolly hat. Sevastopol is the home port of the Soviet Black Sea fleet. Various Soviet air bases are in the area – Adler, Saki, Oktyabr'skoyn – so if you miss Sevastopol you're bound to hit something useful."

"We shan't miss."

"Of course not."

"How many cathedrals has it got?" Dando asked.

"Three. St Sophia's is particularly splendid. Today is her saint's day, so the cathedral should be very full. Also the beaches, of course, since it's the school holidays. We expect large carnage, not to mention the nuclear annihilation of many warships. Now, your alternative targets . . ."

They sat in the aircrew caravan until the phone rang. Quinlan cried: "Kick the tyres and light the fires!" and they sprinted to the bomber. Take-off took one minute thirty-eight seconds. Soon there was little for the pilots to see and to do except to follow the navigator's instructions and to switch fuel tanks.

They completed the exercise, taking care to stay out of Russian airspace. A carpet of cloud covered Europe. They lost height over the North Sea and landed at Kindrick in steady rain.

Debriefing was simple and straightforward.

"We missed the cathedral," Dando said. "Hit the monastery, though. Next to the dogs' home. Do we get an extra point?"

"I'll bear it in mind," Skull said.

"There isn't a cathedral in Sevastopol," Silk said. "Nor a monastery."

"Who cares? There isn't a Sevastopol," Quinlan said. He was hungry. "Not much of a Crimea, either. Are we through?" They got up and went out. Silk stayed.

"How is the cello coming along?" Skull asked.

"You're full of shit. Sevastopol has no cathedral." Silk sat slumped in his chair. It had been a long day. "Neither does Tartu. Remember that? Tartu was our Blue Steel target the day we got bounced by the Swedes. You said it had a cathedral. That was all balls. It's got a big university, one of the oldest in Europe. You never mentioned that. Why not? Are you so queer for cathedrals that you've got to invent them?"

"It's a game, Silko. We've been playing it since long before you arrived." Skull was sorting his paperwork. "The chaps identify Russia with cathedrals. You know: onion domes. So I give them cathedrals. Nobody takes it seriously. You've been reading books, haven't you?" Silk nodded. "A great mistake," Skull said. "We always discouraged it at Cambridge."

"Tartu is in Estonia."

"It is."

"Conquered by Russia."

"Occupied, technically."

"And we're going to wipe out Tartu, and half Estonia with it, in the defence of freedom."

Skull dumped his files in a briefcase. "Now you're beginning to sound like Zoë."

"Haven't seen her for weeks. I can look at a map without Zoë's help. One of our targets is Murmansk East. That's seventy miles from the Norwegian border."

"And you want to know how the Norwegians feel about getting doused in radiation clouds when you H-bomb Murmansk East. Beats me. Ask the reindeer. Nothing else lives up there except two hairy trolls, manners none and habits vile."

"It's all a joke to you."

"Far from it. I know—"

"No you don't. You haven't a clue what our job is like. No penguin has the right to tell us what to do."

"I flew on ops, in '43. We bombed Essen. In a Wellington."

"And when you landed you couldn't speak, couldn't walk, they tossed you into a blood wagon and you were in Sick Quarters for a week."

Skull took out a large handkerchief and polished his glasses. "It was a very hazardous raid. The flak . . ."

"Bugger the flak. You wouldn't last ten minutes over Russia." When Skull held his glasses up to the light, Silk said. "You're scared. You're bloody terrified. A fiver says you can't stand the thought of a simulated op, never mind a real one."

Skull breathed deeply and stood tall. 409 was a very small club. If he backed out now, soon everyone would know. It was only a simulator, a giant toy. "I'll do it if you will," he said.

Silk stood. "What you puke, you clean up," he said.

His years in the R.A.F. warned Silk that he had gone too far: flight lieutenants don't make bets with wing commanders, not when it involves using expensive simulators. He went looking for Quinlan, told him what had happened, asked for his help. Quinlan was amused. "Forget the money," he said. "Call it training. Skull's idea. I'll clear it with the C.O. The rest is up to you. What you break, you pay for."

Silk tried to book time on the simulator, and failed. Other crews were ahead of him. He added his name to the list.

3

Next day Silk attended a couple of lectures on Soviet Air Defence, played squash, spent an hour in the Ops Block going over target routes, got bored and drove to The Grange.

"Her ladyship is in the Music Room, sir," Stevens said. He lifted the cello case from the Citroën. "And Mr Davis is in the mortuary." Silk stared. "Mr Davis the bookmaker, sir. It seems he just slipped away."

"Tough luck."

"Mr Hallett might think otherwise."

Silk saw a small scratch on the side of the car, and rubbed it with his sleeve. Did no good. "I was having a not-bad day until I met you," he said. "What's your game, Stevens? Blackmail? Forget it. You make more money than I do."

"I merely sought to put your mind at rest."

"You failed. Stick to polishing the spoons, do me a favour, stay out of my life."

"Ah, life." They went inside. "What is life? The poet Longfellow spoke well, did he not? *Life is real! Life is earnest! And the grave is not the goal . . .*"

"You're pulling my pisser again," Silk said.

"*Dust thou art, to dust returnest, was not spoken of the soul . . .* It must have taken courage, don't you think, to rhyme *earnest* with *returnest*?!

222

"Move your ass, Stevens."

"If pressed, I would rate Auden higher. *The desires of the heart are as crooked as corkscrews*, he wrote. Is that your experience, sir?"

"You're a smooth sod, aren't you?"

"And you are as curly as a corkscrew."

They stopped and looked at each other, Silk stiff with rage, Stevens calm, one foot on a stair, nicely balanced. "If you weren't carrying that Cabrilloni," Silk said, "I'd smash your face in."

"Further evidence, if such were needed, of your appetite for violence, sir."

Stalemate. Silk strode ahead. The Music Room doors were open and someone was at the piano, playing tidy, unhurried jazz. Variations on Duke Ellington tunes, perhaps. Or maybe Hymns Ancient and Modern played backwards. Silk didn't know or care.

Zoë was leaning against the piano. She wore a blue sleeveless dress. He remembered the time when she had got out of that dress faster than he could unbutton his shirt. Long, long ago. Last year, at least. The pianist saw him, stopped playing, stood up. Before the man spoke, Silk knew he was American: the crewcut, the clothes, the loafers with tassels: ads in *The New Yorker* magazine were full of men like him, over thirty under forty, white, fit and not poor.

"Silko!" she said. "What a nice surprise. Meet Ray Glover, covering Europe for the L.A. *Times*. This is Silko Silk, devastating Eastern Europe for . . . I don't know who for. Not me, anyway."

They shook hands. "I lived in L.A. once," Silk said. "With Ginger Rogers. Nice girl."

"Hell of a dancer."

"Yes. We didn't dance."

"Too bad. A missed opportunity."

"Well, it wasn't so straightforward." He thought of describing the red body rash and knew at once it would be a mistake. He glanced at Zoë. What was this suave West Coast johnny doing here? Christ, that blue dress would fall off in a blink. "Looking well, dear," he said.

"You're a musician?" Glover said. "Why don't we play something?" He waved a hand at the cello case.

Silk looked. Bloody Stevens had dumped it in full view and gone. "I'm hopeless," he said. "Just a beginner."

"You can play *some*thing, Silko," Zoë said. "He's had dozens of lessons," she told Glover.

"You'd hate it. I just make . . . you know . . . noise."

"Play anything," Glover said. "Simple nursery rhyme, for instance. Can you play 'Three Blind Mice'?" He sang the tune: *dah-dah-dah, dah-dahdy-dah.* Zoë joined in. "You do that," he said, "and I'll fool around on the piano."

Silk felt hot. Maybe the rash was coming back. "Honestly, I don't know any tunes," he said.

"No tunes?" Zoë said. "What has Tess been teaching you?"

"Technique. We practise technique." *That sounds bad*, Silk thought. He played an imaginary bow on an imaginary cello. "Hours of technique."

"Play a middle C," Glover suggested. "One note. I'll do the rest."

Silk clenched his teeth. He made a feeble gesture at the cello case. "It's . . ." He shook his head. "The thing is . . ."

"One solitary sodding note, Silko." Zoë was enjoying this. "Don't tell me—"

Stevens coughed. They all turned. He was at the door. "The telephone, sir. An urgent call from the aerodrome."

"Damn, damn," Silk said. "What a bloody nuisance."

"Probably a Micky Finn," Zoë said. "I'll explain later," she told

Glover. Stevens picked up the case. "I don't believe there's a cello in there," she said. "I bet it's an enormous tommy-gun." Silk was halfway to the door. "Apologies," he said.

Stevens led the way. When they reached a telephone, it was resting on its cradle. "The aerodrome must have changed its mind," he said. "What a bloody nuisance."

"Horseshit. Nobody called." Silk stuffed his hands in his pockets and rattled his keys and his small change. "Don't expect any thanks. I can handle pushy Yanks without your help."

"He tips very well, sir. Better than you."

"Good. You can start paying for the claret you steal." Silk grabbed his cello case. "Now bring my Citroën around pronto."

He was too slow. By the time he reached the front doors, Stevens had opened them. And the Citroën was already standing in the drive, with its doors open. Silk slid the case onto the back seat, and Stevens closed the door.

"This place is a dump," Silk said. "It's full of politics and ponces like you. I'd like to bomb it flat." He got in, turned the key, accelerated away, foot to the floor, spitting gravel at Stevens. It gave him little pleasure. It had become a routine exit.

ALL ROGUE MALES

1

The canopy of the four poster had split long ago, and they could see the ceiling. They had thrown off the sheets and their bodies were cooling in the soft breeze from the open windows. She pointed up, and they watched a foot-long cobweb come loose and perform a slow-motion wave as it fell. When it got closer they both blew hard. It wandered off and missed the bed. "Takes more than a cobweb to bother us," she said.

She swung her long legs and rolled out of bed. He watched her stroll around the room, picking up items of clothing. "You're as lithe as a leopard," he said. "Although I'm not sure I've ever seen a leopard in the wild."

She found a green sock. It wasn't his, and it had a big hole in the toe. She threw it out of the window.

"How many poor fools are in love with you this week?" he asked. "Not counting me."

"Hullo," she said, and pointed. "Here comes a vicar,"

"Bloody hell." Silk jumped out of bed and grabbed his trousers. "It better not be the station padre. I'll hide up here."

"Don't agitate yourself, Silko. It's me he's after." She pulled on a pair of slacks and a sweater. "I'll get rid of him."

Silk listened to the fading patter of her bare feet on the stairs. Then he heard voices. He went to a mirror and watched himself knot his tie. "Why are you hiding?" he asked quietly. "It's a music lesson. You used the bathroom. Lesson over. Going home. He's only

226

a parson." He buttoned his tunic and went to the bathroom and flushed the lavatory and clumped downstairs.

"Ah! Flight Lieutenant Silk. A pleasure and a privilege, sir." They shook hands, and Silk knew why Tess hadn't got rid of him: tallish, bald with a grey ruff, bright brown eyes, clerical collar above a burgundy shirt, houndstooth jacket, dark trousers freshly pressed, brogues polished to a deep glow. No ordinary vicar. "Simon Gladstone. A distant relative of the great man."

"Good for you," Silk said. "Well, cello lesson's over, I'll be off."

Gladstone raised a hand. "The Church takes a relaxed view about pastoral duties nowadays. My parish is the Press, the world of journalism. I work where I pray. It makes you one of my flock."

"He says he's doing a series on pilots' hobbies," Tess said.

"Nothing more boring." Silk said. "Nobody's interested in that stuff."

"Skilfully presented," Gladstone said, "it's absolutely riveting."

"So you say. Well, time's up. Cheerio." Silk picked up his cello case and walked out. Gladstone followed him.

"I'm disappointed, flight lieutenant. I see I have underestimated the degree to which you value your privacy."

They reached the lane and stopped. It was a mild, still evening. "What the hell is that supposed to mean?" Silk said.

"Oh, I think you know what it means. If you don't want publicity, I can equally guarantee secrecy. It will cost you a thousand pounds. For the church restoration fund, you understand." Gladstone was still being enormously friendly.

"This is turning into a peculiar day," Silk said. Tess had followed them, and was leaning on the gate. "Don't you think it's peculiar?" he asked her. But Tess was looking down the lane. Silk turned and saw Stevens walking towards him. "Now it's gone beyond peculiar," he said. "Now it's the Mad Hatter's Tea Party. This is Stevens, our under-butler," he told Gladstone. "Have you got an under-butler? No, of course not. Lucky you, they're stupendously bossy. Worse than wives. Look: I don't know where you got the idea that I'm going to give you or anyone a thousand pounds. It's quite ridiculous."

"Of course it is. *Two* thousand is my price for not informing your commanding officer that you and this delightful lady have been banging like a loose shutter in a high wind, to the prejudice of your security status and the defence of the realm. Surely that's well worth two thousand. No, listen: tell you what, I'll make it twenty-five hundred."

"You're not a vicar," Silk said.

"That's irrelevant now."

"May I relieve you of that burden, sir?" Stevens asked. He took the cello case and moved away.

"Tell the C.O. what the hell you like," Silk said. "Mrs Monk and I are studying the cello. That's the truth."

"I have photographs," Gladstone said. "Photographs in which you two are indeed playing duets, but none that the Royal College of Music would recognize. Now *that's* the truth."

"Fakes. Anyone can fake a picture."

"These are moving pictures." Gladstone chuckled. "In every sense. Both cinematic and emotive and active. You make a very athletic subject, flight lieutenant. Prime condition. Three thousand pounds." He might have been a gentleman farmer, bargaining over cattle.

"Tell you what: I'll fight you for it." Silk was unbuttoning his tunic. "Here and now. Bare-knuckle stuff. Anything goes – kicking, gouging, knee in the balls, elbow in the teeth, no limits. Last man standing wins." He gave his tunic to Tess.

Gladstone looked amused. "You're a romantic, flight lieutenant. I don't gamble on fisticuffs. I trade in certainties."

Silk rolled up his sleeves. "I lose, you get the Cabrilloni, it's worth a fortune. You lose, I get the photographs. If they exist."

"Ludicrous idea. Your blood is of no value to me."

"I want yours." Silk raised his fists and moved forward. "I'm sick of bullshit, I want a good hard knockdown fight."

Gladstone's hands were in his jacket pockets. "I am not so foolish as to come unarmed," he said.

"This is stupid," Tess said. Just words: no emotion. "Two grown men fighting in the street. Childish."

"Not me, madam," Gladstone said. "I am left with no option but to consult the station commander."

"I'll kill you first." Silk threw a couple of punches, just out of range.

"I wish you'd both die," she said. "Go off and play in the traffic, it's all you're good for."

Silk edged forward. "Let's see the colour of your blood," he snarled. A line as bad as that had to be snarled. He wondered what he would do if he hit Gladstone once, hard, and the man fell down. What then? Pick him up, the way Tucker picked up the bookie? Gladstone looked a hefty, meaty specimen. Silk's arms were beginning to tire. Then: "Christ Almighty!" he cried, and stepped forward, too late.

Stevens held the cello by its neck, swung it like a sledgehammer, and smashed the soundbox against Gladstone's head so hard that the woodwork shattered and the splintered wreckage lay on Gladstone's shoulders. He collapsed to his knees. Blood cascaded from his bald head. Stevens was left holding the neck of the cello, and he clubbed Gladstone twice. The second blow sent him sprawling.

Stevens dropped the club, stooped and eased Gladstone's false teeth from his gaping mouth. "We don't want the poor fellow to come to any harm," he said. He wrapped the dentures in a handkerchief, and tucked them into Gladstone's jacket pocket. "His remark about moving pictures was in very poor taste, I thought."

Silk had never seen such an act of violence, even in the war, when bombing from twenty thousand feet made violence remote. His mouth was dry; he had to swallow before he could say: "Is he dead?"

"Does it matter, sir?" Stevens asked.

"He's still breathing," Tess said. "See the bubbles."

Without the dentures, Gladstone's face looked thin and weak. Blood-tinged bubbles were leaking from his mouth. "You maniac," Silk said. "That cello was priceless. It was a Cabrilloni. Irreplaceable."

"It was rubbish," Tess said. "I got it from a junk shop for thirty shillings."

"You said . . ."

"Yes, well, I say a lot of things. It amuses me."

Silk turned on Stevens. "You didn't know that."

"I know there is no Cabrilloni in Grove's Dictionary of Music. If you will guard the scene, sir, I shall fetch the shooting brake." He walked away.

"I don't know what the hell's going on," Silk told Tess.

"Well, for a start, your under-butler is not who he seems to be," she said. The bull terrier waddled past her and sniffed Gladstone's head, and was not impressed. It waddled away and collapsed on its belly, all its legs splayed. "Those threats about telling your commanding officer. Does he take such a dim view of illicit sex?"

"Yes. No. It's not so much the sex as the blackmail."

Tess was rubbing the dog's belly. "I'm glad I saw it. You could live your whole life, and never see anyone get brained like that. Like a perfect smash in tennis. And with a cello."

Silk used his foot to scrape together fragments of wood. "We should cover him up. What if somebody comes along?"

"Never fear. I'll set the dog on them."

Silk looked at the sleeping dog, and the bleeding body, and the lovely face of an unworried woman, and he gave up. Stevens backed The Grange's shooting brake towards them at high speed. They loaded Gladstone, still unconscious, into the back. Silk kissed Tess. Why not? Everyone knew. He got into the brake. Stevens drove. "Where are we going?" Silk asked. "Better you don't know," Stevens said. "Do you think you would have punched him?"

"Certainly." Silk didn't like the sound of that. Too brash. "Dunno."

"The cinema has a lot of answer for. Just when a scenario demands swift and brutal action, the hero and the villain waste time in cheap dialogue. I lost patience with your confrontation. Blame my low threshold of boredom."

After about five minutes, there was a long groan from the back. Silk turned to look. Gladstone's face was striped red with blood, and some of the ruined cello still hung around his neck. He made a toothless statement, all pain and saliva. "That's not English," Silk said.

"Polish," Stevens said. "Freelance, on a retainer from K.G.B. in the hope that he'll find someone like you they can blackmail for secrets."

"But he wanted money."

"Yes. He got bored, got greedy, got reckless. End of his career. Forget him."

Silk watched the outskirts of Lincoln drift by. "You're M.I.5, then," he said.

"I might be, but then so might Tess Monk. So might you. For all I know, you two were running a sting operation to get the Pole to break cover. Or perhaps I'm K.G.B. and the Pole is M.I.5. Or neither. We're all rogue males, fighting for our territory. Take your pick."

They drove into the grounds of a private hospital. Stevens went inside. The Pole groaned, and vomited onto his legs, and spat. "Watch your language, vicar," Silk said. "You're not in church now." His own arrogance impressed him.

Stevens came out with three men dressed in white. They put the Pole in an ambulance and drove away. Stevens got in the brake and opened the windows. "Men who are knocked out invariably throw up," he said. "Something else the cinema gets wrong."

"Why the dogcollar?"

"Why not? It worked. He certainly had you rattled. K.G.B. doesn't hire agents with fur hats and bad English."

"Gladstone. That was a nice touch."

"Real name Paretek-Sasak." Stevens concentrated on getting past a couple of tractors towing loads of straw bales. "Too cocky, too greedy. If he'd asked nicely for a couple of hundred, you might have paid."

"No can do. Zoë's got the money, not me. You know that."

"So ask her for it. Tell her you're being blackmailed."

"Oh, sure. Tell her Tess and I . . ."

"She knows that. Knew from the start."

Silk stared out of the window as a field went by. They were burning the stubble: raw red flame under thick black smoke. "Bang goes my marriage, then."

"Not necessarily." Stevens was back to his old smoothness. "By no means necessarily."

He dropped Silk at the Citroën. Tess was still standing by the gate. She was watching the bull terrier gnaw on a large bone. "He's too tired to go inside," she said. "Easier to feed him here."

"He's lazy. You spoil him."

"In dog-years he's the equivalent of eighty. Maybe you'll be glad of someone to bring you a bone when you're his age."

Silk looked at the farmhouse. "Shall we go inside?"

"No. Go away, Silko. I've had enough of men for a while. You're just small boys. Everything you can pick up, you want to break."

He thought about that. "Not entirely untrue, I suppose."

"You owe me for your last lesson." He gave her five pounds and she said: "A quid for the cello."

"A quid. For a Cabrilloni. Fair enough." He paid her, and they shook hands. He half-turned away but he was reluctant to go. "Isn't there anything, you know, happy to be said?"

"Nothing." She was wide-eyed and cheerful. "Nothing is best. Otherwise you're bound to misunderstand it."

He drove to Kindrick, trying hard to make sense of events. All he knew for certain was he wouldn't have to heave that bloody cello about any more. That was one big improvement.

THE MOB FOUGHT THE WRECK

1

When Freddy told Silk he was the tenth assistant deputy director on the right as you went into Air Ministry, he was being modest, for tactical reasons. In fact he was deputy head of the department that administered Bomber Command. When his boss retired, everyone expected Freddie would move up.

His boss came back from lunch. Freddy was waiting.

"There's a direct line between C-in-C Bomber Command and C-in-C Strategic Air Command in Omaha," Freddy said.

"I helped negotiate it," his boss said. "As you know."

"It's not working. Nobody answers the phone."

This had never happened before. The British and American commanders were on first-name terms; normally they talked every day, often twice a day. When one of them crossed the Atlantic he was welcomed in the other's headquarters, and into the most secret operations rooms. Now, suddenly, S.A.C. had shut the door.

"It can't be Berlin," Freddy said. "We're built into the integrated attack plan. If Kruschev got shirty about Berlin, Omaha would be on the phone day and night. Where else? The oil states? China?"

"It's something in their own backyard," his boss said.

"The Caribbean? Makes no sense. Kennedy won't invade Cuba, not after the Bay of Pigs nonsense."

"Wasn't exactly Camelot, was it?"

"Perhaps they aim to repeat Operation Ortsac," Freddy said.

"But that wasn't secret, and it didn't shift Castro, did it? I'm slightly baffled."

His boss informed the P.M.'s office. Freddy called his contacts in the Foreign Office and elsewhere. No joy. Something was up. Nobody knew what.

2

Since childhood, Skull had collected a ragbag of nightmares. Sometimes they left him alone for months or years. Then they lurched back into his sleep, as ugly as drunks. They might reappear so often that his sleeping mind recognized a prancing monstrosity and wearily told it to get out of his dream. It always stayed, until its tormenting jolted him awake and left him clenching the tangled bedclothes, searching for comfort and sanity in the thick grey light of pre-dawn.

He thought he knew what his nightmares were about: it was a fear of losing control, and a terror of confined spaces. When he was small, his sisters had shut him in a wardrobe and gone away. Or maybe he had feared such cruelty and invented the wardrobe. The horror was just as real. Since then he always slept with the windows open and the door ajar. Losing control was different. At school, gymnastics had been compulsory. Skull dreaded handstands and cartwheels and somersaults, any action that threw his sense of balance into chaos.

Flying offered both terrors. It locked Skull in a box and without warning it changed direction, often violently. There was also the risk of exploding, burning and crashing. Flying robbed him of all control. He hated it. Throughout his twenty years as an Intelligence Officer he had flown only twice. In 1939 he went to France in a slow, steady Bombay troopcarrier and was painfully sick. In the middle of the war he was a passenger in a Wellington bomber in a raid on Germany. The flak and the evasive tactics were so intense that he was in a state of utter exhaustion even before they turned for home. He was ill for a week and scarred forever.

"Good news," Silk said. His mouth was serious but his eyes were enjoying it. "The simulator's had a cancellation this afternoon."

"Splendid," Skull said. It was only an imitation, it wasn't flying, it was a couple of hours sitting inside an enormous toy. Silk was a turd, a typical pilot. Just because he could defeat gravity at the taxpayer's expense he thought he was God. "Refresh my memory," Skull said. "Exactly what are we going to do?"

"Exactly what? Christ knows. That's the difference between intelligence and operations, Skull. You expect war to behave reasonably, whereas I know it's always a cock-up." Silk waited, but Skull had no comment. "Fourteen hundred hours," Silk said. "Don't be late. Kruschev's missiles are very prompt."

3

The word simulator was deceptive. It didn't so much simulate as duplicate. Getting into the thing was exactly like climbing into a Vulcan's cockpit: the same size, the same controls, the same feel, the same array of buttons and switches and gauges on all sides. Same smell. Same sounds. Same cramped view.

Silk was in his seat, finishing his pre-flight checks, when Skull arrived, dressed as a wing commander. Silk was in lightweight flying kit. "You'll sweat like a pig in that outfit," he said. "The Vulcan's tropical. Too late now."

"I wasn't told."

"You didn't think to ask." He watched Skull take off his tunic and look for somewhere to hang it. "This isn't the Dorchester," Silk said. "Chuck it behind you."

He got on with his job, talking to the rear crew and to the tower. Skull knew enough to plug in his intercom but he understood little: the talk was too fast, too cropped. Then the engines started and it was like sitting in the middle of a ceaseless thunderstorm. The cockpit vibrated: not much, but Skull sensed disaster and his hands squeezed the armrests. The vibration began to hurt his teeth. He discovered that he was clenching his jaws, and he forced himself to relax.

The bomber rolled. It was raining and the wipers were flinging water off the windscreen with a fury that he found manic. He closed his eyes. "Kick the tyres and light the fires," Silk said. Skull opened his eyes. "Good luck charm," Silk told him. He moved the throttles and the thunderstorm was lost in a volcanic blast. Skull thrust himself back against his seat and the nightmare swarmed about him. Everything was out of control. It got worse: the Vulcan tipped backwards until he was watching the cloudbase hurtle towards them. They smashed through it and gradually he came unstuck from his seat. The engines had faded to a soft bellow. His ears popped. The sun came out. Silk gave him a boiled sweet. "How high are we?" Skull asked.

"By the time I tell you we'll be higher still."

Life became less intolerable. The Vulcan levelled out and the engines settled down to a steady roar, no worse than collapsing surf. "Cruise climb," Silk said. Skull knew what that was: burning fuel to lose weight to climb more easily. "What's our target?" he asked. Silk gave him a map.

A long and very jagged red line ended at the city of Sverdlovsk. Skull loathed it. Bolsheviks shot the Tsar's family there in 1918. Soviet missile knocked down Gary Powers' U2 spy plane there in

1960. Skull didn't gave a toss about the Tsar or Powers: they got what they asked for. What appalled him was that Sverdlovsk was forty miles east of the Ural Mountains. It was in Siberia. It was more than halfway to China. This raid stretched in front of him like a jail sentence. "Where the devil do we land?" he asked.

"First things first. Make yourself useful and lower the blinds."

Skull did. Now even the letterbox view of blue sky was lost. The cabin seemed much smaller. His demons were going to love this.

Nothing terrible happened for a while. Sometimes a small red or green light blinked. Silk clicked a switch and the light vanished. Needles flickered in softly lit gauges. Once, Silk turned a dial, held it briefly, then turned it back to its original position. "What was that in aid of?" Skull asked.

"B.B.C. News headlines."

Skull gave up. He looked at the map. A horribly long way to Moscow, and Sverdlovsk was another seven hundred miles beyond that. Jesus wept.

"Second pilot's job is to switch over the fuel tanks," Silk said, "but I don't suppose you can use a sliderule."

"That's right, I can't."

"Then I'll have to do it. I'm rotten at sums. What's nine eights? Never mind. If I get it wrong there's probably somewhere we can land, some Polish bog—"

Tucker's voice broke in. "The weapon's hot, skip."

Skull's fingers made a small tear in the map.

"How hot is hot?" Silk asked.

"Three degrees above safe."

"Three degrees." Silk scratched his nose. "Three degrees, you say."

Skull cleared his throat. "Blue Steel?"

"Yup. Blue Steel it is. The boys in the backroom keep a close eye on its H.T.P. That's High—"

"I know what H.T.P. is." Skull felt a small surge of optimism. Blue Steel's Stentor engine ran on kerosene and High Test Peroxide. H.T.P. supplied the oxygen to make kerosene burn in thin air; but H.T.P. was more dangerous than T.N.T. It demanded airtight tanks and immaculate handling. A speck of dust might trigger a ferocious reaction. Then the H.T.P. would leak a torrent of exploding oxygen that would ignite everything it touched. Crews were ordered to abandon a flight if the temperature of their Blue Steel's H.T.P. rose by five degrees. Skull relaxed. This might be a very short flight.

"Could be a freak reading," Silk told the rear crew. "Duff equipment, maybe. Any change?"

Pause. Then: "Two point seven, skip."

"Gremlins. They get in everywhere."

"Two point six. Two point four."

Skull despaired. Even faulty equipment was against him. "What difference does it make?" he said. "It's too late to turn back now. If the Blue Steel overheats, we'll go to hell with it."

"Dear me," Silk said. "That doesn't sound like your normal cheery briefing, Skull."

A different voice said: "Morale here in the broom cupboard is very bad. If the second pilot can't look on the bright side, one of us will shoot him." It was Dando.

Skull had a great desire to hit someone. He was strapped into his seat, yet he experienced a clumsy, helpless sensation: he was growing bigger, his limbs were expanding, lengthening, his fingers felt like sausages, his feet were remote. If he shut his eyes, his body might return to normal. It was all very exhausting. He fell asleep.

A shout woke him.

"Hey! What was *that*?" Silk was leaning forward. "At our nine o'clock. More or less."

"Gdansk is that way," Tucker said. "Or maybe Kaliningrad. They're both air defence centres."

"What was what?" Skull asked.

"A splash of sun," Silk said. "It leaked through the anti-flash screen."

Skull looked at the map. The red line crossed Denmark, entered the Baltic and turned south near the German–Polish border. Gdansk was fifty miles away; Kaliningrad twice that. "Our Thor missiles should have taken them out long ago," he said. Silk was working on his sliderule. "Maybe it was a Canberra strike. Or an F-100," Skull said.

"Maybe it was an F-100 getting the chop at forty thousand feet. If it was, Soviet fighters are up in force. Put this on." Silk gave him a black eye-patch.

The elastic string cut into Skull's face. He felt foolish, but Silk was wearing an eye-patch, so he said nothing.

The Vulcan zigged and zagged across Poland, into Czechoslovakia, and turned east towards the Ukraine. Its route was designed to avoid Warsaw Pact military centres, anywhere that was heavily defended. But nuclear bursts flared unexpectedly. The rear crew suggested strikes had been made on probable targets: Grudziadz, Bydgoszez, Poznan, Wroclaw, Czestochowa, Olomouc, Zilina, Miscolk . . . Sometimes blast rippled over great distance and height to rock the bomber. Often Dando told Silk he was jamming the V.H.F. trans-missions of Soviet fighter controllers. Otherwise pilot and rear crew had little to say until they crossed the border into the Ukraine and Hallett warned Silk to steer zero-two-zero in order to avoid the known hotspot of Lvov. That was when the Vulcan refused to change direction, the compass broke, and Hallett's link to the navigational computer in the Blue Steel failed.

Nobody got excited. Each man made his report. Silk said he would steer by varying the thrust and he throttled back the port outer engine. Hallett tackled the compass problem. Tucker tried to revive the Blue Steel computer. Dando found intense V.H.F. activity ahead.

"That's the bitch about high-level penetration," Silk told Skull. "Soviet radars can see you coming, two hundred miles away."

"I know."

"I know you know. I like sharing the misery, that's all."

Skull picked up the map and put it down at once. After Lvov, there were still hundreds and hundreds of miles to fly before they got anywhere near Sverdlovsk. Below was Russia, the Great Motherland, Hitler's Folly. Skull was an Intelligence Officer. He claimed to deal in facts. Was misery a fact? It must be a factor. How could men fly a thousand miles over Russia, hoping to dodge fighters twice as fast and nuclear-tipped anti-aircraft missiles they couldn't outclimb, so as to kill a million strangers in some remote city, knowing all the time that the home they had left was history, was ashes, was dead in a flash? How can men do that without suffering paralytic misery? Skull opened his mouth to ask, but Tucker spoke first. MiG-21s were climbing, positioning for a stern attack. He had them on his radar. Dando's jamming hadn't worked.

For twenty minutes, Silk jinked the Vulcan from side to side. Working the throttles was a crude alternative to using the flying controls but it was all he had. Tucker second-guessed a MiG's attack, Silk dodged its fire. The fighter had to stay level and steady in order to hold its target. The swerving Vulcan flung back a stormy wake of air. Such flying was heavy on fuel. One by one, the MiGs gave up.

"Next time they'll collide," Silk said. "With me, I mean."

Skull said nothing. Constant swaying and wallowing had made him sick. He had filled his handkerchief and it lay on his lap, soaking into his trousers.

"We're off track," Hallett said.

"And somebody down there loves us," Dando said. "We're radar-illuminated. Maximum jamming now."

The jammers were electronic but they generated a range of sounds. Some whined, some crackled, some bleeped. The crew welcomed them as signs that the gear was working. Skull's head throbbed from his vomiting. One particular jammer made a furious, metallic tearing noise, like a train coming off the tracks. Skull's jaws ached. The racket climbed to a screech, almost a whistle, sank and climbed again: a fire siren gone berserk. Simultaneously a mob with hammers was smashing glass, enormous sheets of glass that boomed as they shattered. The mob fought the train wreck. Skull took off his headphones. "No!" he cried. "Madhouse!" He ripped off his eyepatch.

"Put that bloody thing on," Silk ordered.

"Go to hell." Skull tried to undo his seat belt and failed. His hands were shaking too much.

"Sit down. Shut up. You're a crew member. Act like one."

"You maniacs can . . ." Now his head was shaking. At last he got the belt undone, tried to stand, remembered his vomit-filled handkerchief and grabbed it just as Silk's fist hit him in the mouth and knocked him sideways. The loaded handkerchief fell behind his seat. There was a modest bang and all the lights went out.

"Trust you to hit the fusebox," Silk said. "And you owe me a fiver."

242

4

It was only a split lip, but rank has it privileges and the Senior M.O. himself examined Skull, while a medic discreetly wiped away the evidence of vomit. No stitches were necessary. A strip of plaster, two aspirin. Avoid alcohol. Get some rest.

Silk walked him to his quarters. "You forgot to do the debriefing," he said.

"Who cares? It was just a damnfool trip in a simulator."

"Of course it was. Still, you got quite excited, didn't you? Pity it had to be cut short. Tell you what: let's do it again tomorrow, double or quits, how about that?"

Skull tried to kick him, but Silk dodged. Skull was looking ill: white about the chops, strained about the eyes. "You were always a rotter, Silk," he said, "but now you're an utter shit."

Silk gave a grunt of surprise. He had never heard Skull use that word before. "Right first time," he said. "It's a shitty job, so it takes an utter shit to do it."

"You flatter yourself. Scrambling a Vulcan on Q.R.A. isn't a job, it's a charade, it never makes a damn bit of difference, because nobody's going to drop the bloody bomb. You're getting paid to be frightened, like the Soviets, it's a balance of terror. Where's the war in the Cold War? Doesn't exist. *Can't* exist. So – no glory, no victory. Just a perpetual output of fear. What a monumental waste." The plaster had fallen off, and Skull's lip was bleeding.

5

The late afternoon had turned grey and cold. R.A.F. Kindrick looked dull and functional. Well, R.A.F. airfields were not made to look thrilling. Silk decided to spend the night at The Grange. No point in being married to a five-star heiress unless you drank her claret from time to time. He changed into his best uniform, and as he walked to the Citroën he met the rear crew. All three.

"Hullo!" Hallett said. "No cello?"

"I met a Polish vicar who tried to blackmail me for gross moral turpitude," Silk said, "and a passing spy brained him with the cello." He kept walking.

"So don't tell us," Dando called. "See if we care."

He drove through the Lincolnshire countryside, now starting to lose its leaves. Skull's profanity stuck in his mind. He'd have given long odds against that ever happening. Maybe the poor sod was losing his grip.

Stevens came out to meet him.

"Don't say anything," Silk said. "The queen is in the parlour, eating bread and honey."

"Her ladyship is in the gazebo, sir, for which there is no rhyme in the English lexicon."

"I bet there's no rhyme for 'lexicon', either."

"Try 'Mexican', sir."

Silk headed off, then stopped and came back. "Talking of Mexicans," he said, "what happened to the Pole?"

"He's in limbo, sir."

"I see. Dead or alive?"

"Does it matter?"

Silk set off again, in no hurry, wondering what he would do if Zoë punched him in the eye or, worse yet, started crying. It was a woman's secret weapon, sobbing and weeping. He had no defence against sobbing and weeping. A double D.F.C. was no bloody use against sobbing and weeping. He ran up the gazebo steps in order to get it over with quickly, and she smiled, gave him a hug and a good kiss. "I should have knocked," he said. "You might have been up to no good with the American piano-player."

"Not impossible. He's great fun." She had been writing. She scooped up the pages.

"Sounds ominous. Don't tell me—"

"Tell you? I shan't tell you, Silko." She slid the pages into a brief-case. "If I decide to have a fling with someone, I certainly shan't consult you first." He felt as if a large stone was settling in his gut. "You didn't ask my permission," she said. "That would have been a very peculiar conversation, wouldn't it?"

"I didn't know it was going to happen. Anyway, you told me to have a hobby." He looked at the bed. After a long, hard day defending the realm, surely he deserved a reward.

"Listen here," Zoë said. "You must understand that you matter more to me than anyone. I hate mountains. They frighten me. I would climb any mountain to save you. You alone. We had some lovely years when we were in love, and young, and lust conquered all. We're not in love now. I'm very fond of you, but given the choice between a day in politics and a day with Silko, I'll take politics every time. Now beat it. I've got a load of letters to answer and a train to catch." She kissed him, very thoroughly, and pointed to the door.

After that, he didn't want her claret. He drove to Tess Monk's farmhouse instead.

A man was washing the windows, a thin chap with not much hair. He didn't look around when the car stopped. Silk sat and watched; there was nowhere else he wanted to go.

After a while Tess came out. He wound his window down. "Please buzz off," she said.

"He's making a rotten job of it," Silk said. "I can see the streaks from here."

"I'll set the dog on you."

"Dog's asleep. I can hear him drooling. Or have you left a tap running? Who is this bloke, anyway? He's obviously not a window cleaner."

She ran a finger along the line of his jaw. "Clean-cut. It's the only clean thing about you, Silko. Everything else is corkscrew. Well, this is straightforward. He's my husband. Just out of prison."

"You said he was dead."

"Did I? Must have got that wrong."

"Drunk, drove too fast, crashed, you told me."

"You looked as if you wanted to know."

"Prison . . . What was he in for?"

"Fornication on Sundays."

"That's not a crime."

"Then don't tell him. You'll break his heart." She reached in and turned the ignition key, and tweaked his ear and walked away.

Now Silk had nowhere to go, nothing to do, nobody to do it with. He drove back to the airfield, too fast. For once, speed did not dissolve anger. His life seemed to be one battle after another: with Tucker over the bookie, with Stevens over who's boss, with Freddy over . . . he wasn't sure what. And in one quick day he'd lost his girl-friend or mistress or something, and then his bloody wife wouldn't even let him fight about it. What was wrong with Zoë?

He went into the mess. Hardly anyone there, and the only face he knew was the adjutant, who took his pipe out of his mouth and said. "You look like a pig in an abattoir, old boy." He put his pipe back and got on with the crossword. Silk walked out and got in his car and drove back to The Grange. Stevens opened the front door.

"Wing Commander Skelton telephoned," he said. "You should watch the B.B.C. news."

They both watched it. President Kennedy told the American people that Soviet SS-4 Medium Range Ballistic Missiles had been secretly installed in Cuba, that Washington D.C. and other cities were within their range, and that a naval blockade of the island would begin in 48 hours.

"What the hell's going on?" Silk asked.

"I couldn't possibly say, sir," Stevens said.

A HICCUP AWAY FROM WAR

1

The Cuban Missile Crisis was a bombshell with a very long fuse behind it.

The gangster, racketeer and dictator Fulgencio Batista fled Cuba in December 1958. Castro and Ché Guevara led their revolutionary forces into Havana and formed a new government. Washington quickly recognized it, and 1959 passed off fairly smoothly. Castro reduced rents, took over the U.S.-owned Telephone Company, redistributed land. He wasn't a Communist, he was a reformist. He made some angry anti-American speeches, but the U.S. still bought a lot of Cuban sugar. President Eisenhower said he was "perplexed" by Castro's statements and he reaffirmed the commitment of the U.S. to "the policy of non-intervention in the domestic affairs of other countries, including Cuba." Officially, Washington had no big difficulties with Castro – except on one point: it blocked arms sales to Cuba.

Well, the island must be able to defend itself. Castro said he would buy wherever he could. That had to mean the U.S.S.R. or its allies. Now the fuse began to burn.

For all Eisenhower's public declarations, his administration had already begun to think that Castro must go. On the island, hundreds of Batista's men had been tried for atrocities, and many were executed. Large numbers of *Batistianos* fled to Miami, where they plotted to reverse the revolution. In March 1960 Eisenhower ordered the C.I.A. to train Cuban exiles "against a possible future day when they might return to their homeland": the first hint of military force. Eventually, four training bases were set up in Florida, plus others in Puerto Rico, Panama, Nicaragua and Guatemala. The C.I.A. was working on plans to assassinate Castro. And Washington was thinking blockade.

Cuba had to import oil. Soon, under pressure from Washington, the big U.S. oil companies cut their supplies. Inevitably, Castro turned to Russia. Texaco, Esso and Shell operated refineries in Cuba but they refused to process Russian oil. In June 1960 Castro nationalised them. A week later, Eisenhower cancelled the Cuban sugar quota. Russia stepped in, agreed to buy Cuban sugar for five years and to provide $100 million in credit. By the summer, arms were reaching Cuba from the Eastern Bloc and Castro was nationalizing U.S.-owned businesses – 26 in August, all American banks in September, a further 166 U.S. firms in October. Washington banned almost all trade with Cuba. That left Castro with no friend but Russia. Early in 1961 he declared himself (and Cuba) for socialism.

As if to test Castro's wisdom, the new President, Jack Kennedy, approved an invasion of Cuba. In April 1961, the C.I.A. sent 1,400 armed exiles to land on the Bay of Pigs, provoke a rising and overthrow Castro. The Cuban army was waiting. The raid was worse than a disaster; it was a farce. Perhaps it persuaded Kruschev that Kennedy lacked backbone.

In 1962, Cuba was always in the headlines. Kennedy's presidential campaign had claimed that the U.S. suffered from a missile gap. There was no such gap, but Kennedy had created the scare and now he was stuck with it. There were more and more reports of a Soviet military build-up in Cuba, and they were true.

America had installed nuclear missiles in Turkey, aimed at the Soviet Union. Kruschev was furious. He wanted leverage to get the missiles out. The summer and autumn of 1962 saw a stream of

Russian ships to Cuba. Just to transport the troops took 85 merchant ships. Missiles came downriver by barge to the Black Sea and were loaded onto freighters. On reaching Cuba, they were unloaded by night; but missiles were conspicuous, and they were no secret to many Cubans. One mystery is why American intelligence took so long to discover the truth. Another mystery is how Kruschev hoped to construct missile launch sites in Cuba without being detected. Marshal Biryuzov, of the Strategic Rocket Forces, told the Soviet Presidium that the missiles could be installed secretly. To U.S. reconnaissance aircraft, he said, "they would look like palm trees". Kruschev agreed.

The build-up was big and getting bigger: 42,000 Russians on Cuba by mid-October was a lot of Russians. Already, Kennedy had issued warnings, had put 150,000 reserve troops on active duty, had sent more aircraft to spy on Cuba. At last, on 14 October he was shown aerial photographs of construction work that looked like launch sites for medium-range ballistic missiles. More missiles were on ships crossing the Atlantic.

The Joint Chiefs of Staff urged Kennedy to order an immediate air strike on all military targets in Cuba. General Curtis LeMay, the Air Force Chief of Staff, saw the Cuban crisis as an excuse to launch a full pre-emptive nuclear assault on Russia. He believed that the S.A.C. could obliterate the Soviet Union. How much of the U.S. would be obliterated by the Soviet Union in return, General LeMay did not say.

The fuse had been hissing and sputtering and crackling for a long time. Now, in October 1962, there wasn't much of it left and it was burning fast. World War Three was a serious likelihood. To some, an attractive possibility. Wait any longer and the chance might be missed.

Everyone in 409 Squadron assumed that Skull knew the inside story about Cuba. He got tired of telling them to listen to the B.B.C., and he phoned Brigadier Leppard and suggested lunch. "On me," he added.

"Bomber Command is so desperate for news? This Cuba thing's nothing, just a misunderstanding, that's what I've been told to say, although I can't see what's to misunderstand about sixty-three feet of ballistic missile aimed at the White House. But sure, I'll let you pay. Tell the truth, I'll be glad to get off the base. Everyone's hepped up, afraid they might miss the war."

"There won't be a war, Karl. There might be a nuclear spasm."

"Good, I'll tell them that. They'll ask me to spell it."

They got the last booth in the Bum Steer. "What happened to you?" Leppard asked. "Fall out of the wrong bed?"

"I was punched by a pilot, in a simulator. It was a point of honour." *No it wasn't, it was a point of panic.* "Trivial incident." *Unforgettable terror.*

They ordered drinks and steaks. "Okay, here's all I know," Leppard said. "Cuba's been a rumbling volcano all summer. Late August we knew they had Russian surface-to-air missiles, purely defensive, no big deal. Now it turns out they've also got a bunch of medium-range ballistic firecrackers, and they're making launch sites for even bigger bangs, plus they've got MiG-21s and Ilyushin-28s, and heavy helicopters, and coastal defence stuff like gunboats with their own missiles. I may have missed five or ten thousand Russian infantry, they're hard to see in the sugarcanes."

"If I were Castro," Skull said, "I'm sure I'd feel a lot more secure."

"And if you were Kennedy, you'd feel a hell of a lot *less* secure. Suddenly a dozen U.S. cities are within range of nuclear attack."

"So is Moscow, and Berlin, and London, and Lincoln. We've learned to live with it."

"Not the point. It's the *secrecy* that's got everyone spitting blood. Sneaky Commies trying to smuggle their missiles inside our defence. That makes Americans rise in wrath."

"Wrath." Skull took his glasses off and squinted unhappily at the blur of the diningroom. "Russians rose in wrath when Gary Powers' U.2. got shot down a thousand miles inside their borders." Drinks arrived. "Sneaky Yanks," Skull said. Leppard was more interested in his Scotch. "Wrath is bad for the brain," Skull said. He put his glasses on. "Cuba isn't going to launch any missiles. Castro's not going to give the Pentagon an excuse to invade."

"Then why all this nuclear muscle?"

"Why Operation Ortsac? Why the Bay of Pigs? Isn't it just the Cold War to a Latin rhythm?"

"Not a hope," Leppard said. "Either Castro gets his hired guns out of town or all hell breaks loose."

"Goodness," Skull said. "You sound just like John Wayne."

"Well, Kruschev acts like Genghiz Khan. What do you expect? Lassie the Wonder Dog? America doesn't respond kindly to threats."

Skull could hear an undertone of anger. "I wasn't thinking of kindness," he said. "More of intelligent selfishness." He could see their waiter approaching.

"I've got kin living in Washington. Cousins. What does this make them? Hostages?"

It wasn't what Skull had hoped to hear. "The Soviets take a bit of knowing," he said. "For instance, Genghiz Khan wasn't Russian, on the contrary his Mongol hordes *conquered* Russia, they exploited it as a colony for three or four hundred years. One reason why Russia has always been rather sensitive about foreign pressures." Leppard was eating his steak. "And so on and so forth," Skull said. After that, they talked of other things until the meal was over and they were walking to their cars.

"I sometimes wonder how many of our crews would actually drop their bombs," Skull said. He looked at the sky: a perfect autumn blue, made more perfect by a faint sketch of mackerel cloud.

"What's to stop them?"

"Perhaps . . ." Skull hesitated, and took the risk. "A sense of right and wrong."

"Isn't that the same as a sense of duty?"

"Duty to whom? We tell our crews that the West will never make a first strike. So, when they're scrambled for a *second* strike, they know they can't make a difference. The catastrophe has happened. Will they really drop a hydrogen bomb? What will it achieve? Most aircrew are a decent lot. They'll bomb for a better tomorrow, but what if there is no tomorrow?"

"Oh, no doubt about it, Skull," Leppard said confidently. "There *is* no tomorrow. Never has been. Seize the day! And if it doesn't deserve to survive, then cut its foolish throat. Thanks for lunch."

3

The news, never good, got worse.

Kennedy and Kruschev swapped angry messages. The secretary-general of the United Nations tried to cool them down, asking Kruschev to stop all Soviet shipping to Cuba and asking Kennedy not to force a showdown. Both agreed; neither trusted the other. The codeword for American military alertness was DefCon, for Defense Condition. Kennedy upped it from DefCon 5 to DefCon 3, a big jump and a signal to Moscow as much as to the Pentagon. Half the

Russian ships had stopped or changed course in mid-Atlantic; but construction work on the Cuban missile launch sites went ahead. If the work was completed, Kennedy might find he had a much weaker hand in this game of maniacs' poker. He could order an air strike. Cuba was nearby. Kruschev would respond. Where? Maybe England. Why? England wasn't far off, either. Nobody said that thermo-nuclear ping-pong had to make sense.

Skull sat in his office, watching the afternoon sun inch its way across the carpet. That could be the last sunlight half the world would ever see. He picked up the phone and called Bomber Command H.Q. He had once gone trout fishing in the Aberdeenshire hills with an air commodore called Jenkins, now in Intelligence.

"Nobody is in a flap," Jenkins said. "But here's a funny thing. We monitor S.A.C. transmissions, of course, and they've stopped using code for a lot of signals."

"Plain English? I've never known S.A.C. to do that."

"And we know from cockpit transmissions that some S.A.C. bombers are pushing their luck, flying beyond the points where they normally turn back, getting so close to Soviet airspace that Russian radar must think they look like trouble coming."

"It's provocative," Skull said.

"So is firing a ballistic missile over the Pacific. Last night S.A.C. launched an Atlas I.C.B.M. in California. It came down five thousand miles away, in the Marshall Islands, as planned. Russian radar must have picked up the launch. They didn't know it was an unarmed test missile, not until S.A.C. said so. In English."

"And the Soviets believed them."

"Well, they haven't retaliated yet, so . . ."

"Hasn't the S.A.C. got anyone who speaks Russian?"

"Steady on, Skull. Now you're being sensible."

4

If anything is worse than the inexcusable, indelible knowledge of having committed murder, it is the bone-deep suspicion of probably having killed someone, not a stranger, without reason, and being unable to prove that it was a crime or a mistake or perhaps even that it hadn't even happened. Many times before, Skull had suffered under the crushing weight of his own guilt. It was a dream, he knew that. He only murdered in his dreams, because that was where he was already trapped, imprisoned before he was captured. Now he broke out and lay sweating. His heart was playing rapid hopscotch.

He couldn't sleep. He got up, washed his face, put on corduroy trousers and a windcheater, found his glasses, went out and did something he would never have done a week ago: he knocked on Silk's door.

"You're not Lana Turner," Silk said. His voice was flat and tired from sleep. "I ordered Lana Turner. Or maybe Hedy Lamarr. One of the two."

"Awfully sorry."

"Forget it. I had to get up anyway, some bastard was hammering on the door." He yawned. "What's wrong?"

"Well, it's . . . Look, I know we've had our differences recently, but . . . "

"Come in. Haven't seen my wife, have you? Neither have I. Girl friend's gone missing too." He sat on the bed. "Women are an odd lot, Skull. You can't pin them down."

"I keep thinking about Cuba."

"Oh, Christ. Bloody Cuba. Not here." Silk pulled on his uniform over his pyjamas. "Let's go for a walk."

"It's the principle of deterrence I worry about." They went out. "Just when we need it most, it's falling apart."

"That happened to me, once," Silk said. "Lost my marbles. In California."

"Deterrence demands a form of balance. If one side persists in provocative behaviour, that balance is prejudiced and rational analysis goes out of the window." Silk wasn't listening. If Skull didn't care how he lost his marbles in California, then he didn't care what Skull chucked out of the window.

They walked to the camp cinema and back. Skull talked, urgently and fluently. Silk grunted from time to time. They reached his bedroom door.

"You see the dilemma," Skull said. "Fear breeds fear."

"Go to bed, Skull," Silk said. "Go to hell, go to Cuba. Better still, go to Pulvertaft. He likes a good dilemma at four in the morning." He went in and locked the door.

5

There was little flying at Kindrick: just a few air tests to doublecheck the servicing. The Vulcans that had been elsewhere were returned to the base. Aircrew and groundcrew were recalled from leave; major overhauls were postponed. Extra attention was paid to Q.R.A.s, but then Q.R.A.s always got high priority. One afternoon the Vulcan crews sat in their cockpits for an hour and then were released. And that was as far as the impact of the Cuban Crisis went. Bomber Command was on a very discreet alert. Extra police patrolled the airfields, but the bases were not locked up tight: personnel came and went. The newspapers got very excited. Kindrick remained calm.

Skull decided not to take his anxieties to Pulvertaft. The station commander was a group captain looking forward to making air commodore; he didn't question R.A.F. policy. So Skull sat in his office and wondered how two billion people had allowed themselves to drift into a situation where two men, seven thousand miles apart, might blow the planet to bits.

He was drinking coffee when he heard that America had gone to DefCon 2. Just a hiccup away from war.

Doing anything was better than nothing. He called Freddy Redman's office. Mr Redman wasn't there, he was making a tour of bomber airfields, in fact . . . There was rustling of paper. "He should be at Kindrick about now."

Skull went to the window. Freddy was getting out of a car, shaking hands with Pulvertaft. Skull went downstairs, Freddy saw him from a distance, waved, beckoned. When they met, Freddy shook hands and said: "Lunch, sandwiches, you, me and Silko, out there, by the Vulcans. It's a treat I've promised myself for weeks. Can you lay it on? Splendid fellow."

An hour later they were walking along the taxiway. Silk, as junior officer, carried the sandwiches and a flask of coffee. For once, the wind had dropped and the airfield was silent. "Glorious," Freddy said. "Pure fresh air. Beats London, I can tell you."

"Last time I did this I met a Yank on his way to shoot himself," Silk said. "Talked him out of it. Damn glib, I was."

"Captain Black?" Skull asked.

"That's him. Got posted home."

"Where, alas, he did in fact shoot himself. Karl Leppard told me. No known reason."

"He wasn't too thrilled about bombing East Berlin," Silk said. "He had qualms. I had qualms once. Big as barnacles."

"Tell me this, Freddy," Skull said. "How can we have a strategy of deterrence *and* a policy of secrecy at the same time?"

"Nobody knows," Silk said. "All the boffins are baffled, take my word. Now can we talk about sex?"

"You're proposing we drop the secrecy?" Freddy said to Skull. "Let the Soviets know exactly what we've got? The Cabinet would have a fit. The Opposition would have an orgasm. Nato would have kittens."

"And civilization might survive. Just consider—"

"He'll bore you to death, Freddy," Silk said. "I had it from him, both barrels, at four in the morning. God, I'm hungry."

"You can't have deterrence *and* secrecy," Skull argued. "If the Soviets won't attack us because they're afraid of our weaponry, then the more they know, the greater their fear. A secret deterrent is a contradiction in terms!"

"You'd show them everything," Freddy said.

"I'd have a Soviet general living on every bomber base. No secrets, no misunderstandings, no doubt in anybody's mind about what would happen if."

"Interesting."

"Secrecy isn't a weapon. We don't want the enemy to guess what we've got. He might guess wrongly."

"Life is a lottery," Silk said. "Take my wife . . ."

"Let's be specific," Freddy said. "The Q.R.A. system: you'd tell the Soviets how that works?"

"They know already," Skull said. "How many bomber fields have main roads running past them? Anyone with a stop watch can time the scrambles. We *want* them to know."

They had reached a line of Vulcans. "Magnificent beasts," Freddy murmured. "You chaps don't know how lucky you are . . ." He walked to the nose of the first bomber and enjoyed the great sweep of the wings. "Incomparable," he said. "Destined for the scrap-heap all too soon, I'm afraid."

Silk was chewing the inside of his lower lip. His teeth nipped the skin. "Scrap-heap?" He tasted warm and salty blood. "Don't be bloody silly, Freddy."

"No joke, old chap. Vulcans were made to fly so high and so fast that they were untouchable. No longer. Soon you'll switch to low-level attacks. Probably high-low-high: high approach, go low to slide under the radar and release Blue Steel, then high, lickety-split."

"Under the radar," Silk said. "Christ Almighty. They'll be chucking vodka bottles at us."

"Gary Powers was ten thousand feet higher than you when they clobbered his U.2. And that was two years ago."

"*Exactly*," Skull said. There was a note of triumph in his voice. "The Soviets *demonstrated* their deterrent power, so we took them seriously. That's how deterrence stops wars!" He tried to kick a dandelion and missed.

"Nobody's going to scrap the Vulcan," Silk said. "It's a winner. How can you scrap a winner?"

"I'll tell you how," Freddy said. "The oxy-acetylene cutters burn through the wing roots and the wings hit the concrete with a bang that breaks your heart. Now let's eat before you pair destroy my appetite entirely."

"If you scrap the Vulcan we bloody well *deserve* to lose."

They sat on the grass and worked their way through the sandwiches. Nobody spoke.

Freddy lay on his back and watched a highflying buzzard make large, slow circles. Silk chewed a toothpick to tatters. Skull found himself thinking about his pension, felt slightly ashamed for not worrying about Cuba, then felt annoyed. He'd earned a pension, hadn't he?

"In an ideal world, Skull," Freddy said, "life would be a damn sight easier without secrets between us and Moscow."

"But," Skull said. "Here comes but."

"Their bombers aren't a patch on the Vulcan," Silk said. "That's no secret."

"But it's not an ideal world. And one reason we've got to keep our defences secret is the famous four-minute warning. In itself it's fine, we'd certainly get four minutes' notice of an attack. But how many Vulcans could respond?"

"Q.R.A. works," Skull said. "Airborne in under two minutes."

"And how long does it take to prepare the kites?"

"Hours and bloody hours," Silk said. "Fourteen fuel tanks to fill, pre-flight checks. Make the sandwiches, Hoover the carpet. Then you've still got to kick the tyres."

"And remember Blue Steel," Freddy said. "A couple of hours' work there. That H.T.P.: nasty stuff. Can't be rushed."

"There's two hundred and thirty gold studs connecting the weapon to the bomber," Silk said. "Bugger-up one connection and the whole thunderbox has to come off and start again."

"Well done, Silko," Freddy said. "Full marks."

"I read it in *Woman's Own*. Very hot on stand-off missiles, they are."

"We've still got loads of Thor missiles," Skull said. "Thors never sleep."

"But they can't be kept in immediate firing condition day and night," Freddy said. "The fuel is very volatile, liquid oxygen, it leaks out, you've got to keep topping it up. Face it: Thors or Vulcans, the unhappy fact is that if we want to retaliate effectively, we must have several hours' warning first. Not a secret we're about to tell the Soviets, is it?"

"We're all doomed. Well done, Freddy," Silk said. "Drinks on you."

"Far from it, old chap. You see, that's not the whole story. We assume that any nuclear strike would be preceded by a state of mounting international tension."

"That ran off the tongue very smoothly," Skull said.

"Did it? I've read it so often, in strategic planning papers. Written it, too. State of Mounting International Tension: S.M.I.T. Acronyms rule the world nowadays."

"Is this Cuban thing a S.M.I.T.?" Silk asked.

"Definitely. It's given us the breathing space we need to put all our defences on high alert."

"So Kruschev won't attack now," Skull said.

"Worst possible option," Freddy said. "He may be pugnacious but he's not suicidal."

"You sure he knows about S.M.I.T.?" Silk asked. "I mean, if Skull's right, shouldn't we tell Kruschev this is a bad time to blow up the world?"

"Now you're being facetious," Freddy said.

"Am I?" Silk looked at Skull. "Don't just sit there. Have a brain-storm. Have two."

Skull pointed a bony finger at Freddy. "We need a S.M.I.T. to give us the essential time to prepare. Yes?"

"Correct."

"And a Soviet leader would have to be a maniac to order a first strike during a S.M.I.T."

"A very stupid maniac."

"Therefore it follows that an intelligent maniac would strike when there is no diplomatic crisis? No S.M.I.T.? A bolt from the blue?"

"Why would he do that?"

"Silly question," Silk said. "He's a maniac. He can do what he likes."

"World leaders aren't maniacs," Freddy said. "Nuclear war kills everyone."

"Maniacs don't think they're maniacs," Silk said. "Maniacs believe they're doing God's work."

They walked back along the perimeter track. "Puts the whole silly nonsense in perspective, doesn't it?" Skull said.

"They can't scrap the Vulcan," Silk said. "Unthinkable."

A SCANDALOUS ROMP

1

Soon the Cuban Crisis ended. Kruschev agreed to remove his ballistic missiles and Kennedy pledged not to invade or attack the island. Secretly, he also promised to take all the American Jupiter missiles out of Turkey. So: no World War Three this year. Air Force General Curtis LeMay was furious: he believed Kennedy had missed a wonderful opportunity to destroy Communism. The rest of the world stopped holding its breath and got on with its life. This included Squadron Leader Quinlan's pregnant wife, who showed signs of premature delivery; very premature. She telephoned Kindrick late at night. Quinlan was granted compassionate leave and was gone by midnight. Next morning, the C.O. stopped Silk as he went into breakfast. "You're acting captain," he said. "Don't let it go to your head."

* * *

All the crews gathered in the biggest room in the Operations Block, on orders from the station commander. Must be something big.

"One or two impetuous newspapers have announced the phasing-out of the Vulcan," Pulvertaft said. "I can tell you that news of its death has been considerably exaggerated. The Vulcan will be part of Britain's front-line defence for some time to come. Missiles are all well and good, but no missile can do what every manned bomber can do, and that is take orders in flight from commanders

263

on the ground. So your role in the Vulcan will always remain unique. However . . ."

He picked up a clipboard, glanced at the page, put it down. *Nice bit of theatre*, Silk thought. *Make 'em wait, make 'em think.*

"Times change, and we change with them," Pulvertaft said. "Your Vulcan was designed to fly too high and too fast for enemy air defences, and it did. Now their defences have caught up and that superiority has gone. We can no longer fly above the enemy's reach. Therefore it has been decided that you shall fly beneath it."

That stirred them. Pulvertaft allowed the rumble of comment to fade, and said, "Here it is in simple English. You will fly at height to the point of detection, then dive to extreme low level and make your entry below their radar coverage, release your stand-off weapon, and climb to maximum height to exit the area. High-low-high. The Operations Officer will explain more fully."

This he did, and answered questions. What everyone wanted to know was how low was extreme low level. "Certainly below five hundred feet," he said. "Possibly much lower." And where would low-flying training take place? "I can't yet say. Canada and Arizona have been mentioned." Any further questions? None. Everyone wanted lunch.

* * *

Silk's crew were standing around, outside the mess, talking about High-Low-High, wondering how fast a Vulcan could dive from say fifty thou to five hundred without ripping the wings off, when the adjutant came over and introduced Flying Officer Young. "Your co-pilot during Mr Quinlan's paternity leave," he explained, and went away.

"Too bloody young," Tucker said.

"That's what passes for a joke around here," Silk said. "On the other hand, you don't look terribly old."

"Thirty-two. Married, with children. The usual story."

"Another damn Scotsman," Hallett muttered.

"Young isn't a very Scottish name," Silk said.

"I'm a MacAskill on my mother's side. Part of the clan McLeod, from the Isle of Skye, originally."

"Hope you can play bridge," Dando said. "We need a fourth."

"Sorry to disappoint you." Nobody spoke. The crew had lost its Combat status when Quinlan left. Not Young's fault, but to them he represented bad luck. He felt the need to say something, to justify himself. "Mountaineering is my thing. I've climbed all the good peaks in Scotland."

"What a shame," Silk said. "We'll be going into Russia at extreme low level, very boring for you. Bring a good book."

2

Zoë telephoned. She was at The Grange, come and have dinner. A rare occasion nowadays. Not to be missed.

When Silk parked the Citroën, Stevens was waiting at the front door. "Remember me?" Silk said. "I'm still the under-husband."

"Mrs Monk's bull terrier is no more, sir. Chased a rabbit, collapsed. A noble death."

"Did Tess tell you that? She's a pathological liar. I saw her dead husband cleaning her windows."

"Almost true. An exchange was arranged. One shop-soiled Polish agent was traded for Mr Monk. He'd been in an East German jail for seven years."

"Tess married a spy? The windowcleaner was a spook? I find that very hard to believe."

"Good," Stevens said. "That makes it all the easier to forget." He held the door open for Silk to go in. "Along with Wing Commander Skelton, of course."

Silk took off his hat, spun it on his finger, put it on backwards. "I'm sick of your bloody silly hints and riddles. Either speak up or go to hell."

"Nothing is worse than being wrong," Stevens said, "except being right."

Silk headed for the stairs. "I need a drink. I need a bucket of booze."

* * *

Zoë was alone and happy to see him, and still capable of giving his pulse a kick. Dinner was good. Nobody mentioned politics or Cuba or C.N.D. Mostly they talked about things they had enjoyed together, in years past: trips, theatres, films, friends. Beds. All the dozens of different beds they had shared. "I notice you haven't included the punt," he said.

"I never got bedded in the punt."

"That day on the river at Cambridge . . . If I'd agreed, would you really have . . ."

"Yes."

He frowned as he pictured the scene. "Not a helpful setting."

"But that was the whole point of it, darling. We'd have drifted into midstream and collided with dozens of other punts and probably capsized and got arrested for indecent exposure. All quite absurd, I agree, but . . . there was a reason. I had a wild idea that some gloriously scandalous romp would buck up our marriage, and if it failed, at least it would be an afternoon to remember. I'm going to Seattle, Silko."

He tried not to look surprised or hurt. He poured more wine and waited.

"I'm going to join a thinktank on conflict resolution. I'll give up my seat in the House. Time for a change. The constituency needs someone fresh and new."

"Seattle," he said. "Oregon."

"Washington State, actually. You'll come and see me, won't you?"

"I always do, don't I?"

"I know, I know. You got this Vulcan job and now I'm leaving, it's not very kind of me. You can keep the house, of course."

Silk looked about him. "It won't be the same without you. Have I permission to kill Stevens? He broke my cello."

She kissed him on the lips, very firmly. That hadn't happened for a while. And now, when it happened, she was off to Seattle. "You're a good man, Silko. I'm awfully glad we met. But let's face it, apart from our marriage, your life never points in any direction, does it? I'm not saying it *must*, there's no law about it, but ever since you left school you've simply gone from one aeroplane to the next."

"Well, I'm good at it."

"Yes, very good. All the same, I think you fly to escape."

"Escape what?"

She knocked gently on his skull with her knuckles. "Whatever's hiding in there. Now shall we go punting in the bedroom?"

End of serious conversation, thank God.

3

Freddy met Skull at the R.A.F. Club, in Piccadilly. "We shan't need to whisper here," he said. "Half the members are half-deaf anyway. All those years sitting next to roaring engines. All that sudden changing of altitude. I say: Cuba was a close call, wasn't it?"

"You didn't drag me down from Lincoln to get my opinion on Cuba."

"No, I didn't. You know how the Service works, Skull, so you've already guessed why you're here."

"Either I'm being offered a knighthood in the New Year's Honours List, or I've got the chop."

Freddy nodded. "Maybe a bit of both. Not a K, of course. Might get you a C.B.E. Let's have a drink, shall we? Then lunch."

They found a quiet corner of the bar. "I could always join one of the new universities," Skull said. "They offer such peculiar degrees. Lawnmower technology. History of the fox-trot. I could be a professor of war studies at the University of Bognor Regis."

"A chap with your brains? No, no. Total waste. The Service values your analytical brilliance, your penetrating insights, your . . ." Freddy's forefinger made small circles in the air. "Your lust for truth."

"Heaven help us. It's as bad as that, is it?"

"'Lust' was the wrong word. I withdraw 'lust'."

"Last time I got the chop they said I was unorthodox. Lusting after the truth isn't much of an improvement. They sent me to the Desert Air Force. Would you like to hear the truth about the desert war?"

"Look, they've got a table for us." Freddy stood.

"The truth is the flies shall inherit the Earth," Skull said. "The flies already occupy Libya."

They went into the dining room, Freddy nodding and smiling at a few acquaintances. The waiter gave them menus.

"A pint of beluga, a double chateaubriand, and any bottle that says Rothschild," Skull told him. "Since my rich uncle is paying."

"The club doesn't do a chateaubriand," Freddy said. "Their steak-and-kidney pie is well spoken-of."

"I'll have the chops. Lightly grilled. That's a stunning play on words. Chops. Hilarious. Forget it."

When the waiter had gone, Freddy said: "Normally, postings go from Air Ministry via Command and Group to the officer concerned. You know that. So this is an exception. For old time's sake."

"I don't really want a C.B.E.," Skull said. "I'd sooner have the lunch anyway."

"I just wanted you to know that we couldn't possibly leave you at Kindrick, not with your irregular views on deterrence and secrecy."

"Irregular. Is that the same as uncomfortable?"

"Try unacceptable. We can't have a Senior Intelligence Officer casting doubt on our nuclear deterrent policy. You'd corrode morale. Aircrew can't have doubts. You know that."

Skull tore a bread roll in half, and then in half again. He saw a crumb on his left index finger, and he licked it off. "We seem to be in something of a S.M.I.T.," he said. "State of Mounting Interdepartmental Tension. Your department and mine. I can't stay at Kindrick. You can't court-martial me or even admonish me, because if you try, I'll make damn sure Mrs Zoë Silk M.P. knows all the sordid details, and the result will be the kind of publicity that gives your people nightmares."

"And the Vulcan crews' morale doesn't concern you?"

Skull raised his hands, palms upwards. "Since they'll never return from Russia, they deserve to know the truth before they go."

"There you go again," Freddy said. "Swearing in church."

Lunch arrived, and they talked of other things.

Eventually, as they stood outside the club, enjoying some late autumn sunshine, Skull said: "I appreciate the courtesy, Freddy. Now, what's your plan?"

"Send you on a course at a Defence College. In America, perhaps. That's what we usually do with our loose cannons. But you have to promise to behave properly. Don't embarrass us."

"Years ago, when they shunted me off to the Desert Air Force, Air Ministry gave me another ring on my sleeve. Up to squadron leader."

Freddy put his head back and stared at the pure blue sky. "Group Captain," he said. "You want to be Group Captain Skelton."

"Analytical brilliance. Penetrating insights. Your words."

"Blackmail," Freddy said. "Don't go back to Kindrick. Stay at my place. I'll get all your stuff sent over. And do us all a favour, Skull. Learn how to lie, will you?"

"Yes, of course, at once, fluently," Skull said. "How did that sound?"

Freddy flagged down a taxi. Another problem solved.

* * *

Freddy arranged for Skull's stuff to be packed and taken to his house, but he forgot about the Lagonda. Skull immediately caught a train to Lincoln and a taxi to Kindrick, collected the Lagonda from the Motor Transport Section, and he was quietly driving away when Silk saw the car and came running. Skull stopped.

"You weren't at our briefing," Silk said. "We had an idiot flight lieutenant Intelligence Officer who doesn't know Arthur from Martha. Where are you going?"

"Nowhere. Freddy's place. He's putting me up for a while."

"Oh." The Lagonda's huge engine began to grumble, and Skull

made tiny adjustments to the choke. "You mean you're off," Silk said. "Leaving for good."

"Good or ill."

"Well . . . that's bad news, that's all I can say. I mean, stone the sodding crows, this whole damn place is falling apart. Bloody hell . . . You weren't much good, Skull, but at least you never let the bullshit baffle you."

"Raw cunning, Silko. It's as easy as falling off a bicycle. Try it, sometime."

A quick handshake. Silk watched the Lagonda go. "Nothing lasts forever," he said aloud. "More's the pity." It sounded like bad advice from a stupid friend who meant well and should have shut up.

4

The flight was a routine training exercise: a trip to Benbecula on the Isle of Lewis, where No. 81 Signals Unit would test Dando's air electronic warfare kit.

Six-monthly servicing. No sweat. Even the weather was friendly, for late autumn. Patchy cloud, the odd shower, light winds.

Silk captained the bomber, with Young in the right-hand seat, and Silk flew it for the first twenty minutes, until they were high above the commercial airliner routes and heading for the Atlantic south of Ireland. Then he gave the control to the co-pilot. Hallett would navigate them around Ireland and north to the Western Isles of Scotland. Young could drive the bus. Quite soon, Silk regretted it. Young flew well; too well. There was nothing to tell him, nothing to do but think.

Silk thought about Skull. It couldn't have been an ordinary posting. Movement orders normally took days, or weeks; they didn't happen overnight. The odds were that Skull had got the chop again.

He'd been shat on from a great height. This was such a bleak thought that Silk forced it out of his mind, searched for a happy replacement, and got Zoë. She could easily capture his mind with a royal flush of memories; but Zoë was moving to Seattle. The better the memory, the bigger his loss. He kicked Zoë out, and in came Tess Monk, riding her bike. She'd chucked him out. He forgot her. What he couldn't get rid of was this act of forgetting. Everywhere he looked, he lost people, one after another, bang crash wallop, and it hurt. He turned to Young. "So you're a mountaineer, are you?" he said. "You must be mad. Explain to me how you're not mad."

"Ah, well now . . ." Young didn't turn his head. His flying was rock-steady. Maybe this was a test, an attempt to distract his attention. He checked the major dials and indicators: all correct. "Good mountaineers have a love of the mountain, they understand the rock and work with its shape. Bad climbers treat the mountain as hostile, and they fight it and lose, sometimes they die. Ten years ago, the newspapers said Everest was conquered. Wrong. Nobody conquers a mountain. What happens is it lets you share its space for a while." He checked the fuel gauges. Okay.

"Still, it's dangerous," Silk said. "You wouldn't do it if it was safe."

"I wouldn't be on a Vulcan squadron if I wanted a quiet life."

"Nothing lasts forever, not even Vulcans." That got no reply. "We're the last in line," Silk said. "After us, empty skies." Still no comment. "Make the most of it, I say. What's the best mountain in Scotland?"

"Not Ben Nevis," Young said. "Too many tourists in gym shoes. It once had a hotel at the top. Imagine that. A hotel . . . I prefer the Northern Highlands. There's a peak called Suilven . . ."

At that height, through the cockpit window, Scotland was

unseen. When Young got a course change from the back room and gently banked the bomber, Scotland might be glimpsed. From eight miles high it looked as flat as a map.

Talk about mountaineering whiled away the time until they reached Benbecula and then it was all business: steady cruising at fixed heights and speeds and bearings while Dando switched his black boxes on and off, and 81 Signals Unit got washed in their electronic energy. Then Young turned north. Their flight plan took them clockwise around the coast of Scotland, and finally south to East Anglia and Kindrick. Routine trip. Not even a mock interception by Hunter fighters. Maybe Fighter Command had lost the hangar key.

"Good," Silk said to Young. "I have control."

Young sat back and poured himself some coffee. Silk got a course change to 075 degrees: just north of east. "Landfall at Cape Wrath," Hallett said. Silk did nothing. Hallett repeated the new bearing. "Tell you what," Silk said. "Let's go and look at the scenic grandeur which our second pilot so much admires. What's a nice juicy sea loch near here?" he asked Young.

"Sea loch . . . Let me think . . . Well, Loch Laxford is due east of us, maybe a bit south."

"I need a course to Loch Laxford, Jack."

"Give me a second, skip."

Silk put the Vulcan into a wide, descending spiral. When he got the new course he was down to thirty thousand feet. "You know this isn't on our flight plan, Skip," Hallett said.

"No, I don't," Silk said, "but you whistle the opening bars and I'll pick it up as we go along."

Not even an old joke: a very old joke. Nobody laughed. Nobody spoke as Silk kept circling and losing height. At ten thousand feet he straightened out and made a shallow dive towards the mainland. When he entered Loch Laxford he was down to five thousand: still a mile high. "Damn letterbox windscreens," he said. "No good to man nor beast." He banked, steeply this time, and flew out to sea. When he returned, the bomber was low, and getting lower. "Nav radar to pilot," Tucker said. "Altitude six hundred and falling."

"You talk to them," Silk said. "I'm too busy driving."

He flew into the long, twisting valley of Loch Laxford at a leisurely 250 knots and 400 feet above the water. There were islands, not big, not high, and the land on either side was rugged but not threatening. "I see what you mean," he said. "Quite delightful." In shadow, the loch was grey; in sunlight it was green and blue. Loch Laxford was five miles long; the Vulcan covered it in a little over a minute.

"Mountains ahead," Hallett said.

"We see them," Young said.

"Which do you recommend?" Silk asked him.

"Ben Stack. Go dead ahead, follow the road, four or five miles, you can't miss it, I mean give it lots of space, it's two thousand feet high and close to the road." Young heard the rapid-fire tension in his voice and told himself to be calm.

"Altitude four hundred and fifty," Dando said.

Ben Stack was a magnificent hulk, and Silk showed it respect by keeping a quarter-mile distance as he circled it. The Vulcan had used a lot of fuel; it performed better now it was lighter. "Impressive," Silk said, "but not majestic. What's next?"

"Steer one-nine-zero," Young said. "Skip: are we doing a low-flying exercise?"

"Mountains ahead, thirteen hundred feet," Hallett said.

"We see them. That's Ben Strome, steer east of it," Young told

Silk. "Look for the lochs, they're near sea level, it's safer there." Silk nudged the Vulcan away from Ben Strome. Young said, "Is this an official low-level job?"

"What a lot of heather. Let's say it's a pioneering low-level job."

The Vulcan swept around the flanks of Ben Strome and turned south, briefly chasing its shadow across acres of peat bog.

"Mountains coming up," Hallett said. "Many mountains, and high."

"That's Quinag," Young said. "You must be extra careful here."

Silk skipped over a couple of lochs and a road, and lined up the Quinag range. "Doesn't look much," he said.

"Please, please, do a circuit. Look it over first."

Silk dropped his speed to 200 knots and prowled all around Quinag. "See what you mean," he said. "Several peaks."

"Five high ones, up to twenty-six hundred feet. Steep isn't the word. On a good day, the view of Eddrachilis Bay is . . . I wouldn't swap all of England for it."

"Isn't that a little loch?" Silk dipped a wingtip to improve their view. Sun glinted on water, deep in the black heart of Quinag. "There's a big valley leading up to it. That's a glen, isn't it?"

"With a sheer wall at the far end."

"Vulcans climb walls. Didn't they teach you that at your O.C.U.?"

He banked and flew at Quinag, opening the throttles until the speed neared 300 knots. The glen was vast. It seemed to swallow the Vulcan. More throttle, but no more height. Young had the illusion that the bomber was skimming the stream that led to the little loch, an illusion created by the rising sides of the mountains as they narrowed the glen. He told himself it would be a painless death, smeared over two thousand feet of vertical sandstone. That was when Silk gave full throttle and pulled the control stick back and the Vulcan stood on its tail and left Quinag standing.

They levelled out at five thousand feet. "Always a pleasure," Silk said. "I could get to enjoy this mountaineering game. Now where's your favourite peak? Where's Suilven?"

When Young first set out to climb Suilven, he didn't know it was perhaps the most remote mountain in Britain. He took a day just to cross the wilderness surrounding it. Broken peat bogs, flat jungles of deep heather, erratic sheep trails that faded to nothing; and the weather was foul. He camped under the awesome heights, streaked silver by the run-off of rain. Next day, typical Highland weather: beautiful. He climbed the mountain and walked its ridge, a dozen roller-coaster miles, much of it knife-edged. When he wasn't terrified he was bewitched. Then the rains returned: another wilderness slog. Three secret, sacred days.

Silk did Suilven in eight minutes.

After that he did the An Teallach range, wandered around the coast and did the Beinn Alligin ridge, hopped over Wester Ross and stooged down Loch Carron and up Loch Alsh, frightening the yachtsmen, and did the Five Sisters of Kintail.

"I don't want to spoil your fun, skip," Hallett said, "but this ultra-low-level stuff must be drinking our fuel like there's no tomorrow."

"Glencoe," Silk said. "Can't leave out Glencoe."

"You do Glencoe," Dando said, "and we might not reach Kindrick."

"Glencoe tops are probably fogged in," Young said. "They often are."

Silk took the Vulcan up to three thousand. "You drive," he said. "I'm knackered."

"Steer one-six-five," Hallett said.

The identification letters and numbers on the fin of the aircraft were easily readable. Bird watchers on Ben Strome had binoculars; they looked down on Silk's Vulcan thundering past and abandoned any hope of seeing snow buntings, peregrine falcons, greenshank or golden eagle. They scrambled down the slopes and looked for a telephone. Theirs was one of a stream of complaints that reached Air Ministry.

While the Vulcan was still cruising south, Freddy phoned Pulvertaft, gave him the ident and was not surprised to hear that Silk was the pilot.

"How low?" Pulvertaft asked. Freddy told him. "The man has a death-wish," Pulvertaft said. "He's a menace. I'll place him under close arrest the minute his wheels touch down. I don't want to prejudge, but he'll be stripped of his commission and go to prison, that I can guarantee."

"Wait. We still have a little time," Freddy said. "Do nothing. It's not as simple as it looks. I had enough trouble with Skull. Silko could be infinitely worse. I'll call you again in fifteen minutes."

He talked to a few colleagues, veterans of crises, and then got back to Pulvertaft. "Agreed, Silko's got to go. But absolutely no fuss, no close arrest, leave the Provost-Marshal's office out of this."

"Surely we should make an example."

"Never forget: his wife is Mrs Silk M.P. Very big in C.N.D. They'd love a big court-martial, they'd squeeze every drop of juice out of it. Nuclear Pilot Goes Berserk: I can just see the placards. No, we tread very softly-softly. When he lands, have a car ready. Take him at once to Bomber Command's medical centre, the place where we test would-be Vulcan pilots. Someone will meet him. And pack his kit."

* * *

The man who met him was Group Captain Evans.

"Silk," he said. "Slippery stuff. I thought I might see you again. Hoped not, but . . . here you are."

"Here I am, sir." It was dusk. Hours ago, sweat had dried on his face: low flying could be hard work. A wash would be nice.

"We're worried about your eyesight, Silk. It's not good enough, is it? Anyone who goes looking for trouble, the way you did, and finds it, must have rotten eyesight. Agree?"

"I could do with a drink, sir."

"You still owe us for half a bottle of claret. Follow me."

They went to his office and Evans gave him a whisky and water. "So you're leaving the Service," Evans said. "Retiring on medical grounds. In fact you're out already – the paperwork was completed while you were still in the air. Slightly irregular, but I'm sure you can see your way clear to accepting the change."

Silk stirred his drink with his finger, and sucked the finger. "I can barely see you, sir. And I don't know what's become of that bottle."

Evans gave him another half-inch of Scotch. "The first time I saw you, I warned you that Vulcan duty was no piece of cake. I told you that any weakness was terminal, it would eat away at you until you cracked. And here we find you playing silly-buggers at sea level in the wildest corner of the Scottish highlands." There was no anger in his voice; only flat amazement. "What went wrong?"

"People kept disappearing," Silk said. "And I worked it out – I've got fewer years ahead of me than behind me. And they'll scrap the Vulcan soon. I knew I'd never get another chance like today. That's all. Now I'd like to wash my face."

When Silk came back from the bathroom, Evans said: "The best thing for all of us would be if you were to disappear. Go a very long way from Britain. I've looked at your file. You must know people in Air America."

"Barney Knox was my boss. The last I heard, he was in their California office. Los Angeles."

"The West Coast." Evans looked at his watch. "Eight hours difference. It's worth a try. Here's their number in L.A."

Silk took the slip of paper. "You know everything, don't you?"

"It's reciprocal."

Silk made the call. Naturally, Knox was glad to hear from him. Surprisingly, his old job was available. "Preferably somewhere not a million miles from Seattle," Silk said. Knox suggested Vietnam; plenty of Air America work there. Silk said he thought Vietnam was quiet now the French had gone. "Think again," Knox said. Silk took the offer.

He handed the slip of paper to Evans but he didn't release it. They stood in the middle of the office, each holding the end of a piece of paper. "You had this ready," Silk said. "You didn't write the number and give it to me. It was all prepared."

"I spoke to Knox an hour ago. He was waiting for your call."

Silk let go. "I feel somewhat manipulated," he said.

"Well, you manipulated Bomber Command, Silk. So now we're quits. We've booked you onto a plane to L.A. tonight. Ticket and passport will be at the check-in. Hungry?"

They walked down the corridor, to the mess. "Vietnam," Evans said. "Jolly good. Don't come back soon, will you?"

AUTHOR'S NOTE

Hullo Russia, Goodbye England is a fiction based on fact. The reader is entitled to know which is which.

The major events are true. References to Bomber Command's operations in World War Two, the formation of Vulcan bomber squadrons by the R.A.F., the policy of nuclear deterrence in the Cold War, and the American attack on Cuba at the Bay of Pigs, followed by the Cuban Missile Crisis of October 1962 – these all happened in much the way I have described. However, there was no Vulcan squadron numbered 409, and no R.A.F. Kindrick in Lincolnshire. Air America was only one of many C.I.A.-owned airlines; for the sake of simplicity I allowed it to represent them all.

Accounts of the design and performance of aircraft are as accurate as I could make them. This includes details of the Blue Steel stand-off nuclear weapon, the Thor ballistic nuclear missile, the A.E.O.'s jammers (Red Shrimp, Blue Diver and so on), simulators, Micky Finn exercises, electromagnetic pulse, nuclear targets in the Soviet Union, and Vulcan training flights to Benbecula and to Rockall, including the presence of Russian trawlers engaged in electronic snooping on Nato activities.

The characters are fictional, although some of them have been around for years. Skull and Air Commodore Bletchley first appeared in my novel *Piece of Cake*, and then turned up again in *A Good Clean Fight*, while Silk played a big part in *Damned Good Show*, as did Zoë. Silk's morale-boosting tour of American war factories, and his visits to U.S. Air Force flying schools, are invented; so is the hectoring interrogation he gets when he rejoins Bomber Command.

But Silk's generous treatment by Ronald Colman fits the facts. During the war, the British colony in Hollywood was very hospitable to passing R.A.F. aircrew, and I have not exaggerated the warmth of the welcome that beautiful stars gave to young pilots.

The eyepatches are not fiction. The Vulcan cockpit had windshield blinds which could be used to hide a nuclear flash; but as an extra safeguard against total blindness, aircrew were indeed issued with an eyepatch. By 1962, Quick Reaction Alert (Q.R.A.) and Operational Readiness Platforms (O.R.P.) were standard procedures on Vulcan squadrons. When bombers were scrambled, the thrust of their engines was truly massive: on one base it repositioned the town rubbish dump, unwisely sited near the perimeter fence. Ejection seats – "bang seats" – were provided only for pilot and co-pilot. In time of trouble, the rest of the crew were expected to bale out through the door in front of the nose wheel – by no means an easy exit, given the height, speed and perhaps damaged condition of the aircraft.

The title is apt. If the policy of nuclear deterrence failed and Vulcans were sent to retaliate, they would never turn back until their task was done; and then turning back would be pointless, because every home base would have been obliterated. Few aircrew, if any, seem to have lost any sleep over this bleak scenario. Perhaps their maturity and experience shaped their outlook. Many had served in Bomber Command since the early days of World War Two, when they flew such vintage machines as the Battle or the Hampden. Silk's arrival on 409 Squadron brought the average age of Quinlan's crew below forty. This situation was not unknown. Bomber Command liked seasoned performers in its nuclear aircraft.

The Cold War needed no invention: the reality of M.A.D. –

Mutual Assured Destruction – was chilling enough. Reports by the Conservative Medical Association and the Royal College of Nursing are fact. Captain Red Black's task – to bomb East Berlin while, within a minute, it was being destroyed by two Thor missiles – was part of the strategy known as "cross-targeting". An official history of the Cuban Missile Crisis comments: "The pilot assigned this task is remembered as the individual who sweated the most during cockpit alert."

I had no need to embroider that Crisis: the bare facts provide ample material. It is true that the telephone link between S.A.C. H.Q. and Bomber Command H.Q. fell silent; that S.A.C. signals were transmitted in plain English for the benefit of Soviet ears; and that B52s flew threateningly close to Soviet borders. In mid-Crisis, S.A.C. – without warning the Soviet Union – launched an Atlas intercontinental ballistic missile over the Pacific, later revealing that it was unarmed. At about the same time, the U.S. radar network reported a missile launch in Cuba, aimed at America – a radar technician had mistakenly inserted a test tape into the system. Luckily someone aborted the process of knee-jerk retaliation. That was not the only cock-up.

General Curtis LeMay was, by his own account, the most hawkish of hawks. On the other side, Kruschev was indeed persuaded that Americans would mistake Cuban missiles for palm trees; and Russian forces (to protect the missile sites) turned out to be far greater than he had expected. Generals always need more troops, sometimes to protect the troops they already have. By contrast the British response to the Crisis was laid-back: R.A.F. nuclear bombers were not sent to their dispersal fields.

The acronym S.M.I.T. is invented but the policy it stood for is not: British (and American) nuclear defence was based on the assumption that mounting international tension would allow time to prepare for war. Preparation is one thing; action is another. The survival of Great Britain might well have hinged on whether or not Prime Minister Macmillan was on the road. There was a vital link between his Rolls-Royce and the Automobile Association. All messages to and from Macmillan's car-phone – cutting-edge technology in those days – went via the A.A. network, normally used to communicate with its motorcycle patrolmen. If Russia attacked Britain, the A.A. would find the P.M. and tell him.

A generation is growing up which did not know the Cold War. They may find it hard to imagine what life was like for aircrew on a Vulcan squadron: endlessly rehearsing the task of penetrating deep into Soviet air defences; knowing by heart the street plans of Russian cities; shaping their lives around the possibility that a scramble order could, at any moment, send them airborne to wipe out those cities, with very little chance of return. *Hullo Russia, Goodbye England* can convey only a fraction of the flying skills, the high endeavour and the mental strength that the job demanded. The scramble order never came. Nuclear deterrence worked. We should be thankful.

* * *

While working on *Hullo Russia, Goodbye England,* I was fortunate to meet Air Commodore Brian Sills. He flew the Victor nuclear bomber in the period that included the Cuban Missile Crisis; later he was Station Commander at R.A.F. Waddington, where four Vulcan squadrons were based, and he regularly flew that aircraft. His expert advice has been invaluable in helping me to avoid pitfalls and inaccuracies. Any errors that appear are entirely my fault.

THE ROYAL FLYING CORPS TRILOGY

WAR STORY

Fresh from school in June 1916, Lieutenant Oliver Paxton's first solo flight is to lead a formation of biplanes across the Channel to join Hornet Squadron in France. Five days later, he crash-lands at his destination, having lost his map, his ballast and every single plane in his charge. To his C.O. he's an idiot, to everyone else – especially the tormenting Australian who shares his billet – a pompous bastard. This is 1916, the year of the Somme, giving Paxton precious little time to grow from innocent to veteran.

HORNET'S STING

It's 1917, and Captain Stanley Woolley joins an R.F.C. squadron whose pilots are starting to fear the worst: their war over the Western Front may go on for years. A pilot's life is usually short, so while it lasts it is celebrated strenuously. Distractions from the brutality of the air war include British nurses (not much luck); eccentric Russian pilots; bureaucratic battles over the plum-jam ration; rat-hunting with Very pistols; and the C.O.'s patent, potent cocktail, known as "Hornet's Sting". But as the summer offensives boil up, none of these can offer any lasting comfort.

GOSHAWK SQUADRON

France, 1918. A normal January day on the Western Front – no battles, and about 2,000 men killed. Behind the lines, at an isolated airfield, Major Stanley Woolley, R.F.C., commanding Goshawk Squadron, turns on a young pilot who has spoken of a "fair fight" and roasts him: "That is a filthy, obscene, disgusting word, and I will not have it used by any man in my squadron." Woolley's goal is to destroy the decent, games-playing outlook of his public school-educated pilots – for their own good.

THE ROYAL AIR FORCE QUARTET

PIECE OF CAKE

In 1939 the R.A.F. was often called the best flying club in the world, with a touch of the playboy about some fighter pilots. That soon changed. *Piece of Cake* follows the vapour trails of Hornet Squadron as it takes a beating in the Battle for France and regroups for the Battle of Britain, which is no piece of cake either. The Luftwaffe is big in numbers and confidence, and patriotism alone cannot save a man in a spinning, burning Hurricane.

A GOOD CLEAN FIGHT

North Africa, 1942. Dust, heat, thirst, flies. A good clean fight, for those who like that sort of thing, and some do. From an advanced landing field, striking hard and escaping fast, our old friends from Hornet Squadron play Russian roulette, flying their clapped-out

Tomahawks on ground-strafing forays. Meanwhile, on the ground, the men of Captain Lampard's S.A.S. patrol drive hundreds of miles behind enemy lines to plant bombs on German aircraft. Cue revenge.

DAMNED GOOD SHOW

When war pitches the young pilots of 409 Squadron into battle over Germany, their training, tactics and equipment are soon found wanting, their twin-engined bombers obsolete from the off. Chances of completing a 30-operation tour? One in three. At best. The hardest part of any war is not winning but slogging on to avoid defeat. Bomber Command did that. A wickedly humorous portrait of men doing their duty in flying death traps – fully aware that in those dark days of war there was nothing else to do but dig in and hang on.

HULLO RUSSIA, GOODBYE ENGLAND

After a stint running guns for the C.I.A., Flight Lieutenant Silk, a twice-decorated Lancaster pilot, rejoins the R.A.F. to fly the Vulcan, a nuclear bomber. This is probably the best aircraft in the world. It makes sex look like gardening.

But there's a catch. The Vulcan exists to retaliate against a Russian nuclear strike. Silk knows that if his squadron gets scrambled for real, there will be no England to return to. In the mad world of Mutual Assured Destruction, the Vulcan is the last – indeed the only – deterrent.